SOUVENIR (IN A KILLER'S WORDS)

Chapter 1: The lady in the lake.

I can remember it like it was yesterday and one day not so long ago, it was. Some stories are hard to tell, others are hard to hear, this mismatch of hatred, love and murder is a bit of both. So, take the weight off your feet, sit back, and relax, if that is at all possible. My name is Colin Stevens, and this is my story.

The night was black, lit only by the distant faded light of an otherwise silvery moon. If not for the clouds the vista would be crystal clear and shining like a spotlight, illuminating the town brighter than London's West End Theatre District or Blackpool's golden mile of lights. Depending on which part of the north/south divide you happen to find yourself being from. This night however was different and for good reason, something needs to be hidden, something needs to remain a secret. One person will do anything that is possible to hide their actions, they are doing something in private that they believe nobody but themself needs to know. Yet before very long, everyone in this small country holiday town with a population of only 5,000 people will be only too aware and gossiping about what went on at this lake. Tomorrows' news, happening today, happening now.

Small gaps in the seemingly endless blackness let through small shards or rays of moonlight that shine down directly onto the boating lake, lighting it up and making it visible to the naked eye and as a result a sight and a delight to behold. Without them the lake would remain invisible, black as ever and hidden in the shadows of the darkened clouds, masked from view, and shrouded in mystique.

For the moment at least the weather is dry if a little overcast, but for how long could be anyone's guess? The weathermen have given their usual report, "Dry and sunny with the possibility of clouds and rain," how can they go wrong? The clouds, forming since mid-afternoon have all convened and joined together forming one large nimbostratus and waiting patiently for their chance to spill their ill-gotten gains onto the earth below. Pretty soon they will be dampening the atmosphere and muddying the ground before washing away any possible evidence that may have accrued. Before too long the said rains will come, of that there is no doubt, this is England after all. When they do, the silence will be drowned out by the pitter-patter of toxic acid rain falling from the sky before disappearing with a fizzle into bubbling puddles of water.

Not too long after this spectacle and certainly before the early light of dawn gleams its magnificent shine, the birds will sing in unison their morning chorus to welcome the brand-new day. All hell will break loose and, in more ways than anyone could ever imagine, or even begin to contemplate. Death is an enigma, hard to come to terms with and always closer to hand than one could think. It's as free as a wild stallion on the open plains of an American prairie galloping into the sunset, totally free and oblivious to anything around it, nothing can change it or stop it in its' tracks. Or subsequently, like a juggernaut of doom, or a runaway train thundering down the tracks on its' way to oblivion and getting there fast, taking down all in its path.

Pushing through several unforeseen obstacles, it is gradually making its way to this one place at this exact time, here and now as if it were its destiny, its one true goal and its sole purpose in an otherwise meaningless life. Yes, death and all associated with it is most definitely at hand. Anyone in its' path should bow down to fate and accept the consequences by joining the list of statistics that grows with every passing day. But that is my opinion, you will have to work out for yourself what it means to you.

Right on cue, and as expected, the blackness gives way and is suddenly disturbed and lit up by even more bright light, as two headlights add to the glow of the moon's rays. A black Toyota Corolla pulls through the double gates of the park and heads directly towards the lake. The entire park is a pedestrian only, no-drive zone for everyone barring the rangers and keepers that need to go about their business. But this rule, or law is not stopping whoever it may be from doing whatever they need to do, why would it? It's now just a little after 3 am and nobody else is around to see them or stop them so they just carry on with what they are doing, after all it's their business, nobody else's and they don't seem to have a care in the world.

Whoever it is, there are no second thoughts about what it is they are doing; indeed, they have no cares or worries as to whether it's legal or illegal. Without a doubt it is obviously the latter, or why the secrecy, why in the darkness and more importantly, why here and now? They are fully aware of their actions but appear to have no guilt, it is obviously not a feeling they possess, what would it prove in any case, if anything at all? It's just something that must be done, and this is the only time for them to do it while escaping the hustle and bustle of activity that would stop them later in the light of day when joggers, dogwalkers and mothers taking their kids to the swings would be in abundance and looking on inquisitively at this strange activity taking place.

 For now, though, the only other life around is the lakes' resident ducks, most of them are asleep with their heads resting across their backs and even if they weren't, they are not going to tell a soul about what they may or may not have witnessed. One or two may be going against the grain and swimming backward and forward, toing and froing. I guess even some ducks can be insomniacs, why should it be limited to the humanity? They may be the noisiest animals in the park by a country mile, but they keep a secret well and tonight they are not talking. All you need to do is feed them bread and your secret is theirs, they will love you forever, and you them, I mean, who doesn't love a duck or feeding them at least?

 As kids surely, we all loved being taken to the park to feed them and they most certainly loved us coming. Who doesn't love to see them all converge on the one area of the lake where you stand with bread in your hand waiting impatiently to be fed and making the mother of all noises until you throw the bread to them?

It is so easy to get side-lined and go off track and I believe that is exactly what is happening here, so where was I? Ah yes, my black Toyota Corolla.

When it reaches the lake, it comes to a halt by the edge. The red glow of the brake lights is clearly visible for a few seconds before darkness strikes again and the noise from the engine disappears as it is turned off. Leaving the area once again in peaceful silence and lit only by the shards of moonlight as it had been before what had been such a rude disturbance.

The driver's door opens, and a silhouetted figure emerges. From its' burly shape and size, it's quite easy to make out that it is a man. He walks to the rear of the car and presses the release button to open the boot. Once the catch releases, the boot springs open, and he reaches in with both hands and grabs something. Lifting whatever it is up and throwing it over his shoulder he moves slowly towards the lake and tosses it in. Whatever he was throwing in was either light or he had the strength to make it look as though it was. The splash it made when it entered the water was so loud it took even him by surprise and in doing so answered both questions in one go, it wasn't light, he was strong! His power was mightier than even he could have imagined when he was just a puny little oaf of a boy all those years ago. All the long hours at the gym, working out has certainly paid dividends, but not getting ahead of myself, we will learn more later.

Looking around furtively to make sure nobody had seen or more particularly heard anything and making them wander along to see what could or had made such a racket, after all it was an almighty splash. But to no avail, luckily as all was just as still and quiet as it had been before he had turned up. He of course wouldn't have known that because he wasn't there. He could ask the ducks; they wouldn't have heard the song "Feed the birds" but maybe they could earn from it. I bet today the cost would be slightly dearer than the tuppence charged by the lady in Mary Poppins'. Movies were a part of his life, especially horror and tales of murder, and to some degree he was currently deeply embroiled in his own murder mystery, how cool. He could only guess and assume that every normal person would be in bed at this time giving it zeds, deep in slumber and relaxing in preparation for work the next morning. That was exactly where he should be and would be heading to as soon as he was finished here and discarded what needed to be tossed away but was it incriminating evidence or fly-tipping? The truth would soon be known.

Whoever it was and whatever they were dumping was obviously illegal or else why would they feel the need to hide and use the cover of the dark? The full extent of the truth and just how illegal would only be revealed by the rising of the morning sun and its' light shining down on what was now there waiting to be discovered.

Fresh on everybody's lips it will be talked about, incessantly a little later by all the loose tongued gossipmongers that will have nothing else to talk about, or so it would appear. Almost immediately after checking once more and for a final time that no-one was spying on him, the man got back into his black Toyota and drove off in the same direction as he had come from a mere few minutes previous. It was no time at all before it pulled out through the park gates before disappearing into the dead of night, how apt to use the word dead was thought, how appropriate indeed.

Chapter 2: One man and his dog.

It didn't take long for it to be found, I never expected it to. I mean, if I wanted it to go undiscovered, I would have dumped it in the woods or buried it like most serial killers would have, hidden away from prying eyes, but that really wasn't my aim. I was more than happy for her to be found, then I could sit back and listen to all the news and have the added satisfaction of knowing it was all about me.

Three hours later and with the sun three-quarters of the way up in the sky an old man was out walking in the park with his dog when he came across the lake and saw what he believed to be a shop mannequin lying face down in the water. The little shitheads will steal and discard anything, he thought to himself, they are getting worse by the day and all down to lack of supervision of their parents and not caring what they are up to. To some of them it's easier to let them loose to run riot than try to control them and risk their wrath. Anything for an easy life. On closer inspection, though, the alarm bells starting ringing in his head, his hatred for the little-buggers or litter-buggers as you will subsided. Suddenly, the anger in his face turned to horror as he realised that it was not a mannequin at all, it was in fact a human body.

 He felt queasy immediately as this was the first dead body he had ever seen, and the blood drained out of him quicker than if being sucked out by a vampire at full lust. He needed a phone to call the police, where was his mobile? Shit! It was still on charge by his bed! He started to run as fast as he could, he knew where there was a call box, but his run turned out nothing more like a doddery jog, with his faithful hound following at his heels. It was fun for the dog, more exercise, and he was having a whale of a time chasing his owner but for the poor guy it was a complete nightmare and one that he didn't want to live but was kind of forced to by the circumstances in which he had found himself.

At one awkward point the dog nearly tripped him up by running across his path and getting under his feet. Luckily enough he managed to straighten himself up at the last second and in doing so saved an accident that could have had repercussions for both himself and the dog. At his age any accidents take that little bit longer to heal than they ever used to, and he was quite a portly guy so if he fell on the dog then…. Well, it wouldn't be nice or pretty by any stretch of the imagination and certainly a lot worse for the dog.

When he reached the phone box, his legs were shaking uncontrollably from the sudden burst of exercise and his hands nervously quivering from the sight he had just seen in the lake. He took a few deep breaths to control himself and managed to slow his breathing enough to compose himself enough to dial 999. Luckily the thugs and mindless morons hadn't smashed up this phone box like they have so many around town, why do they feel they have to do it? Why indeed? there can be no answer but one day it may come back to haunt them when in their own moment of emergency, they can't find a working one. It would be a fitting revenge against themselves but alas not for the loved one they would be trying to save.

After dialling he heard a friendly voice asking him if he needed police, fire, or ambulance to which he replied, police please. A few seconds later he was put through and spoke to a constable who took all the details, and he was told someone would be there, at the lake in five minutes. He headed back pronto or as fast as his tired old legs would carry him, another doddery jog. He had no idea he was so out of shape until now, these things have a habit of rearing their ugly heads at the most inopportune moments, yet again the dog was having none of it, just loving his exercise. He didn't want to see the body again, who would, but he needed to be there when the police turned up. He positioned himself with his back to the boating lake, so he didn't have to see the horrible sight again. He felt the urge to turn his head, his eyes being drawn to the lake, but he squared his shoulders and held firm, resisting the temptation. No! He didn't want to lose his breakfast!

He could hear the sirens almost immediately and could even make out that they were getting closer and closer with every passing second. Before the five minutes were up, he saw an array of blue flashing lights as two police cars screeched to a halt directly in front of him. He had to squint at one point and hold his hand over his eyes like the peak of a cap as the lights were so bright. He then saw a couple of policemen climb out of each car and look around weighing up the scene before they came over to him to hear what he knew if anything.

He was glad they were there as he felt a little on edge beforehand, wondering if anyone was around looking. By anyone he meant of course whoever had committed this heinous crime, if in fact that's what it was but he had already talked himself into believing that to be a fact. He had heard or read somewhere that killers like to hang around and see the after-effects of what they have done. He just put it down to nerves and what he had just witnessed, and now the police were there he thought no more of it as the feeling of ease and reassurance took over from his earlier nervousness.

He was asked a series of questions based on the circumstances he found himself in, there were no real set of questions to be asked as it was such a strange predicament, not normal in any way, not to him anyway. It may have been his first time and he was clueless how things were done, or any business was conducted but the police had been through it on many occasions previously and they guided him through it effortlessly and gave him pointers at times when he became stuck for something to say or struggled for answers. He remained there talking with the officers for about twenty minutes answering all their questions before being allowed to go, he headed off with his trusty hound in tow.

 He left the police with the gruesome, unpleasant, and thoroughly unenviable task of recovering the body so forensics could work out who she was and when, and how she had died. They were sure as hell that she died elsewhere and was then placed in the lake, their experience told them as much, but they would have to wait for the coroner to confirm it. It's so easy to write down answers or possible motives in a notepad but proving them, well that's for the real experts. Although he really didn't want to see it again his morbid fascination took over, kind of like a car crash when you just can't help but look and he had one last look before he left which made him shudder at the thought of what someone could do to someone else, and why? But there were no answers, how could there be? and he darted away as quickly as he could to make his escape and try to make the rest of his day as normal or at least as normal as was possible, but not before taking that last glance, urrggh, he shuddered to himself one final time and went on his way.

It was certainly not how he planned his day starting as he left the house to take the dog for its mandatory morning walk. The dog had done everything that it needed to, and he was not in the mood for any more walking, so he headed home. A nice cup of tea is what the doctor ordered, and he was ready to sit and enjoy it in the warmth of his living-room, and as far away from the park and the horrible sight as he could possibly get.

Chapter 3: Colin who?

Life is a rollercoaster; I believe that is what they say. Personally, I have never been one for fairgrounds although I have visited a few over the years. The rides just made me sick and left me feeling unsatisfied. I needed a bit of a boost, something in my life to give me the buzz that other people felt while spinning or twisting on the rides. Their cheesy smiles or the big grins on their faces was something I never got, until now, so this was how it felt?

It had been two days since the police had fished the body of what turned out to be a dead girl from the lake, and although nobody knew who she was or anything about her, she was on everyone's lips and the only real topic of conversation worth giving a second thought to. The next best was the story of a cat that had got stuck up a tree and had to be rescued by the fire service, so the girl in the lake was head and shoulders above it as a story really. Her story also made the headlines and was plastered all over the front page of the Gazette, the local newspaper, the story of the cat in the tree, however, did not and was relegated to page nine, life in a small town, hey. It was reported that she'd had her throat cut and had been dead for several days before being dumped. It was also reported that she had been sexually abused, possibly even after death, but this was for the moment only speculation. What kind of sicko, or completely fucked-up retard would do that to a dead body....? Or a living one either, that should go without saying too, but especially a dead one, how the mind boggles. The world is one fucked up place and getting more and more fucked up as time elapses.

Colin Stevens walked through the doors that led into the offices of Allen & Co, the mortgage brokers where he had worked for several years, ever since he had left school, and after graduating top of his class in every subject. He was a very bright boy, and everybody wanted him. Hence, he had his pick of job offers but settled for this one as his chances of promotion were high and had been a major factor in his choice. Promotion leads to more money, more money leads to a better lifestyle and a better lifestyle leads to well anything. The world could be his oyster, all he had to do was want it bad enough, and he did. Maybe one day he would take the next step and move on but for now he was content, he had worked himself up a few of rungs on the ladder and the next one was the top rung, picking up the golden pot and taking over from Mr Allen. Assuming of course that the old bastard would one day retire, or die, he had no preference as to which, he just wanted to be top dog and along with it have the power he craved, but the stubborn old bastard was certainly not playing ball. Maybe, and it was something he had contemplated from time to time, that just maybe he could give him a helping hand or a push so to speak in the right direction. After all Mr Allen had lived out the most part of his life and was now just going through the motions, albeit with a healthy bank account. Colin felt his best years were yet to come and didn't want to lose them by settling for what he had, that just wasn't him.

There was a buzz around the office, everyone was talking about the girl in the lake and although he was trying his hardest to avoid them or the subject completely, he couldn't help but be dragged into their mindless gossip and guesswork. "Isn't that terrible Mr Stevens," a voice would say. "What happened to that poor girl!" It continued. "Yes, very," he replied while trying his best to get away to the sanctuary of his office where he could be alone and get on with his own life without having to play-act that he had a care in the world, or in his own inevitable words, a flying fuck about a stranger that had been found in a lake.

She was as much of a stranger to him as she was to everyone. Had he seen her before? Of course, in fact he'd last seen her just a couple of days ago, and he was probably the last person to have seen her alive, probably, no strike that, he was the last to see her alive. But he had no idea of her name and no wish to learn it, hence a stranger she remained. He learned what they learned and when they learned it, but he had the added advantage of knowing it was him they were all talking about and that gave him a thrill. It made him feel special, but in his own inevitable way, he was losing sight of reality in his quest for infamy and taking things up a notch to an entirely new level.

When he reached just under halfway along the corridor a voice came from a few paces behind him saying, "So it's happened again Colin, another poor girl cut down in the prime of her life, just like the others." It made him jump and startled him for a second or two until he realised it was Mr Allen, his boss. "Good morning, Mr Allen. Yes, I've just been reading about it, you can't get away from it, can you?" Colin replied. "All the girls are obsessed with it, they just won't stop talking about it," Mr Allen responded, "I guess they are all scared it could be them next, things like this don't happen here. They are usually just things you read in the papers. And if it's not them it could possibly even be someone they know or is close to them." he finished." We can only hope it doesn't distract them from their work too much because we have a lot on today." Colin informed him.

Mr Allen smiled his usual smile, which at times could rip the skin off an elephant and calmly said "I don't think it will Colin, let's give them a few minutes to get it out of their system, once they have bored themselves with the small talk, they will be fine and then they can knuckle down to work. I'll see you in my office for our meeting in about 15 minutes if that's ok with you," he said as he walked away. "Yes, I will do…." Colin started to reply but stopped half-way through as Mr Allen was gone or at least he had stopped listening anyway, just like he usually did as his attention span was shorter than a goldfish's memory, maybe it was an age thing or possibly a deliberate act of not caring, who knows. If it was the latter of the two then he played it well, after all it was his firm, he founded it and he had every right to do things as he so pleased but as it goes, he wasn't a bad boss, really. He was firm but fair and could be tough as the next man when he needed to be, so all-in-all, a very dangerous man to get on the wrong side of or try and take on, there was only one way that could turn out and it didn't look good for anyone but Mr Allen.

After the meeting was over and not a lot was really sorted as was the norm, just two men talking tactics that would probably never be implemented, Colin headed back to his office and closed the door, he wanted some privacy and didn't leave his office for anything other than toilet breaks all day. He had two of them, one in the morning and one in the afternoon and the rest of the day he spent sat at his desk reading the paper and memorizing the article on 'The girl in the lake' word for word, taking in the local news that meant a murderer was on the loose. Was he a murderer? Really? He never saw himself as a murderer, a killer maybe as it was just a little experiment he tried, but when he thought deeply into it, only then did he realise that yes, he was, and he kind of liked the attention it was drawing, if only they knew it was him that had done it, they were closer than they could ever have imagined to the one person they were all yapping on about.

 A sly, wry grin appeared on his face, and he felt special to be the only one to know exactly what had happened to the lady in the lake. From her disappearance through her torture and finally to her reappearance, albeit dead. They may be the ones' talking about her but from her initial abduction all the way through to her senseless murder, her blood was on his hands, so to speak. Although he had cleaned it off rigorously and there were no more visible signs, her blood was still on his hands and no matter how many times he told himself the fact he never got tired of hearing it. It was his work and his work alone; nobody could take that from him.

At the end of the day and feeling a tad guilty about not doing a shred of work, yet not guilty enough to make him want to make up for it and stay behind to play catch up and do some, he left his office and headed out like a sheep with the rest of the flock. He held his head low and stooped down slightly so as not to catch anyone's eye, it was attention he didn't want as he really wasn't in the mood for small idle chitter-chatter, meaningless conversation with people he had no interest in speaking to. He walked down the corridor with all the others in the flock and stepped out into the car park and took a good lungful of fresh air. It was a blessing as he had only been breathing in his own exhaled carbon dioxide all day and no fresh air whatsoever, it felt nice, it felt clean.

He went to bay 4 of the car park, where there was a space reserved for the office manager, that was him. The company only had limited parking spaces and he was fortunate enough to be granted one of them with MR Allen taking another. The rest, no more than 10 or so spaces were shared on a first come- first served basis between the rest of the employees. It really was one hell of a debacle on certain days when everybody chose to drive into work. After successfully managing to avoid any unwanted attention, Colin climbed into his black Toyota Corolla and drove the short distance home.

Chapter 4: VW Golf or Toyota Corolla?

Forget Porsches, Jaguars, or Mercedes-Benzes, even super-cars like Ferraris or Lamborghinis, why spend tens or sometimes hundreds of thousands of pounds on glorified shopping transporters, when a small but conventional family saloon will do the job just as well and at a fraction of the cost. Some people have more money than sense, but I am not some people, I am me and that is my choice.

Colin Stevens had always been a fan of economy cars, both for their initial price compared against so-called super-cars and then the value of them in running costs, a double whammy in his eyes. Although not many would admit it, he did, he loved the VW Golf, he made no secret about it and often spoke about them with great affection. Even though he had not actually owned one himself, he had driven a couple. Some friends or acquaintances had purchased them in the past and he had been allowed to borrow them on a couple of occasions when he needed them, and he felt that they were such an easy, comfortable drive. Although he had an affinity to the VW Golf his favourite car of all time had always been the Toyota Corolla, ever since he had seen his first one at an early age it was the one make and model he always wanted to own, and he always knew he would fight tooth and nail to own one when he could afford to buy one for himself, the shape, the slickness, everything about it he loved, most definitely the car for him.

It had taken a couple of years of scrimping and saving with a couple of sacrifices of things he really wanted thrown in, but he finally managed to get the money together and he headed down to the Toyota dealership. He knew that this way he would enjoy it more as he had put in the time and effort to earn it, also the sacrifice to warrant ownership, thus enjoying it was his right and something he felt he had to do, he wanted to do, he needed to do. The car is calling out to be driven and he was just the guy to do it.

There were some Corollas on the forecourt, not many, but enough to give him goosebumps knowing that before too long one of them could, no scratch that, one of them would be his. He stood there for a few minutes admiring them all lined up together just like an identity parade down the police station and he had seen a few of them in his time, from both sides of the law. He had the choice of a few colours but there was only one for him and when he caught sight of it, he knew immediately. There were two red ones, a yellow one and a green one but Colin had never been into summer or spring colours, it was not what he was about at all, he was into darkness and more gothics than light, he was the dead of night and black was the only option he was interested in. He'd already seen it, even though it was tucked away behind the others it stood out more to him than any of them. It was the most majestic black Corolla he could have wished for; the search was over; he had found the perfect one. It was jet black with tinted windows, and he fell in love with it at first sight, he had to have it and signed on the dotted line that very day. He was now the very proud owner of his very own black Toyota Corolla, a dream come true for him but a nightmare for anyone who got in his way.

Colin drove as he lived, 100 miles an hour and never giving way to anyone, he saw it as a sign of weakness or at least he felt others might try to take advantage if he conceded ground even in the slightest, so he never did. He had been pulled over by the police countless times and accrued so many speeding tickets that he had genuinely lost count, but he really didn't care as he never paid them anyway, choosing instead to just throw them into the glove compartment of his car as he had seen on so many U S tv cop shows. So far it had worked as he hadn't been called to trial so he must be doing something right or else he was just darned lucky that the police never followed up on their earlier enquiries. Who knows what they may have found on him if they had, who knows indeed? Or it could even be they knew both who he was and where he was, but they were biding their time before choosing the perfect opportunity to nab him, it seemed feasible although it really didn't make that much sense. Now it was a game of cat and mouse, a game of waiting, not just for him but for them too. The fact that he went by more than one name he seemed to believe was to his advantage and may keep them one step behind, for now at least. Every time he was pulled over and it wasn't a cop that had arrested him before he would use one of the different names on a new driving license, he had plenty and used this system to keep one step ahead of them, but if it turned out to be one of the cops that had already pulled him over he would use his Colin Stevens license so as not to bring any new attention to himself, attention he could really do without. All he had to do was remember which Cop he had shown which licence to, that was proving a tricky prospect each new time, but for now he was on top of it.

Chapter 5: Connie Jones.

Connie was lovely, she was strong-willed enough not to take any shit I gave her, but she was brave enough to be in the room with a convicted killer and all in the name of a story for her paper. In what was deemed at the time a man only world, she was a woman trying to break through the sex barrier. I thought I could help her out by giving her a boost, all the while helping myself at the same time. Two birds, one stone so-to-speak, and it seemed to work, barring a couple of tiny mishaps but that can happen to anyone, anytime.

Connie Jones worked as a reporter for The Independent newspaper, a position she had held for several years. Waking up in the morning was no longer the chore, or problem it had been during her previous jobs, it was now a pleasure and a highlight of each day for her. It was a good reason for her to rise with the sun and the larks in the morning, she was both happy and content. Sure, there were one or two days thrown in that never met the standards of others, but shit happens. Is that not par for everyone in all walks of life and it does you good to have a little moan every now and then, that's what she told herself, anyway. But overall, she loved her job, she lived for it and more than that she was very good at it and her efforts were starting to get her recognised and rewarded as being one of the best newcomers to the reporting world or media.

Today was a special day for her personally. As a reward for all her hard work and recognition she was being let loose and was out of the newsroom on her way to prison to do an interview with convicted killer and serial rapist, Colin Stevens. Dubbed The Cotton Mill Rapist, a name he detested, by her peers and others in the media he had requested her in person as he was a fan of her work, or at least the work he had read of hers, thus far. He believed if anyone could do his story justice and get him known again and stop him rotting away like an unattended corpse, then it was her.

She couldn't believe her luck when her Editor called her in to his office and told her that Colin Stevens had wanted to do an interview and she was the only one he would talk to. She was surprised and a little wary because she had never met him in person before and only knew about him from what she had read in the papers, so why her and why now in particular? She was both excited and a little fretful or apprehensive in equal measures as she had never met a serial killer or a rapist before, or at least not to her knowledge. It's possible there could have been one or two somewhere down the line but if there were she had no idea of who or when and they hid it well, and now she was killing two birds with one stone or one person if you like as Colin was both, a murderer, and a rapist.

Chapter 6: What is a serial killer?

Am I or aren't I? I guess you could argue the facts. I never saw myself as a serial killer until I read the definition and yes, I was one, without a doubt.

Connie looked at the piece paper that she held firmly in her hand, written on it was the definition of a serial killer that she had printed off the internet, she had studied it in a hope to get a feeling for how Colin may be or could feel when she meets him, she really had no idea what to expect from him as this was all new to her. She hoped she wouldn't crack or faulter in any way or show signs of weakness, but many experienced reporters had come and gone before her who was to say she wouldn't go the same way. She started reading the letter for the umpteenth time, just trying to get all the information into her brain and keep it there, time was not on her side, and she was fighting a losing battle that she so drastically wanted to win. Once the pendulum starts to swing, where it lands is anyone's guess, but for now she could really do with a helping hand on where it comes to a stop. Tampering is not an option cheating just makes the innocent as guilty as the criminals and that was not what she was about and certainly not how she wanted to be remembered. She read on……

"A serial killer is someone that murders 3 or more people, usually in service of abnormal psychological gratification, with the murders taking place over more than a month and probably including a significant period of time between them.

Psychological gratification is the usual motive for a serial killer but can also involve a means of sexual gratification, even with the corpse known as necrophilia. According to the FBI, motives of serial killers can include anger, thrill-seeking, financial gain and more commonly just attention seeking on their own behalf.

The murders can be similar in style for one killer and the victims often have something in common: I.E., demographic profile as in similar appearance, gender, or race." On occasions, the killer is known to have taken a small souvenir of his crime, maybe a lock of hair, a drop of blood or in this case a button from the clothing of his victim.

She'd added the last bit on herself in red pen as a reminder to herself, to make it stand out as it was personal to the subject she was going to be interviewing him about, and didn't want to forget anything, or just leave it to chance. She wanted to be as professional as she could, to do such a flawless job that it would be impossible for them to leave her out of future stories and other such events. Even though they denied it on many occasions, it was a man's world she worked in, and a woman had to be exceptional to make it and that is what she was aiming for, this was what she was ultimately striving for, being exceptional in every way possible or at least making them believe she was. When she was younger her father told her she would be exceptional at whatever she did and she didn't want to let him down or prove him wrong, she had come too far to let that happen now.

Chapter 7: Welcome to Salworth Prison.

What can you do in prison but obey the rules and keep the guards sweet? If you break them, you are punished, yet you are still expected to be around and see the same faces every day. A smiling face is so much better than a miserable grump any day of the week. If you don't break the rules and stay on the straight and narrow, then the relationship is better for all involved.

Some people take exception to being bossed around, of course they do as they have not had people run their life for them before. These are the ones that rebel, even if they know only too well it is futile in the long run. Rebelling is something I just wouldn't do as I need to live as ordinary a life as I can. Privileges, no matter how small are better than no privileges at all.

Once they are caught and incarcerated, serial killers just seem to disappear into the system somewhere and are left to rot away slowly, but Colin decided he wasn't prepared to let that happen to him, hopefully never but certainly not yet. He wanted to be in the limelight again even if it was his one last shot of fame, he felt at one point he had earned all the gloss and glamour and potential fear that came when people mentioned his name and he was ready for the infamy once again. Connie Jones seemed to be the only way he thought it was possible to relive it. She had the nous, the brains and judging by her work the ideas and not to forget the platform of The Independent to be able to pull it off. Hopefully, she would prove worthy and live up to the hype he had so graciously afforded her.

It had been a good while since his arrest and conviction, so long in fact that he had drifted so far out of the limelight and was in such a dark place that he was hidden in the shadows or even the shadows of shadows. A dark place indeed with an unending bleakness that he could see only getting bleaker unless something drastic was done, and fast. Nobody was going to do anything for him anymore, it was up to him, and possibly now Connie, a lady who he had never met. He was putting his trust in her hands, all his faith in her. He had let himself down on so many occasions, hopefully this time it would be different and the choices he had made in picking her were the correct ones.

He was hoping he hadn't left it too late to put himself back out there again or at least his name as physically it wasn't possible for him personally to be there and get people talking about him again, mentioning his name just so people didn't forget him, he longed for the fame, he missed being the centre of attention. As with all serial killers he felt he had earned it so what gave people the right to just forget and move on with their lives, after all he couldn't.

With serial killing it is all done for the thrill and the fame of it and the renown that it may bring so they can bask in their own glory and marvel at what they have done, and always without fail at somebody else's cost. Once that is gone or taken, precious little remains for them and they retire back into the shell from which they originally emerged faster than a tortoise in danger backs into his, kind of like a prison cell really. Forgotten and lost like little children out on their own for the first time without their parents, they have no idea of how to survive and yet somehow manage. They need a direction to turn and how can you turn anywhere in a ten-foot by six-foot cell and everywhere you look are the same four walls. You can hang any picture up to disguise them but underneath they are still just the same four walls no matter how much you try to pretend they are not.

Colin Stevens stood up in his cell looking into the mirror, not made of glass as normal mirrors are, but a piece of shiny silver foil stuck to the wall with Sellotape which was peeling slightly at the edges and beginning to curl over. Glass was not permitted in the cells, at least not without guard supervision for obvious reasons. He shook his head and laughed a hearty laugh as he wondered how it had ever come to this.

He was two years into a life sentence for kidnapping, rape, and murder. He did what he did for the fun of it and just because he had the urge at any moment. He always knew he would get caught at some point, but it didn't stop him, if anything being caught spurred him on and gave him an added incentive but either way, he was fine with any outcome. With the way the case was turning against him at the time he felt he had made the right decision to hand himself in to Detective Martin Jackson when he did. He had no intention of running or hiding and looking over his shoulder at every noise he heard for the rest of his life, walking around petrified to live as he saw fit, it just wasn't in him to be fake when all his life he had played things for real. It would be a big mistake and let down to his own high morals or high expectancies to change now, so why should he bother and turn against everything he ever knew.

He was looking forward to today and had been for several weeks, ever since he decided he was going to do it, to tell his story. Today he was meeting with Connie Jones of The Independent, she was doing an article for the newspaper all about him and how he became the monster that he had turned into. Monster was their word and not his, but he could understand why they would think it. He was getting no financial gain whatsoever from telling his story and didn't want any, this was nothing to do with the money but all about him and a chance for him to quench his thirst for infamy. Just the simple opportunity for him to tell his story and let the world know who Colin Stevens really is and was but will probably never get the chance to be again.

He was going to tell her everything, leaving nothing out and maybe even throw in a few new facts that had never been made known before, just for good measure but only if he took to her and he saw no reason why he shouldn't. Depression had taken its' toll and it had been cutting into him like a knife for months. To subdue the pain, he needed the attention that he had lost over time and maybe, just maybe, that attention could drag him back from the edge of despair and stand him back in the realms of reality and possibly even put a smile back on his face. A face that had not had reason to smile for as long as he could remember. His frown most definitely needed to be turned upside down.

Connie Jones pulled into the parking space that had been allocated to her by the prison governor and turned off her engine. It was a good two-hour drive to the prison from her home, door to door and she had stiffened up a little on the journey. She climbed out of the car and walked around the car park for a few minutes, just to stretch her legs, once she had puffed a few nervous breaths out just to calm herself down, she felt ready, she was ready. It was a beautiful sunny day, not that she was going to see much of it being inside the prison but it's always nice to have sunshine or at least know it's there if you need it.

She returned to her car and opened the boot, pulling a bag forward to the edge and reaching in she pulled out a tape recorder and a stretch of wire. She plugged the wire into the recorder and pressed play and then spoke into the microphone, "Testing, testing, one two, one two. Connie Jones reporting from Salworth Prison on my way to interview Colin Stevens." She then pressed stop, rewind and then played it back. "Testing, testing, one two, one two, Connie Jones reporting from Salworth Prison on my way to interview Colin Stevens." it repeated. "Perfect" she said to herself and then checked the battery, it was fully charged. Failing that and in case of emergencies she had what no reporter should be without, her trusty notepad and pencil.

Colin was collected from his cell by one of the guards and was taken on a ten-minute walk through the prison confines to a room located on the second floor of the west wing. On the way they had to leave the south wing he was housed in and cross the courtyard to reach the west wing. He saw daylight and it was nice for him to feel the sun on his face even for that short amount of time, it was both blinding and perfect, simultaneously. When they finally reached where they were going, he was taken inside a room. There was nothing special about it just a ten-by-ten room with a desk in the middle and a window on one of the walls. Oddly, the window didn't face outside but onto the corridor of the building which may seem strange but was only there, really so the guards could look in on their prisoners rather than for lighting purposes. He was placed at the desk and told to wait as she wouldn't be too long.

Before the window was put in there had been a few incidents where the guards had been unable to see prisoners who had been fighting until it was too late and irretrievable damage had already been done. A few broken bones, some stab wounds and even bite marks were not uncommon, any weapon of choice really, if they can get hold of them of course. One lawyer was even stabbed with a shiv made from an old toothbrush that had been filed down to a point by one of his disgruntled clients after he was given a life sentence without parole when expecting only ten years, he was not a happy camper, and it was the only way he knew how to express his contempt. Colin had no intentions of hurting Connie Jones but with his track record nothing was guaranteed, and he couldn't blame the guards for making sure that they safeguarded her security. They had to err on the side of caution rather than take any unnecessary risks, it had backfired on them in the past and they were not willing to let it happen again.

 As he sat at the desk, the guard that had brought him from the cell said "Don't try anything Colin, we will be watching you at all times and it only takes a second for us to get in. You will be tasered with no hesitation so play nice and be a good boy, don't make us have to hurt you." Colin just nodded. He had been tasered on a few occasions and he really didn't like it, just thinking about it made his body shiver just as if someone had walked over his grave, boy did it hurt and not something he wanted to go through again.

Connie was a little nervous as she was walked through the prison by Steven one of the prison guards. He would unlock a gate, walk her through and then immediately lock the gate behind them. They must have gone through at least 10 gates with each one clanking closed with an earth shuddering noise just like the last, and walked down 10 long unwelcoming corridors, each one just as daunting as the last and all painted in a battleship grey colour as if they had got the paint as a job lot from the navy. Suddenly, Steven stopped and said, "here we are Miss Jones." They were standing by a door and Connie could see through the glass in the door that a man was already in the room and sitting at a desk. She could tell by the pictures she had seen of him that it was Colin Stevens, his hair was so much shorter, more prisonlike, but his facial features were the same. Her heart skipped a beat as the reality of it all hit her, she was only a few feet away from a convicted serial killer and with a little trepidation she walked into the room saying to herself, "This is it girl, this is what you have been waiting for. Don't fuck this chance up, just don't fuck it up or you may never get another."

As she entered the room Colin looked at her and smiled, he stood to greet her and shaking her hand said, "Hello Connie, nice to meet you at last, please take a seat." Spoken as if it was a room in his house, which it was, really. She sat down and he, like a true gentleman, kept standing until she was seated and then sat down opposite her. Connie replied, "Thank you and you too, I was a bit nervous I must admit. I half thought I would see you strapped down like Hannibal Lector in the movies, I really didn't know what to expect at all, this is my first trip to a prison."

Colin laughed before replying, "No nothing like that, I am well settled and it's all very informal here. The real psychos are still locked in their cells and are only allowed out at midnight for the witching hour." Connie laughed and shook her head, she thought it would all be very serious and didn't think Colin would have a sense of humour so, she felt a little more at ease with each passing second. He seemed human and nothing like she had pictured him.

She pulled out her tape recorder and after asking him if it was OK, to which he nodded yes, she then pressed play and spoke into the microphone, "Interview with Colin Stevens at Salworth Prison, Friday 16th June, 10:15 A.M. Those present are me Connie Booth, reporter for The Independent newspaper and convicted rapist/ murderer Colin Stevens. She then placed the tape recorder on the table in between them and waited, she waited a few minutes for Colin to begin and just sat back in her seat, made herself comfortable, well as comfortable as she could in the circumstances and she waited, and waited and then she waited some more. All in all, it took Colin about 10 minutes to say his first words. Why he waited she had no idea but thought he must have had his reasons. She put it down to the fact that he wanted to get it right and just like her, not mess it up for himself either.

C.S.   "Sorry for the delay Connie, just making sure of stuff. Before we get fully started, I must be honest and say although I remember a lot of what has happened some things are a bit of a blur and I had to get some help as to what happened and when, during my early years especially. Also, you may hear some things that are not easy to listen to, if you are in any way squeamish then we can stop now. I will be as honest as I can and try to leave nothing out. What you use from it is up to you, I will bow to your media judgement as to what needs to be included and what needs to be discarded."

C.J.   "Yes, that is fine Colin, I wouldn't remember everything in my life without a few pointers or reminders here and there to steer me in the right direction. I am a woman of the world and I have never seen myself as being squeamish at all, try me, give it your best shot."

C.S.   "O.K. then Connie, that's the formalities over with, let's get going, is there anywhere you would you like me to start?"

C.J.   "Not really, just where it all began Colin, why don't we go as far back as you can remember. Right back to the beginning and we can work our way through."

C.S.   "I won't start with once-upon-a-time or no crap like that and there will be no happy ever after I can assure you. If you need either of them then you are in the wrong place, this is not a fairy story. If you really want or need them, you can add them yourself at a later date maybe to enhance the story if it gets boring...OK here goes nothing..... or everything, who knows."

C.J.   "One thing I would like to ask is, just so I know what angle you are coming in from, have you ever regretted or felt you were wrong to do what you did to them?"

C.S.   "Without a doubt I know only too well what I did was wrong, oh God yes indeed I do, but I can't say I regretted it, not in the slightest because I did it so many times, and each time enjoyed it more. If anything at all and I am not saying yes here but the first one, possibly. If that hadn't happened, then who knows? We may not have been here now, but we are and that's how it goes, it's way too late to change anything now, that moment has come and gone."

I guess everyone has heard of the saying throwing away or breaking the mould at least once in their life and probably more. No matter what the meaning or true intention it is usually used loosely as a description of something that is so perfect that it cannot be bettered, so why would anyone even begin to try, but everyone does at some point in the hope of bettering a flagging relationship in a failing world. It is normally reserved for a hero, a friend or possibly even a loved one but can at times even though it may be very rare used to describe an inanimate object. Possibly a mini fridge where a man could keep his beer cool in preparation for the big match or a woman's plaything before she plugs it in and gives it a full charge to make it last through an orgasm are there just to name a couple. I believe there has never been a better case than there is in front of us now for doing the exact opposite, they should have thrown away or broken the mould before the creation of Colin Stevens, not after and for completely different reasons. If God truly existed then he would have stepped in and stopped the creation of what can only be described as a demon in human form.

After was way too late, it's like closing the gate after the horse has bolted, it serves no purpose whatsoever. Colin Stevens was an accident just waiting in the wings to happen and often did but could have so easily been stopped had the correct choices been made at the right times. Or rather he was a purpose waiting to happen because anything Colin Stevens did was no accident and usually involved eternal suffering for someone else, especially if they were female, young and pretty but most of all blonde.

Chapter 5: Sarajevo.

I was too young to know exactly what was happening around me. Although I was aware that there was some danger, I guess I never fully realised just how much. My parents and to a degree, my brother kept me as safe as they possibly could, until they disappeared. I never found out what had happened to them until later in my life and it just made me sad. Sometimes I wondered if knowing did me any good at all, but the fear of not knowing was much greater.

The real Colin Stevens was born Karol Jovanovic in Visoko, Bosnia, a small town just outside of Sarajevo, the Bosnian capital. Visoko, apparently world famous for its' pyramids believed to be the oldest in the world, but only if you are Bosnian and from Visoko, had been home to the Jovanovic family for decades. He lived with his mother Seraphina, his father Thomaz, and his elder brother Klaus.

Thomaz Jovanovic was working on the engine of the VW Golf he had acquired from Tvornica Automobila Sarajevo nearly 2 years earlier. It was a slow burner, but it kept him occupied when there wasn't much else to do. They were about to scrap it and therefore finish its' usefulness in the world by putting it through the crusher, so he offered to take it off their hands and vowed to restore it and return it to its' former glory. How? He had no idea, he had never worked on a car before, he just said what he felt they needed to hear in order for him to get himself a free car. He had the gift of the gab and wouldn't be surprised if there was Irish blood in his veins, maybe one day he will research his family lineage and find out for sure, but for now he would wait. He knew how to be convincing even if what he was saying was total bullshit and he and whoever it was he was giving it too probably did as well. In fact, after finally looking he found there was no Irish blood in the family whatsoever so he must have been born with the gift and could talk for his country, for Bosnia.

The VW Golf wouldn't start and apparently had not been driven for several years. It had also been placed at the back of the compound where nobody ever goes, it had been left to rot and rust before Thomaz saw it and against his wife's better judgement, decided he wanted it and had to have it at any cost. Well not exactly at any cost as money was extremely tight, in fact everything was tight in and around Sarajevo. Whatever they wanted for it he would bargain them down until they agreed to let it go for free or at least close to free as possible. If nothing else, it would give him something to do, something to work on and keep him occupied until he could manage to land a real job. It had been so long since he had been employed by anyone, he was thinking he would never be useful again. Feeling sorry for both himself and his family as all he wanted to do was provide for them and it made him feel like a complete failure as he couldn't even do that. Although it wasn't his fault in any way, he was a proud man and felt the pain and anguish.

 In the end no bargaining was needed at all as Tvornica Automobila were more than happy to get rid of such a piece of shit without having to dispose of it themselves. It saved them from an unnecessary trip to the scrapyard and said yes take it by all means, so long as you have the transport as they couldn't deliver. It was not by all means the best car in the world, but it was a car, and it was free, he had to look at the broader picture. It may have taken a few days but eventually he managed to talk one of his mates into towing it for him and it was dropped at his home where it had sat motionless since.

He had worked on it most days for the last two years, come rain or shine, summer or winter, whatever time he had to spare and even some he didn't. Time was precious but so were his family and he knew that he had at times neglected their needs to work on a fucked-up heap of shit that didn't even start, but one day, one day he will prove the doubters wrong. Sometimes he would work on it for only a few minutes but other days he would spend hours rubbing it down, cleaning it and filling in any cracks on the bodywork. So much so in fact that it was starting to look smart and like a proper motor again. If only I could get the engine to start, he thought to himself. How far he had come was amazing and everyone told him so but getting it to start would be up there with his best achievements or higher, like producing his two wonderful boys although it would only play second fiddle to them, it would possibly be next on the list, but don't tell Seraphina, she would be well-pissed if she knew that was how he felt.

From the vantage point where he was working which was just outside the door to the block of flats in which they lived, Thomaz could see his youngest son Karol shooting any unsuspecting passers-by with the stick he pretended was his very own AK47 assault rifle. It wasn't an ideal environment in which to raise children, but they were surviving and praying to God every night that the war would end, and only then could they live in peace, surely that wasn't much to ask. He saw Karol disappear for a second as he bent down and picked something up off the floor and watched as he ran into the block of flats holding his hand across his chest. He wondered what was up and was just about to head inside to check everything was alright when Karol re-emerged, picked up his stick and continued playing war as if nothing had happened. Maybe if he had trusted his instincts and followed him inside then he could have staved off a lifetime of misery for many people. Although he had no idea at the time, Karol's life turned in a completely new direction that day due to this one option. Choosing to turn left when he should have gone right so to speak, and Thomaz could easily have helped if he hadn't ignored his own nagging doubt. Should he have zigged instead of zagged, but Thomaz was never to know and by unlucky circumstances was never going to get the chance find out.

Thomaz' big worry was that one day, when his two sons Klaus and Karol were old enough, they would be conscripted into the army and forced to fight in this goddamn vile war and be maimed or worse, possibly even die for a cause they knew nothing about or even cared for. But with a bit of good fortune and plenty of praying to God, the war would finish before they reached the minimal age to be conscripted which was 14.

Praying to God was something Thomaz took very seriously, and the entire family would all dress up in their best clothes and go to church as a family on a Sunday morning. Even though the church had been damaged by war and scarred by its' remnants and no repairs had been made to it yet due to the funding shortages wartime can bring, and yet somehow it still felt to him like God was there for him when he wanted to be heard. It was a sacred place not just for him and his family, but also for just about everyone else in the village. It was the only place that was full to over-brimming week in week out without question, the power of believing gives one the strength one needs in the most demanding of times.

Both Klaus and Karol were being home-schooled as their school had been destroyed in the bombing and for the same reason as their church had not been repaired, also because a private education costs money, so that was not an option. Money is a scarce commodity in and around Sarajevo. Not just Sarajevo in fact, all over Bosnia people were doing whatever they could just to get by, to survive and when survival instincts kick in who knows what anyone is capable of. Although they were both quick learners the added distraction of being home slowed them both down considerably. Nothing to do with the teaching being done by their mum, she was doing everything in her power to help and doing it well, but more to do with the fact home schooling is nothing like a proper classroom education. There were far less distractions in a classroom, especially for two such young lads being taught in and amongst all their toys and personal belongings. They didn't have much but what they did have was right there. It was so easy for their minds or even their hands to keep wandering off on some weird and wonderful adventure or another and their mother to keep asking them why they couldn't keep still. It was almost as if they had ants in their pants, which they found to be very funny, and they used this as another distraction.

Although she was angry with them, she couldn't stay that way for long as it was just nice to hear them laugh. Laughter was also a disappearing commodity and slowly drifting away and becoming a thing of myth. Dirty faces filled with frowns were the new order of the day and more commonplace than ever before. One day it will change they kept telling themselves, maybe one day they will believe it too.

Food too was scarce, and meals were made up of whatever was available on any given day, anything that they could pick or catch which, all in all, was not very much. Occasionally there would be a small treat here and there, like an apple if they could scrump one from the farmer without getting caught, or if they were very lucky a chocolate bar to share between them but only on the rare occasion that a little money found its' way to them, but it had been a long time since they'd had one of them. A staple diet usually consisted of rice or potatoes and some other vegetables that came to hand. Maybe on the odd time here and there, they happened to catch a rabbit or squirrel then the protein off them came in very handy, it was like a slap-up feast. They could almost taste it already as they watched their father skin and prepare it and he could see the excitement that was in their eyes.

It's the simple things in life that can bring the most pleasure. Sitting down as a family to eat each night meant everything to him and when that included the extra protein a little portion of meat can bring then so much more the better. Karol would often disappear upstairs after dinner and practise gutting and skinning one of his old teddy-bears like his dad had done with the rabbit but with the knife he had found on the street. The one he kept hidden in the underwear drawer in his bedroom the secret he kept hidden from everyone, even his brother. The knife he had found as his dad had been distracted while working on his car and not noticed he had disappeared inside with it hidden under his T-shirt. Little knowing of course that he had been noticed.

His father had an idea something was amiss and had been waiting for him to slip up, but even at such a young age he was devious enough to stay one step ahead and had no intentions of losing his now favourite new possession. He kept moving it if he felt his dad was getting in too close but always returned it to the drawer until he could find a more secure place. Although Thomaz had no idea what he was looking for or even where to start he hoped he would catch Karol off guard, but he never did, he had to admire Karol's tenacity even if he was a little peeved with the sneaky, conniving bastard, but he hid it well or so he believed, Karol on the other hand was only too aware what was happening and his dad's words were falling on deaf ears.

At getting on for nearly 4 years of age, Karol had seen more than any 3-year-old should ever have to see. Death, murder, genocide, torture, mutilation, rape and more blood and gore than anyone else would or should see in ten lifetimes. The soldiers would come into town starving and horny and take whatever they wanted. Food, drink, valuables, money or even the local women were not sacred to them. The women were often raped and battered in front of them and left for dead as they moved on like a swarm of locusts hunting their next victim. So much for these being the guys that we're supposed to be protected by, the self-titled heroes. It was dog-eat-dog and funnily enough even the dogs joined in as food was that scarce and they would hang around for any discarded scraps, but not long enough to become one themselves.

 Karol's daily haunts were bomb craters where he would hang out and play pretend war using a stick as an AK47, just like the ones' he had seen the soldiers use so many times, He liked throwing a stone or two as if they were grenades by pulling a pretend pin out, throwing it as far as he could and ducking from the devastation and carnage a real one may have caused. It was all a great adventure to him but a complete nightmare for his parents when their only aim was to keep him safe and yet there were so many dangers. He knew how to pretend so well because he had seen the after-effects from when the real grenades had exploded and the devastation they caused and the blood and guts then were not just a figment of his imagination, they were true to life memories.

When Seraphina Jovanovic called in her three favourite guys for tea, the three being Thomaz her husband and her two sons Klaus and Karol, it was exactly six o'clock on the dot, as had come to be expected from Seraphina. Her timekeeping was impeccable and she somehow managed to do it all without owning a watch.

Six o'clock was the usual time for them to sit together as a family to eat. Even if they had their own adventures or tasks in the days or lay in bed alone at night, at least they had the hour or so it took to finish tea together as a family. But more than just time together, it was a special family time that you could never get back if ever missed. So many families never got the chance to sit with their loved ones as they were taken too soon and quickly became just another statistic of the war.

You could almost set your watch by her timing as she was never late. Occasionally she had been a tad early but only by seconds but without fail she was never late. Tonight, they were having a stew made from leftover meat and potatoes. Not much of a last supper perhaps but then again, they had no idea of the events that were about to unfold. There was no clue that the meal they were about to sit down to was going to be their last together, I mean how could there be? They sat down together, they talked while they ate, small talk, laughing at something trivial. Then afterwards, cleaning dishes away to the sink, washing up, everyone doing their bit. Sitting a while together before Seraphina taking her youngest up to his crib but letting the oldest have a little longer. Tonight, rightly, or wrongly fate was going to throw this small-town ordinary family such a curved ball that by the time it had landed on the floor three of them would be dead and the youngest would be an orphan.

Karol was certainly no stranger to the horrors and torment of war as has been made clear already, with the destruction he had witnessed, but on this fateful night his resolve was about to be taken to a whole new level as a misguided, loose mortar shell landed on the family home exploding and destroying everything in its' path and ruining his chance of any sort of normal future. His mother Seraphina, his father Thomaz and his brother Klaus were all killed outright but Karol somehow survived. He was upstairs in his crib in the only part of the house that hadn't collapsed. He was buried for nearly 22 hours in fallen debris and loose rubble until rescued by neighbours who had no idea that he was alive until they heard his muffled screams and sobs and so began the mad rush to dig him out before he too became a victim.

After they had heard his faint sobs it took them nearly 5 hours to free him from the ruins and a further 2 days to find the remains of the rest of his family and to free them from their temporary graves. When they finally reached him, they were shocked that someone could survive in the conditions and covered in that amount of rubble. It turned out that although he had been unlucky enough to be caught up in the blast in the first place, he was lucky by the position he finished up, it saved his life. His crib was shock-blasted about 10 feet across the bedroom floor and came to a halt against the far wall, the only wall that remained upright after the blast. Also, the base of the crib snapped, dropping down and forming a V shape into which Karol slipped and the sides of the crib caved in to form a protective layer against the masonry and debris that was piling on top.

The conditions were cramped, and he was in pain, but he had air to breath, fresh air was getting into his lungs and somehow it was helping him to breath, a real lifesaver, if only he had some water. When his rescuers, or neighbours as they turned out to be managed to reach him and free him, they were doubly shocked, one by the lack of injuries he appeared to have suffered and two by the vice like grip he had on his Teddy-Bear. Either he loved that Teddy more than anything or he was stuck in a reassuring comfort pose with the only thing that was there to help him through such a seemingly impossible situation.

Fear was still abundant in his eyes, and he was not letting go at any cost. In the end it was decided that they just had to let him take it with him in the ambulance as he was rushed off to hospital.

Three weeks earlier.

I was changing, I could tell that much myself. I may well have only been little more than an infant, but I was growing up faster than my mind would let me believe possible. Whether it was real or not my teddy bear was talking to me, or was it? Could it really have been that I was on the slippery road to Crazyville, or was it just a place in the back of my mind that I went to be alone, my sanctuary?

Paranoia was beginning to creep into Karol's life as he was under the impression that someone, although he had no idea who or why was trying to steal his knife. His father was acting guilty, whether he just felt it, or the knife had told him he wasn't sure, but he sensed it and there was no way he was going to relinquish control of the only possession he had gained for himself with no help from anyone and kept moving it from one place to another, just in case. It was his and his alone. Yes, a bad case of paranoia was really taking over him and the first real signs of rot were setting in, establishing themselves in the part of his brain usually reserved for sanity.

He was changing and not for the better but worst of all he seemed incapable of doing anything about it, he was being swept along on the crest of the wave, every time he fell off, he picked himself up, dusted himself down and vowed never to be caught by it again. It worked to a point, but life is so complicated and so out there that one can't help but fall into its trap at some time or other and Colin was falling hook, line, and sinker without a hope of being rescued. The future Colin Stevens was being moulded by the shell that is Karol

Jovanovic although he had no idea of what was to come, he was just being swept along and going along for the ride.

Wrapped up in the socks in his chest of drawers was a decent first choice but only as a temporary hiding place and without a doubt not a permanent solution. He knew it wouldn't take a rocket scientist or genius to find it, especially laundry day, so he started thinking of new places, more secure places that he could find to stash it. After a few different options which were quickly discarded for reasons not even worth discussing he came up with the brilliant idea of his favourite Teddy-Bear. If he could manage to cut a small hole in the body, he may well be able to slide the knife inside and he would be able to hold it close to himself and know exactly where it was always. His favourite Teddy-Bear guarding his favourite possession, yes that was the way for him to proceed, a plan he saw with no drawbacks. Surely nobody would ever believe that such a cute Teddy Bear could hide a secret, especially such a dark secret as an army issue knife that could have possibly killed many people and may yet kill many more.

After using the knife in question to make the small incision he then pushed it up into the torso of the Teddy and it fitted perfectly, no lumps, no bumps it looked just like an everyday Teddy Bear that a kid or sometimes an adult would love and cherish. He held it close to his chest and gave it a squeeze and there was no inclination that anything was hidden in the belly of the beast, well his cuddly Teddy anyway, it could never be classed as a beast. Every night he would go to bed clutching it and hugging it as if his life depended on it and when he was out, he would place it lovingly in his crib as if it was waiting for him to return.

So, when he was found and rescued by whoever the kind people were and then taken to hospital clutching his beloved Teddy-Bear, he had ulterior motives. He did love the Teddy, that part is not disputed but he loved the knife more and without the Teddy-Bear's help the knife would have vanished and been lost in the annals of history, forever, and Karol was not ready for that to happen, not now, not ever.

Karol, of course, had no idea where his parents or brother were, he guessed they had gone in another ambulance or else they would be waiting at the hospital to greet him and give him a big hug and be happy to see him, happy to see that he was okay. Little did he realise their true fate or the fact that he would never see them again.

He was whisked off to hospital in the ambulance as soon as he was pulled from the rubble and his rescue completed. Once he arrived at the hospital he was treated for his wounds, which proved to be only superficial considering how well buried in the rubble he had been, but he was kept in for observations overnight, just in case, and who would take him in anyway, all his relatives had been killed although this fact he didn't find out till much later. In the hospital he kept calling for his mummy but of course she never came, and nobody dared to tell him that she wouldn't ever come again because she had died as had his father and brother too, I mean how can you tell that to anyone let alone a three-year- old?

In time he would learn to forget.

How unlucky the Jovanovic's were that night was not to be known for a few weeks or at least until the official army reports had been issued and only then was it made a public fact that their house was the only one hit that night. The bomb that hit their house was from friendly fire as they call it, but what can be friendly about dying, whoever or whatever kills you, it's not something a friend would do or ever even consider, not for a moment. The report issued also stated that if the bomb had landed a mere twenty yards away it would have landed in the street and avoided them and everyone else. In that case casualties would have been zero instead of the count of three that they had on their records, alas it didn't, and the official count of three still stands. In the result of friendly fire, the person or persons involved were not told, ever. It was bad enough having to kill anyone even in time of war let alone knowing you are responsible for innocent people and fellow countrymen/women and children at that, losing their lives and having it on your conscience as well. Accidents happen at the most inopportune moments, but that is what they are, accidents. It would be a pointless exercise blaming someone for something that was never meant. What would be the point?

Now an orphan, Karol was taken into care and placed in the protection of the Children's Welfare Society. Although he was moved around constantly, he spent most of the next 6 months in homes for war-orphaned children in and around Sarajevo until it was deemed unsafe for him to remain due to the ongoing dangers of warfare, and he was put up for adoption, solely for his own protection and safety. Anywhere away from here is the best place for him now whether he believed it or not, he of course didn't have any choice in the matter, it was out of his hands. His future now was placed in the hands of complete strangers who apparently knew what was best for him, but did they really? He now had to depend on complete strangers, when depending on family hadn't turn out too well for him, why should this be any different, life is shit he kept telling himself, he could see it, he could feel it and one day he will believe it for real.

Every new day was exactly like the last, complete Deja-vu. He would wake up, have his breakfast, usually a piece of buttered toast and a cup of watered-down tea, no milk, and then immediately afterwards he would be told to vacate the premises and not return until tea-time. That would give them just enough time to spring clean the place from top to bottom and keep it in a habitable condition. He would be given a sandwich and a bottle of water and be expected to walk the streets for the next 6 or 7 hours. What he chose to do in that time was entirely up to him so long as any repercussions didn't make it back to them. He like everyone was on a three strikes rule. If the cops were called on you three times, for whatever reason, then you were kicked out and would have to relinquish the room and nice cosy bed and then be left to fend for yourself. That was your chance, or three chances and if you wasted them, that was just tough luck and you never got another. They would wash their hands of you preferring to spend their valuable time and what little money they had on somebody that in their words "Wanted help and wouldn't abuse their trust."

He spent most of the day hanging around with some of the other kids from the orphanage and getting into minor scrapes, but nothing too serious and managed, with a good deal of resilience and an even bigger slice of luck, to keep himself in care and hold onto the cosy bed that he was given. Then one day from out of the blue a couple from England, John and Adele Stevens saw his picture, fell in love with him and wanted to give him the home he craved, the home they felt he deserved after hearing his story. They had been having problems conceiving and decided adoption was the way forward.

Although there were plenty of children available for adoption in England, they took it upon themselves to go further afield and help a child from a different country and free them from the horrors of war. Karol was that child and they wanted more than anything to help him. Although they were taken by surprise at how quickly the process had progressed, they were also excited at getting a son sooner than they ever imagined they would. Maybe another person around the house may ease the minor problems they were having, the back chatting and snide remarks that were creeping in and it seemed to do the trick. They channelled all their love and affection into him, and things calmed down for a while at least.

Things were starting to look up for Karol and he was getting swept along with all the excitement, what could go wrong and all the psychotic thoughts he had while he was in Bosnia had died down, for now at least. Maybe it would have been easier for them to see what could have gone right. Sure, it would mean moving to a strange country also learning a new language, but it was decided for Karol this was his best option. Possibly the only option to avoid him falling into the criminal underworld that was rife around where he lived. He had done well so far especially under the circumstances he had found himself in, but the experts were seeing signs that he was getting more and more frustrated with every-day living and put it down to a rebellion against the system and being kicked out of what he classed as his home. As always, frustration goes together with trouble, so those supposedly in the know could see no other option. It was only small things at first that go unpunished but afterwards they hit you hard and make you pay, before finally dumping you on the compost heap of shit called real life to normal people.

We have all been there at some point in our lives and although we promise ourselves, we will never return, it is inevitable really that one day we end up right back in amongst all the crap we try our best to avoid and pretend does not exist. Shit happens as they say, but so does life and to give in would be a travesty to all the hard work put in to stay on the straight and narrow. Work hard, play hard but never lose sight of reality, easier said than done in a few cases especially when reality is not real and just a made-up fantasy in ones' mind. That is how Karol felt almost all the time, unsure, scared and confused and now alone in a scary new world, he had to adapt and quickly before he was lost forever. If he didn't do it for himself then no-one was going to do it for him, he would no doubt have ended up being just another statistic in a hate filled world of lies and debauchery that is downtown Sarajevo. A vicious, war-torn hovel for anyone, but especially one so young as he.

Chapter 4: A new life.

I loved Helena, she was the only one that told me anything, she kept me informed as and when things happened and never ever said it in a frightening tone or voice. Everybody else just made up the numbers of dead wood in my life. They locked me in my room and to them, that was their job done. I would go as far as to say if all women were like Helena, then I would not have turned out like I did. She would have rescued me from my ever-spiralling journey and put me back on the path to righteousness, she was that special.

I believe she wanted to adopt me herself but was told it wasn't feasible. It would have been a mercy adoption, being governed by heart rather than reality and in any case, they already had a couple lined up. The rest they say is history.

The adoption went as smoothly as it could possibly have and Karol travelled to England accompanied by Helena Savic, a social worker from the paediatric department who was there to ensure the handover went to plan. She also helped to break down the translation barrier built as strong as the great wall of China that had sprung up between them, she just told herself although it was strong, nothing was impenetrable. Helena was lovely, she was softly spoken and never shouted, not even once and would often hold his hand to comfort him when he felt scared and reassure him everything was going to be OK. If she believed it herself or not was another thing but he saw no need to doubt her as she had not lied to him yet or at least as far as he was aware.

Once in England, he was introduced to his new adoptive parents at Heathrow Airport, they had travelled from their hometown to meet him. From that moment on 4-year-old Karol Jovanovic ceased to exist and 4-year-old Colin Stevens was created to live out the life that had been taken from Karol and transferred as his own.

When they arrived at the house that he was to call his home he was a little shell-shocked and frightened to say the least as this was a complete change for him and the entire situation had him quivering with fright. Both of his new parents were doing their best to make him welcome, by giving him big hugs, and kisses on the forehead as they would walk by in the hope it would help him settle in quickly, but to no avail. He was really struggling and was finding it hard to cope with the change. The language barrier was overwhelming, and he thought he would never get the hang of the English language and why should they learn Bosnian as they didn't have any plans to visit his homeland. He just wanted to go back even if it meant trying to survive on the streets, why was the choice made for him by someone he didn't know and would probably never meet, just a name at the bottom of a document, a signature.

Helena, the social worker explained to John and Adele that he would need a little time to settle in, she explained that it wouldn't happen overnight and in some very rare cases could take upwards of weeks or even months. She said she would hang around for as long as needed but would take a back seat to give them the chance they need to make a bond and help them translate when needed. So, they also backed off a little to let him do things at his own pace, and to bide his time and let him settle in a way he felt more comfortable. She also told them that by trying to force him would only cause resentment and rejection, something she or they didn't want for Colin or themselves, especially after all the effort to get this far.

It took a few weeks for Colin to start settling in a little better and although he was still slightly edgy and nervous at his new surroundings, he was more open with both John and Adele. He had learned very basic English taught to him by his new parents and he was beginning to realise he was safe where he was and there was no gunfire or explosions going on around to be fearful of, a world of love and smiles but a few cross words thrown in here and there, but he learned to ignore them. After a while as the memories faded, Colin learned to forget that his family had died in such horrific circumstances, or in fact that he'd had a family or a life in Bosnia at all. Age was on his side, and he had a new life to live. A second chance that many were never blessed with. He remembered certain things, at different times but they were too vague to determine when or where they had happened in his life, if in fact they had happened at all and were not just stories made up to appease him.

He started feeling secure and for the first time in a good while he started feeling loved. He was sent to school which was a whole new experience for him as he had never been to one before. Home schooling was a thing of the past and learning became his life with no added distractions, he wanted to know about anything and everything. He was a very bright boy and picked up English very quickly, then, slowly but surely losing the Bosnian accent that he had lived with for the first 4 years of his life began to sound like he had been born local and had always lived local.

Things went swimmingly for about two years until around the time the arguments restarted. John and Adele's problems had flared up again and they argued over just about anything that could be argued about and then some. Their drinking got out of hand and that's when the violence and abuse started, and Colin was caught right in the middle of it all and taking the full force of both their anger as a double whammy. When he would try to protect his mother and stop her taking a beating then he would get hell for from his father and likewise, when he tried to protect his father then he would get hell for from his mother. He just couldn't win as it was an impossible position to be in no matter what he said or tried to do it was always the wrong choice and before long a lot of their resentment and hatred was deflected from each other and focused mainly on him. He was the smallest and weakest, it was easier to prey on him than each other, survival of the fittest and that certainly wasn't him.

He mostly heard their shouting and screaming from behind the bedroom door where he had on countless times locked himself in for his own protection. He was sad and couldn't help but show his emotions, he cried nearly every day and through his tears, which made things blurry he could see the bruises that had been inflicted on his arms, legs, and body from the constant beatings he had taken, through no fault of his own. Just a case of being in the wrong place at the wrong time. He should really stop getting involved but feared if he didn't then someone would be killed.

Four years later.

Four years is a long time in any scenario but in my case so much happened that I just couldn't keep track of it all. I had lost my family, been torn away from my homeland, and taken to live with two strangers. I had to try and adapt to new surroundings where I also had to learn a brand-new language. Once all that was sorted and things were looking up for me, well. Lightening does strike twice. I lost another family, albeit in different circumstances, and now, once more I was alone again and wondering what was going to happen. I felt the time had come for me to take my life into my own hands again and fuck all the do-gooders that pretend they are trying to help when all they are really doing is collecting a whopping great big wage at my expense, fuck them all.

It had taken a while but all of Colin's worst fears came true in the blink of an eye, he woke with a start, a tense nervous feeling took over his entire body, he was in a strange bed, in a strange room he didn't recognise. He tried to adjust his eyes the best he could, but he couldn't get a clear view of anything, it was all just a blurred vision. He had no idea at the time as he lifted his head off the sweat-soaked pillow that his vision was blurred because his eye socket was fractured from a blow, a hard crack he took from the back of the hand of his adopted mum last night. She was only small and slight of build, but boy could she hurt. He didn't think there was a single person alive she didn't have the capability of damaging. He dropped his head back down on to the pillow as his neck was rather stiff and had a crick in it. He lay back and stared straight up at the ceiling, what is happening he asked himself, where am I? And then the memories came flooding back one by one and all he could think was, oh Christ, once again I am alone.

He may have had no idea where he was exactly, but Colin certainly knew why he was there, there was no getting away from the horrors of the previous night, no matter how hard he tried to blank them out. He raised his head from his pillow once more, a pillow still soaked in sweat resulting from the full-on terror of an 8-year-olds' nightmare. After all he was only trying to protect his father as any son or daughter would do. He felt a lump in his throat, so took a deep breath of air in to try and compose himself even just for a second, but in his mind all he could see was the knife being thrust into his fathers' chest cavity time and time again. All he remembered thinking was thank God it wasn't the knife he had hidden or else they would take it away and he had owned it too long to let it just be taken away from him. Obsession is a strange old trait, once it is inside you there is no getting rid and it was most definitely inside him and growing like an infectious disease with every passing second, minute, hour. He was treading a dangerous path, a very dangerous path indeed.

Colin felt warm, but not in a good way, not a happy warmth, feeling miserable and slightly damp down below. When he lifted the blankets, he could see a wet patch in the bed round about the area where his genitals had been resting. He had urinated, not a lot, but enough, how much is too much really when it comes to pissing the bed, he thought to himself. He made excuses for himself as one might, but still felt it was not normal behaviour and so he wouldn't tell anyone. He would just leave it for them to find and by the time they did he would be long gone, that was his plan anyhow. The fear he had lived through last night was still there and just thinking about it all made him even more terrified, and for a split second he wondered, where was she, could she be there, hiding in the shadows just waiting for her moment. After all he was one of only three that knew exactly what had happened and maybe, just maybe she would do anything or everything she could to stop him talking and in so doing, maybe condemn her. She had done plenty to him before so what was to stop her now, she had no cares or worries left in the world and the life as she knew it was basically over so she could do what she wanted and when she wanted to who she so chose and that could easily mean him.

Of the three people that knew the true events of last night. One, his father was dead, so he couldn't say a thing. Two, his mother had been taken away by the police and who knows if they had released her or what she had been capable of making them believe. And three, himself, an eight-year- old kid unsure and still confused about anything and everything. He knew what he had seen but didn't know why it had happened. What could he say that could make anything better and what could he do, either way he had lost one parent and was more than likely going to lose the other one as well? Colin had a smart head on his shoulders, especially for one so young but on this day, rightly or wrongly he was somehow forced into becoming a man at the tender age of only eight. He decided to keep quiet and not say a word to the police as he felt it would only result in complications for both himself and his mum. He didn't give a flying crap about her but felt stoking the boiler may have deeper repercussions for all involved. After a fair bit of deliberation and pacing back and forth across his room his decision was that he must run away and hide for as long as he possibly could. If he couldn't be found then he couldn't be questioned, it seemed the most feasible option.

He walked over to the door and tried the handle. It was locked from the outside. He had a feeling it would be but thought he would try it anyway. Not knowing what else he could do, he moved back and sat himself down on the edge of the bed, avoiding of course the wet patch, he had enough of that for a lifetime although he felt it may not be the last time, he did hope. He may have to be an adult in some ways but in reality, he was still just a kid.

All he desperately wanted was for someone to tell him last night was just a nightmare and hadn't really happened although deep down he knew it had. Or even for someone to give him a big hug, just to pull him into their chest and tell him everything was going to be fine, but again, no chance. They were all running around like busy ants trying to work out what was best in his interests and what to do with him next. Why was his life, and possibly his entire future all down to these strangers he had never met before? He wanted out and to have the chance to make his own decisions and was willing to do anything to get away. He began to hatch a plan, it may take some time to implement it, but he was darned sure he was going to try his best to get it up and running as soon as was humanly possible, now in fact.

He had a feeling that whatever they felt was in his best interests were not really what he had planned for himself, and he was the only one he could rely on for protection. He had a sly smirk on his face and shook his head in disbelief at the irony of it all as he wondered, how am I supposed to protect myself when I couldn't do a thing to save my father or stop my mother from doing what she did. He felt like a complete failure and at that moment he made a vow to get stronger, both physically and mentally and never let harm come to himself or anyone he loves ever again, if he loves again that is, nothing in life is guaranteed as he knew only too well. Colin Stevens the little boy from Bosnia had spent four years metamorphosing into Colin Stevens the adult from England, well as adult as an 8-year-old can be but he grew up a fair deal there and then. It was a case of do or die and he was ready to do no matter who it affected or who it may kill, even himself.

Chapter 5: Who are you?

I had done my homework on Connie and felt I knew just about everything about her that I needed to know. She answered my questions intelligently and better than that, truthfully. I knew from the very first moment I spoke to her that she was the right one. I was kind of proud of myself for choosing her, I have been wrong on occasions, but this was not one of those times.

Back in the prison interview room, Colin thought he would take the chance and find out a little more about Connie and what she stands for, who she really is from her own mouth and not what he had learnt or found out for himself from others.

C.S.   "Thought I would just throw this out there like a fishing line hooking a catch but, who is Connie Jones?"

C.J.   "I am a nobody really, just a young girl trying to make it in a man orientated world but fortunate enough at the same time to love what she does and accept it if I don't make it."

C.S.   "You certainly aren't a nobody, I would never have asked you here if I felt you were and by the work of yours' that I have had the pleasure to read you will make it, in fact you should have already made it."

C.J.   "That's very good of you to say but also by saying I should have already made it and I haven't could mean my chances may be limited due to my gender. I have no doubt whatsoever of my ability and although I can improve, I know where I am now and how long it has taken me to get here while watching others elevated to superior positions without justification. Anyhow we are veering away from the subject in hand, and I really don't want to turn this into a case of sexism."

C.S.   "It's just that we have talked loads about me, and I just wanted to know a little about the Connie Jones sitting here in front of me. Who you are, what you are about? What are your likes and dislikes? or else I may as well be talking to anyone or even the walls of my cell, as usual and believe me when I say it, I have talked to them on more than one occasion. More like a daily occurrence really. Please, can you give me anything at all?"

C.J.   "That's a fair point, I never thought about it like that. My name is Connie Jones as you know, I am 24 years old and have been a reporter for The Independent for several years. I am not married but I do have a boyfriend who also works for The Independent, his name is Alan, we met on the job and hit it off straight away. In fact, he tried to talk me out of coming to see you today. God forbid, I even tried to talk myself out of coming as well."

C.S.   "So, why did you come if he says no, and you even say no yourself. The warning signs must have been there, why not listen to them."

C.J.   "I haven't got where I am today by bowing down to every Tom, Dick and Harry that comes my way and having my tummy tickled by them. If that was the case, then I would be left behind with zero chance of success. I do my own thing when and where I want, within the boundaries of the law of course and maybe that's where we are different, you have gone the other way, there seems to be no boundaries as far as you are concerned."

C.S.   "I was right in my initial assessment about you, there is a fiery spirit hidden somewhere in there, waiting to escape. Kind of like a caterpillar that's been cocooned for the summer and now become a butterfly that is flying away to freedom, you want to hit the heights."

C.J.   "And I was totally wrong about you, I thought I would be talking to a tough guy serial killer and all you are talking about is beautiful butterflies, ha-ha, sorry for laughing but it is kind of funny."

C.S.   "I would stick to my guns if I was you Connie, if you show any weakness now then you will have your tummy tickled for the rest of your life. I learned that years ago and vowed never to take anyone's crap anymore, that is why I am like this, I took it and then I took some more, eventually I cracked, until I felt I was left with no choice. I had to find my own direction in life so that is what I did, not everybody's cup of tea I grant you, but it was mine, I found that out for myself, I had to. I guess to a degree we are similar, you pushed yourself in a direction you felt you had to go and so did I. Just the two directions are exact opposites of each other."

C.J.   "I had to, this story is big for me and means everything. I have never been given this kind of opportunity before, hopefully it will lift me a few rungs up the corporate ladder but that is only if I don't completely fuck it up myself. Once I get your blessing to publish it, I will need my editor's permission to take it to print but only after accepting my own admittance that it is worthy of being put out there. I am my own harshest critic sometimes so much so that it is not healthy, I wouldn't say I was totally sane but then again, I wouldn't say I was mad either."

C.S.   "I was the same, no matter how much anyone hated me, I made a point of hating myself more and even if they liked me, I wouldn't believe it, it was like they were plotting against me. I was and still am a very sceptical person, I don't think I will ever lose the feeling."

C.J.   "Scepticism is not a good trait for anyone to have and yet we all have it in us. Just some of us give it the push it needs to show its' ugly face and others don't."

C.S.   "I have enjoyed learning about you Connie, I know so much more now than I did twenty minutes ago. Shall we get back to the nitty-gritty of the real stuff now, what else do you want to know?"

C.J.   "Anything you have to say is what I want to hear so carry on please from where you left off...."

C.S.   "Something about my mum, well my adopted mum anyway, what can I say about her that you don't already know, you appear to have done your homework Connie."

C.J.   "Anything at all, I am sure there will be something in there that I haven't heard before."

Adele Stevens settled in for the first night of what could prove to be a very long stretch in prison, a very long stretch indeed. She would most likely be in for twenty years although it could be as little as fifteen depending on how lenient the judge turned out to be. Domestic abuse was his forte, or so she had heard and that could possibly work in her favour. Her claim of self-defence was her only hope and her lawyer was going to play lavishly on it and mention the abuse at every given opportunity. The fact that she was just as violent and abusive had nothing to do with it as he was unable to defend himself. This was going to be easier than she had planned, or so she thought.

She had never been incarcerated before or even known anyone apart from her husband that had, and his time was only one night for drunken behaviour in the local police station. She'd had no forewarning of what to expect in jail and was going to have to wing-it as best as she could. Over the years she got so good at winging it and got so settled into prison life that she saw problems when the time came that she would eventually be eligible for parole that she wouldn't know what to do or how adapt and settle back into normal life. Like so many before she had been institutionalised and could see no way of undoing the damage it had caused.

It gave her so many sleepless nights and added to the fact she had chosen to cut all ties with Colin, something she hadn't chosen to do lightly and would be in his best interests as well as her own she thought. If she stays in contact then there may even be the chance of him being deported back to Bosnia, but at least if she keeps away, he may be able to stay and live out some form of life here, a safe life away from war torn Sarajevo. Something that although she and John had tried their best at first, in the end they had failed miserably to provide for him, and it was all down to their inability to get along with each other after the alcohol and drugs started taking effect. They were a right pair of fuckups and now Colin was paying the price for their mistakes, their shortcomings.

Meanwhile back at the prison:

C.J.   "It couldn't have been nice having your mum cut all ties with you, and also knowing your father wasn't around, who did you turn to for help, if anyone?"

C.S.   "I really didn't give a shit what she was doing at that point, she was a big part of the cause of it all and now she was gone, hopefully forever as far as I was concerned. I think I felt a little relieved if I am honest. I just decided to go it alone and rely solely on myself. It was too late for anyone to help me, or that is how I saw it. At least by being reliant only on me, I could blame only myself."

C.J.   "Still, it's a big responsibility and a lot of weight or burden for an 8-year-old to have to carry around. Especially with knowing it could be for the rest of your life."

C.S.   "I just got on with it, what else could I do but I did change then, I felt a big change in me and how I felt."

C.J.   "In what way, how did you change, exactly?"

C.S.   "I lost respect for women around that time, not just my mum although she was the key factor. I was also pissed at never getting the chance to vent my anger or tell her in any way how much I hated her. She was just gone out of my life completely. I started hating them all but mainly blondes and slim blondes at that. The ones that reminded me of her. That's where it all stems from, anything after that was my choice but that was the catalyst, where it started and the new stage in my life began. Colin Stevens the boy was quickly becoming Colin Stevens the psychotic rapist and future murderer that sits in front of you now"

C.J.   "What about Marie Calvin, what did she do to get you so riled and make you want to finish her off as you did. You near enough decapitated her in what was a most vicious, hideous attack."

C.S.   "Simple, she just wouldn't shut up when I told her to, she just kept pushing and pushing. I really didn't plan it, I had no intention of killing her, it just happened. I was just so frustrated at her constant bickering that I just snapped and cut her throat. I guess that I was so angry that I had no idea how hard I was pressing and even got a shock myself when I saw her after the red mist had died. Funny thing is I even contemplated letting her go not long beforehand, but by then it was obviously too late. She couldn't go anywhere."

C.J.   "What about before then, the Christmas party and the 'blow job' she gave you and then spurning your advances. That must have played some part in your choice to get even with her."

C.S.   "I didn't just want to get even with her, I wanted to make her pay for it over and beyond. She had made me out to be a laughing- stock time and again in front of people I was supposed to be respected by, she had them all laughing at me, they were people that should've shown me total respect, but didn't and it was all down to her. In fact, I will tell you some things about that bitch now, if you want to hear them."

C.J.   "Marie Calvin? oh yes please, I would love to hear about her."

Colin started to introduce Marie into the conversation and started by telling Connie about the night at Adams and Co when he asked her to come to his office.......

Chapter 6: Marie Calvin.

Me and Marie had a love/hate relationship, I loved her while she hated me, he smiled whereas Connie just ignored it so he pressed on. I was smitten and would have done anything for her but, unfortunately apart from one drunken night when she made me feel special, she let me know exactly how she felt. She took exception to the fact I was so open with our relationship. What relationship? she would often ask. She turned out just as bad as the rest of them or possibly worse as with the others there was never any pretence. If someone takes you in their mouth then that is a relationship, am I wrong?

As Marie Calvin sat at her desk, she had only one thing on her mind. It was nothing to do with the mountain of paperwork that had been sitting on her desk and steadily building higher and higher all day. The paperwork she had moved from the left of her desk to the right and back again but only to make herself look busier than she was. None of it was urgent and all of it could be done next week so that was her aim, enjoy the weekend and start afresh on Monday morning.

What was going through her mind was; if she could negotiate her way through the next fifteen minutes without any major incidents or occurrences then she would have survived another week at Allen and Co. The company where she worked in admin. as an office clerk. Her job was very boring, and we are not breaking into a Martha and the

Muffins song here, but it paid the rent on her apartment and got her all the mod-cons she needed and wanted.

It was Friday and it was 4.25p.m., the start of the weekend was imminent, or was it. Marie loved Fridays, she always had, everyone was happier it seemed on a Friday and preparing for the 2 days off. The weather never got to anyone no matter how bad it was, and nobody moaned about anything as they were too busy planning for the action-packed fun weekend. She was all set and ready to head off too and so nearly made it, but she hadn't factored in the idea that Colin the office manager would want to see her and asked to speak to her privately. His timing couldn't have been more off if he tried, sometimes she wondered if he did things like this just to spite people. She wasn't a big Colin fan, a fact she had never hidden, and he knew it too, maybe this was his revenge for her spurning him again. There was something creepy about him, he hadn't done anything to warrant this feeling, but she just felt as if he was not all there almost as if he had a screw loose. But he was her supervisor and she had to do what he said and do it with a smile on her face as if she was happy to help no matter how she felt about it deep inside.

When he came over and asked if he could see her in his office, she shrunk a little, like a tortoise does when retiring back into its' shell when startled or trying to protect itself from its' prey. She just wanted to go home and start the weekend like everyone else, but for the time being anyway that would have to be put on hold. Colin sounded serious for some reason and after a couple of minutes of contemplating what he could possibly want she headed off to his office all the time hoping it wouldn't take too long. When she arrived, he was standing in the doorway waiting for her. 'Thank you for coming Marie, come in and take a seat' he said as he moved only ever so slightly, and in so doing forcing her to brush past him and into his office meaning she had no option but to rub her breasts across his pouted chest. It was a very awkward feeling and situation to be put in, but he was her boss, so she let it slide for now and considered taking it up with Mr Allen, maybe on Monday, but for now she would give him the benefit of the doubt, but only just. He was pushing his luck and she was pretty sure he knew it.

She sat in a leather chair identical to Colins' and positioned on the opposite side of the desk to him. As he started to speak, the phone on his desk rang so he excused himself and answered it. Hi Mr Allen, Marie heard him say, can't it wait I am with Marie now. Oh, ok then I will be right there. Marie could tell by the tone in his voice he was not happy at the disturbance, but this was the big boss, the one guy at Allen and co. you had to bend over to please and Colin knew it, everybody knew it, without him Allen and Co. would never exist. Everyone but it seemed Mr Allen knew it as he felt he was a good boss. Ruthless when he needed to be but fair with his staff and anyone that was able or willing to help him make money. Anyone else, the ones found not to be making him profits were expendable and as a result so many employees had come and gone and so many more will probably will also.

"I am so sorry about this Marie, I will be right back, please wait won't you, I should only be a minute or two." he said. She wanted to leave but was intrigued to find out what he wanted to tell her, it sounded important, and even Mr Allen seemed to know what it was about. Hopefully and if she was lucky, it could mean a promotion or pay rise or even both. Her thoughts were rushing ahead of her, and she said, "sure no problems see you soon". To which even she thought O.M.G. that sounded so corny, God knows what Colin would read into it. He could read sex into you telling him to fuck off, but that was just the way he operated. Good as gold when in company and butter wouldn't melt, but get him alone and who knows which Colin Stevens you may get? For now, though he was being pleasant and acceptable.

She spent the best part of ten minutes alone in his office, just waiting. She wanted to snoop, and even started to look around, but every time she got the courage to move and delve deeper, she heard some noise or another and sat back down quickly as if she hadn't moved at all. Colin eventually returned and apologised for the interruption. He appeared human and seemed in some way normal, which was odd for him, it was a side of him she hadn't seen before. With hindsight she should really have seen the warning signs if she hadn't let her guard down enough to give him the upper hand that is. He appeared nothing like the drunken letch he had been at numerous office parties and most of them ending in her trying her best to keep away from him and avoid him. But then again, she was sober too. Maybe she had read too much into things, she started having her doubts as to why he was being so nice.

"What it's about Marie is Mr Allen and I have been very impressed with you and your work, and we were considering you for a promotion." Colin began. "Wow, thank you for your confidence in me," Marie butted in. Colin continued, "It would be for a trial month at first but if all went well and we have no reason to believe it wouldn't, then a pay rise would come into effect." "I am very flattered, can I think about it, I don't want to sound ungrateful, but it is quite a big step for me." said Marie. "Yes, of course, take the weekend, consider your options, then get back to me on Monday with what you decide," Colin replied

On saying this Colin reached down and pulled out a bucket of ice with champagne and two glasses. "I had rather hoped you would say yes straight away, so I got this as a sort of celebration. It's cold and ready to drink, would you like one." He asked. What harm can one glass of champagne do she thought to herself, the offer of promotion doesn't come along every day, "Yes please I will, and again, thank you. I am sorry for not answering straight away." she said. Taken aback slightly when eyeing up the champagne flutes, Marie remarked that she had the same ones at home. "A woman of taste then," he said as he poured two glasses out and placed one in front of her and the other, he took a drink out of and sat back down. She sipped slowly from her glass and thought to herself she had never felt so relaxed in Colins' company before, maybe he wasn't as bad as she thought he was, could it be the alcohol or was there more to him than she had given credit.

After a couple of glasses of champagne and some pleasant conversation and possibly some flirting on both of their part, she made her excuses and told Colin she had to go. As she stood to leave Colin walked around the desk, thinking he was going to hug her goodbye she prepared herself for the awkwardness it would leave but was shocked as he walked past her and shut the door to his office.

I don't see that there is any reason to leave now Marie, what can you get at home with nobody waiting for you that I can't give you here and now. She noticed a complete change in him, there was something sinister in his voice. He had turned from Jekyll into Hyde in the blink of an eye, and this was the reason she feared of what he was capable of. Frightened she tried to walk past but as she did, he grabbed her and pulled her back. She screamed but his response was eerily frightening, "No-one can hear you; everyone has gone home. It's just you and me and these four walls. Oh, and by the way Marie, if you think Mr Allen can protect you that was him on the phone saying he had to get away and asked if I would lock up for him, that turned out well for me." Colin said with a vicious tone in his voice.

Marie, near to being paralysed with fear, and trembling felt Colin touch her. She pulled away and tried to fight him off, but he was too strong. No longer the weak child he once was, now he was a strapping man full of muscles and pure power. She fought as best she could, but Colin using his brute force simply picked her up and placed her on his desk as if she were merely a parcel.

Her panic, her screaming, her fighting, were all futile as Colin who was far too heavy and strong pulled out a knife and pressed it tight to her throat. "One more struggle and that's you fucked bitch." He said as he reached down and raised her skirt with his other hand. Reaching up he grabbed her underwear and in one tug ripped them away exposing her glistening vagina to the world, or rather for his own private viewing. As he looked down at her private parts he felt his cock throbbing with anticipation, it was hungry for pussy, and she was the food. He placed his hand between her legs and started to rub the vulva, making her wet. She really didn't want to help him in any way and tried to stay dry but when someone is doing that to your sensitive region it's like an involuntary reaction, you have no control. She tried to block it out but that was impossible so she did the next best thing she could think of and pretended, she pretended that Colin was Brad Pitt or George Clooney. Thinking about the pair of them had gotten her through many situations in her life, but none like this. With a loud roar Colin then moved on top of her menacingly and without a single word readied himself to do her harder and rougher than he had ever fucked anyone.

Marie was resigned to the fact of what had happened, what was happening, and what was yet to come because her lack of strength had stopped her fighting and she just gave in. She thought if she did then he may not harm her any more than he had up to now if it was possible and anyway, he was Brad Pitt, her mind told her as much. As she felt him penetrate her and then hurt her and hurt her and hurt her with one vicious thrust after another, she closed off her mind and prayed to God it would be over with as soon as his lust had gone, and reality had retaken its' rightful place.

She could hear his heavy breathing, snorting and animalesque grunting, then she felt his hands disappear into her top and roughly fondle her breasts, squeezing them like he was kneading bread. She tried to picture a happy place, somewhere away from the reality of what was happening, but it proved impossible. Sobbing uncontrollably while still hoping, praying, this nightmare would be over and finish before it had started. What lasted only a few minutes in real time seemed a lifetime to Marie until she felt him cum inside her and fill her with his semen, his horrible demon seed. He took one last deep breath, and she felt his cock throb a couple of times as he thrust twice more to finish off what he had started, and a grin appeared on his face as if he had just satisfied someone other than his own fantasies.

When he was done, Colin calmly climbed off her, pulled up his pants and adjusted himself before walking out of the door to the office, leaving Marie in tears and fearing in case he returned. After about 20 minutes or so Marie moved cautiously towards the door and out into the hall. She continued walking to the front door of the building and hopeful escape into the street, but as she reached it Colin appeared. No please she begged, leave me alone. But unexpectedly Colin just unlocked the door and opened it for her to leave, even holding it for her like a gentleman that she knew he wasn't or never fucking would be. As she walked out the door he said to her," I would keep shtum if I were you, who is going to believe a slag like you that everyone has seen putting herself about on more than one occasion over a respectable office manager whos' only crime is liking someone too much. Think hard and long about it, Marie because If you want a fight then you can have one, otherwise this is the end. You embarrassed me and now I made you pay. An eye for an eye, I see us as even. What about you Marie, the ball is in your court now?"

She never answered or looked at him in any way, instead, keeping her gaze straight ahead and walking like a woman with a mission. Like fuck we are she thought to herself as she walked away from the building, you keep believing what you want but like hell are we ever going to be even. She could feel the weight of his stare in the back of her head and moved away as quickly as she could. She didn't turn her head, not even for a second and just got into her car and sped off to what she believed was relative safety or in other words as far away from that monster, as far away from Colin Stevens as she could possibly get.

When Marie arrived home, she had no recall whatsoever of the journey. Her mind had completely blanked out everything except for the heavy breathing and the remembrance of that bastard fucking her. No, she thought to herself, it takes two people to fuck. All she could think of was that nasty animal or total monster raping her and she trembled as she fell in a heap on the floor holding her head in her hands while rocking gently back and forth resembling a lunatic strapped into a straitjacket in an asylum. Only she wasn't mad, perhaps livid but she most certainly wasn't crazy. She needed to be strong for her own sake, she needed to stand tall if she was going to make it through this situation. It was harder than she ever could have imagined, but for reality's sake she had to try.

Although she didn't know for sure, she thought that what she was feeling was delayed shock. She had heard about its' effects but had never had any reason to feel it before for herself and hoped to God she never would again. She felt abused, she felt unclean but most of all for some unknown reason she felt ashamed and guilty. A natural feeling apparently with anyone that has been through an ordeal such as rape, but why feel guilty, nobody knows and possibly never will. It's just the way it affects different people.

Why had she not just walked away? What if she hadn't drunk the champagne? Could she have fought harder? Was she sending off signals to him that she hadn't intended? All these were questions she asked herself time and again in the hope of trying to make any sense of it all. But in the end, there are no answers and sense as always plays no part in someone's psychotic intentions. All she felt was total and utter guilt although she knew she was totally blameless, it still did not stop her feeling remorse or hatred but sadly not only for him, but also for herself, she hated herself.

She went into the bedroom and took off everything she was wearing, throwing them all in the bin. She wanted to burn them, just burn them all but held back enough to think about possible evidence. One thing was for sure, she was one hundred percent certain she would never wear them again, ever. For a few minutes she lay naked on the bed, curled up in a ball, holding her head in her hands. Feeling sorry for herself as well she should, she cried and cried and cried. After a while, when the tears had dried, she walked into the bathroom and entered the shower. She washed and scrubbed and cleaned every part of her body, especially the parts he had violated. Her breasts, her vagina inside and out but also her ears in a bid to rid herself of the sounds still ringing in them, the snorting and grunting of his breath as he fucked her, he raped me, he raped me, he fucking raped me she sobbed once more. She was quite rough with herself but was determined to scrub away every trace of him and what he had done to her. She had in fact been so rough that she needed some cream to ease the pain slightly. Smearing it on the tips of her fingers she rubbed it inside and out, the relief was instant, cold like an ice-cube, but instant.

Still somewhat in shock she left the shower running and went back into the bedroom. Whether or not she knew it was running she had no idea and really didn't think about it or even care, she just walked away. If someone asked her what her name was, at this precise moment she probably wouldn't be able to tell them. She climbed onto the bed and rested her head on the pillow, staring at the ceiling before finally drifting off into a deep slumber.

She had no idea just how long it took her to fall asleep but when she woke the next morning, she had hoped it was all a nightmare, and a tragic dream she'd had, but her wishes were soon quashed. She looked in her bin and saw her clothes in it and then heard the running water of the shower. She realised it was no dream and started thinking about what she should do next, what were her options, how much would her water bill be? The least of her problems maybe but anything to distract her mind from the reality. She was going to have to report it to the police that was for sure (the rape and not the water bill), so she took a few minutes to compose herself and think about what she was going to divulge and what parts she was going to leave out. Anything that may see her in a bad light in fact, but no she thought, I have done nothing wrong. I will go with the truth, the pure and total truth. As she had heard said by Judge Judy so many times, you need a good memory once you start lying. Because once you tell that initial first lie you must remember it, and then all the subsequent lies that link up to it and they can run into the hundreds but tell the truth and you only need to remember one thing. It's not rocket-science, just common sense and it's amazing how many people slip into the viper's pit and end up losing themselves in the lies and treachery that it all brings.

Chapter 7: Self harm.

I cut myself, I won't lie, and it made me feel happy. The pain was part of the overall enjoyment, and so I decided to share my feelings. That is when it all kicked off big time. That is when I became me and forgot who I was or who I thought I had ever been or wanted to be. I had given myself a new goal in life and intended to see it through to the end, good or bad, whatever the end may have been.

After his encounter with Marie a little over an hour ago, Colin felt great. There was a beaming smile on his face, a bound in his otherwise awkward gait and a feeling of invincibility running through the blood his veins. For the best part of that hour, he had just sat in his office thinking about Marie and how beautiful her body was while reliving the events in his mind. He finished the champagne that they had been drinking before calling it a day and decided to head home.

He turned the lights off and the building plummeted into darkness, he then fumbled his way to the front door where there was at least a little bit of light shining in from outside. He then locked the door with the key he had been entrusted with before walking the few yards to where his black Toyota was parked. He was over the limit he knew all too well but couldn't care less. Nothing was going to bring him down, not today, not now. He was not only drunk with the effects of alcohol but also drunk on the power he now felt.

He climbed into his car, started the engine, and proceeded to drive away. He felt he was doing well but hadn't realised just how much he was swerving all over the road. If he had been seen by the police, he would surely have been pulled over. He also drove straight through a red light without even realising it was there and touched the curb with his wheel on a few occasions. Eventually, and luckily without any major incidents he arrived home and parked the car against the curb, or at least what he thought was against the curb. It was at least a foot and a half away and looked like it had been abandoned, rather than parked.

As he walked into his home, he stripped himself completely, underwear included, and strolled naked into the kitchen and sat at the table. He was still partially aroused from the events of earlier, he had taken Viagra to help keep himself hard and it was still having affect so, he started to caress the shaft of his cock. Gently at first but it quickly turned into full-on masturbation. He was still high on the emotion he had felt when doing her, so much so in fact that he ejaculated within a minute and covered the leg of the table with his semen. Once he had come down from the high of the moment, he realised that he had his knife in his hand and was pressing it into his own throat. Why he had no idea, but he guessed maybe just to see how they must feel when he does it to them. He felt both empowered and petrified in equal measures, empowered, and aroused by the feeling of danger, but petrified of being able to do it without even knowing it was happening. He had no idea that he had picked it up and it took a while to catch on.

He pulled the knife away and admired the blade, still as shiny today as the day he had found it and still just as sharp. He placed the edge of the blade on the inside of his arm and pressed down, breaking the skin before moving it across the forearm and making a clean cut. He did this three times all parallel to each other and watched as the blood oozed out of the wounds.

Placing the knife on the table he used his hand to smear the blood all over his arm and then rubbed his face making it crimson in colour and all bloodied. He did the same with just about every inch of his body and then moved to the full-length mirror in the hallway to admire his handywork. He felt strong, he felt powerful. So powerful that he flexed his muscles and let out an almighty roar as if he were Tarzan of the jungle but more like a wild scream than a chant. Now he knew just how an artist felt when taking a step backward to admire their handywork, seeing and taking in the full glory of what they have created for the first time.

He had been self-harming for years but was always careful not to cut himself in places where it could be seen by others. He would always cut in places that could be covered up, like the arms, the legs or stomach and so easily hidden from prying eyes or so-called do-gooders who have no intention of helping and just want to interfere as much as they fucking can. A thought came into his head, maybe he should have started on them, that would have shut the bastards up, one way or another, but it was way too late now. If going back in time was an option, though. He thought to himself.

He looked at the clock and it read 5.46 a.m. He had sat there naked and covered in blood for most of the night, not moving at all just soaking in the atmosphere and living for the moment when he decided it was time to clean up and ran himself a nice warm bath. He scrubbed and cleaned until all traces of blood were gone and then checked in the mirror again to be sure, he was as clean as he could be and then headed off to bed for a well-earned rest. He didn't really want to wash off his own personal artwork but felt he had no choice as he had work and it would look strange to turn up looking like a beetroot, imagine that and what would they say. Once the thought was there, he so wanted to do it just to see their faces and hear their gasps, but not this time, maybe later.

Marie broke the silence in the prison, Colin was still a little high on the story he told her, she asked him:

C.J.　　"The things you said about Marie and her supplying the wine and the glasses, was that true or not?"

C.S.　　"Total bullshit, I made it all up although those dozy bastard coppers started to believe it for a while. Idiots, they shouldn't give badges to clowns that are just not worthy of them."

C.J.　　"So how did you do it then. How did you set her up?"

C.S.　　"I managed to get hold of her key for long enough to have a copy made. I then simply waited until she went out opened her door and walked right into her house and took the glasses. Same with her card, took it when she was unaware, ordered the champagne and slipped her card back in, she had no idea at all and by the time she would get her statement I would have been finished."

C.J.   "All the keys that were found at your place, who did they belong to?"

C.S.   "They belonged to me, I had copies made where I could get away with it. They opened the doors to some of my workmate's houses and the others were taken from the victims. There isn't one place I haven't been in when they weren't home or with some even when they were."

C.J.   "To get this straight, you have been in peoples' houses both while they have been in and when they have gone out."

C.S.   "Yes, absolutely."

C.J.   "And for what purpose, I mean why would you do that, what would get out of it?"

C.S.   "Mind games really, I moved a few things around without them seeing, some of them thought they were going mad and even came to me to talk about it. The effort I went through not to laugh right in their pretty little fucking faces, I think I deserved an Oscar, it was a scream it really fucking was, hilarious."

C.J.   "Quite an elaborate plan, so how did it go so wrong."

C.S.   "It was going great guns until that wanker of a cop Jack Williams heard me in the shop. I thought he was in the car when I threatened her (Marie) and he stepped in trying to be a fucking hero. I gave him a good hiding, that part of it felt good."

C.J.   "Very devious of you, when did you learn to be so devious, can you remember?"

C.S.   "It wasn't nice being left on my own as I said before but just something I had to learn to live with and just get on with it. It made me stronger and less likely to accept bullshit from anyone, I grew up that day and made a vow to protect myself at all costs."

C.J.   "At all costs to everyone else though, not yourself, it never really cost you anything did it?"

C.S.   "You may look at it like that, but at the time it felt like survival of the fittest and strongest. If I was strong, I would survive whereas if I was weak, I would crumble. There was no way I was going to crumble, not again. I stood tall and bowed down to nobody after that. Anything that was thrown at me, I just took in my stride."

C.J.   "Do you mind if we take a little break Colin, I need to powder my nose, so to speak. When I return, I would like to hear more about the young 8-year-old Colin, if that is OK with you."

C.S.   "That's cool, you rock on. I am fine so I will wait here for you and try to remember all I can."

Connie turned off her tape recorder but left it on the table and walked out of the room. Steven the prison guard came over to her and asked if everything was alright and she replied "Yes, just needed a toilet break and my throat is parched, any chance of a drink of water if you have one, please." He showed her the way to the bathroom and apologised that it was a men's room, but it was all they had and said he would stand guard outside to stop anyone entering while she was inside. When she had done what she needed to do she was taken back to the room where Colin was waiting, which was just as well because she would never have found it on her own. Prison is like a maze of linked rooms one after another and all connected by corridors, so many corridors, every one of them looking exactly like the last. She sat back down at the table and got ready to start her tape recorder when Steven walked in with two bottles of water, one for each of them. She thanked him and then pressed record...

C.J.   "Thank you for waiting shall we continue where we left off..."

C.S.   "Okay then, not a problem, here we go...... I was sat on the edge of the bed wondering what to do next, I just wanted to get out, where I didn't care, just out and away from their incessant questioning so I tried the window......"

Chapter 8: Eight again.

Once I finally realised what it was that I had to do, everything just sort of fell into place. Each decision became easier than the last and apart from one or two minor mishaps, I sailed through life without worrying about consequences for any actions I undertook. Life was becoming a piss-easy ride the more I didn't care. So why should I care when it was easier not to.

Eight-year-old Colin lifted himself off the sweat and piss-ridden bed and moved toward the window, he needed a new way of escape. The door was locked from the outside. He couldn't see if anyone was on guard in the hall but if they were he would most likely be heard and caught before he had even put his escape plan in action.

He had no intentions of hanging around until the police came as he knew they would, eventually. Whatever story he told them and when he told them, he needed the chance to embellish for his own gains, but he was more than sure he would say nothing at all if he could get away with it. He also carried the potential to hurt his mum and although he hated that bitch more than anyone else in the world right now, he was more than just a little bit frightened of the power she possessed over him and what she would do to him if she knew it was him that spoke up against her. He was quite sure she already knew but wasn't willing to risk the consequences of her being freed and to come looking for him. He needed as much distance between them as he could get.

He tried the latch on the window, and it opened without a key. The window slid up and down, freely on its' runners and Colin put his escape plan in motion. Gathering up whatever he could carry, but nothing too clumsy or heavy and placing them in his rucksack, the only real possessions he felt he still owned. He climbed through the open window and after a tentative look around to see if there was anyone watching, which nobody was, he darted quickly down the street as fast as his little legs could carry him. He didn't want to count his chickens or tempt fate in any way, but he couldn't help but think to himself, well that was easy. Maybe a little too easy in fact and he was waiting for something to go wrong. An arm possibly to grab him by the scruff of the neck or reach out and tap him on the shoulder, but it never came.

He had no idea where he was going to go, just away. Anywhere that they couldn't reach him or hurt him because that is what everybody seems to want to do to him. Have I really been that bad to make everyone hate me he used to ask himself and still does on occasions, but only when things aren't going so good for him, and he starts feeling sorry for himself?

 He didn't slow up until he had gone round the corner at the bottom of the road and disappeared down an alleyway where he checked his bag and looked at what he had with him, hoping he hadn't been stupid enough to leave anything important behind. But he need not have worried. Before setting off on the pathway to freedom and whatever life may bring the way of an eight-year-old on the run he just needed to check for his own piece of mind. Not just on the run from the police, or from his mum, but from himself and the second life he had made but was now taken away just like the first one in Bosnia that was long forgotten. Soon maybe this one would be just a memory too and stop being the nightmare that it is.

When loading his rucksack, he just threw in what he felt he may need and didn't really think about it so really had no idea what he had put in, even though it was only minutes previously. He had a small amount of cash, although not so small to a child his age. About £30 in total, his entire life savings, a pencil, and a pad in case he needed to make notes, one toilet roll for emergencies and the thing he loved more than anything else and was his favourite travelling companion, of course, his trusty knife. It always did as it was told, went where he went and more importantly never answered back.

Colin and the knife had been through so much together even at such an early age. He had found in it 1993 when he was just three years old and playing war on the street outside his Sarajevo home. Discarded by a dead or dying soldier, he had found it just lying in the street. It was glistening in the sunshine and drew his attention away from the stick he was using as a fake AK47 assault rifle while rat-a-tat-tatting any unsuspecting passers-by. They all laughed along with the game and said awe how cute no matter what they were thinking inside. Some even held their hand to their heart and pretended to be wounded which made Karol happy, oh the fun to be had with something as simple as a stick. They were probably all thinking what an annoying little twat, he was sure, but nobody had said it, not to his face anyhow.

But by now the stick had served its' purpose as the knife was so much better, it was real and far outshone any of his favourite toys. This was the genuine article, made from shiny metal and not just something he had to pretend with, just in private and not outside where it would be snatched off him in a shot. He felt if anyone saw it then they would want it and that made him obsessed and possessive. Although he was only three, he was bright enough to know his mum and dad would never let him keep it, not in a million years. But for them to take it they had to find it first, so he was going to have to be cunning. He hid it inside his T-shirt and ran into the building where they lived. On reaching his bedroom he took out the knife and put it in the chest of drawers under some of his underwear and totally hidden from view or any nosey people that might be prying. If he even knew who Gollum was, then Karol was in possession of his very own precious, just as the character from The Hobbit had found his ring Karol had found his knife.

The knife remained mainly hidden for the next few months and was only brought out when he knew nobody was around to see him. He would hold it up and admire the blade, its' shininess, its' sharpness, and the very dangers that it brings. When it was out it was like nothing else mattered, as if he was in some kind of trance and the bond between him and it was getting stronger. He had several small scar marks where he had touched the blade to his skin, but always under his clothes and always out of view of anyone that may want to take it from him. He would also at times use it to cut up his Teddy Bear while pretending to copy his father's culinary skills in skinning a rabbit or squirrel or whatever else they could catch around their home and have for tea. There were a few close calls where he was almost caught with it but always managed to get it hidden again, just in time. He could still picture parts of his old life, just little morsels but other parts were either a blur or long forgotten.

Closing his rucksack, and with everything he needed inside, he had done a good job in getting it together. Colin then casually walked out of the alleyway and onto the street passing many people and just hoping no one would recognise him. He headed off down the high street and into the train station. His £30 could get him somewhere, anywhere far away he was sure, but he needed that money for other things he was sure and decided to chance hopping on the first train that came along and would worry about not having a ticket if the time came. He got past the guards very easily, as someone was asking directions he calmly or as calmly as his pounding heart would let him, strolled onto the platform, and headed towards the train.

Once on the train he settled into a seat and trying not to bring any attention to himself, sat quiet as a mouse so as not to make anyone wonder why a small child was travelling on a train on his own. If any nosey bastards did ask, he would simply say his auntie had gotten him to the train station and his parents were meeting him at the other end. What could go wrong … easy thinking for a worldly conniving little bastard.

Lucky for Colin and although he had no idea as he was hanging on edge of his seat the entire journey in anticipation of being caught, but this was a guard free train. With costs mounting and cut-backs inevitable the driver of the train was also the guard and the ticket inspector. Maybe one day he will sell the tickets in the office before taking his position in the drivers' seat but we're not quite there yet but getting closer than ever.

On disembarkation, getting out of the train station was so easy, he just pretended he was with someone or other and strolled out with them. Nobody was going to question a young child or think he was a stowaway, why would they. If you have confidence in your own ability, then you can get away with anything. This is what Colin learned that day and has gotten through life by sticking to this one simple rule, just act like you know what you are doing. Colin from this point on simply disappeared somewhere into the system. He lived but he didn't exist. He got by on what he needed and nothing more. He took what he could make use of and left the rest for some other deserving soul to find. If he ever got too greedy then it may lead to his downfall, so he just took what was necessary and no more.

Chapter 9: Reporting a crime.

I had no idea what Marie would be up to after the "incident" in my office, I didn't even stop to wonder for a second. If I had known she would go straight to the police, I may well have had second thoughts but unfortunately for me, thinking was not something I thought about if you can excuse the pun. I seriously expected the warning I gave her to be enough and she would simply roll over and play ball. I couldn't have been more wrong, and who can blame her really, well I can, and how I did?

When Marie arrived at the police station, she explained to the desk sergeant why she was there and was immediately escorted to an interview room where because it was such a delicate topic of conversation, she was to speak to a female police officer called Jane Collins. She didn't care who she spoke to, male or female but for argument's sake she went along with it. She had been sat in the room for about five minutes when the door opened and in walked a woman, slight of build, dressed in a grey skirt and white blouse.

She had heard the clip-clop of heels along the corridor and wondered to herself if this was the woman she was supposed to see. When the footsteps stopped and the door opened, she had her answer, yes it was. Hi," said the woman "I am Inspector Jane Collins You must be Marie, I believe you have an alleged rape to report, please take your time and tell me everything you can and try not to leave anything out, no matter how unimportant you feel it may be, Sometimes the most meaningless of details can be the most important and on occasions even a case solver." She knew Marie wasn't interested in the nitty gritty details of solving a crime but once she had started telling her she felt she just couldn't stop, she just went into policewoman mode. Marie just nodded without saying a word, as Jane Collins expected she just wanted justice for what may have happened to her.

Marie's mouth was feeling uber dry, so she asked for a glass of water which Inspector Collins after excusing herself, left the room to go and get for her. She returned about two minutes later and placed a glass of water in front of Marie and sat back down opposite her. After Marie had gulped it down, she began to tell her story about Colin, work and the meeting that turned into an horrific experience at knifepoint and eventually, violent rape. She told everything from start to finish and even added in the rejections she had given Colin at the office parties over the years, even the one time when being drunk and stupid she had given in to peer pressure and taken Colin into one of the offices and performed oral sex on him. She said she had done it more out of pity than anything because she had felt sorry for the way the other girls had been treating him. Just the one time she had done anything but there had been several rejections gone his way since then as he started to freak her out with his persistence and pushiness. Only then, when it was too late did she begin to see what the other girls saw in him, he was certainly touched in some way, crazy and even a little scary.

"How may rejections? and how did he take them?" asked Inspector Collins. "I would say at least 5 or 6, maybe more, in fact no more in fact. He was ok at first but after I did what I did to him, he changed. It's almost as if he felt I was his personal possession, and he became angry if I turned him down. But I tried to explain what I did was a mistake, just a drunken moment and wouldn't be happening again, but he wouldn't have it and every party he would try again and again to continue what he called our relationship. I got so fed up with it that I stopped attending any office parties if only to avoid any contact or misunderstandings that may arise. When I was next in work, either on the Monday after a weekend or after the holidays if I was off everyone kept telling me he would just walk around the floor like a man on a mission asking everyone where is Marie? why hasn't she come? Every time they told him I didn't turn up because of him, he thought they were lying, and that I was just avoiding him, each time he came looking for me. It was becoming grating, my nerves were shot, and I was fed up with making excuses for not being there. I really wanted to go but felt it would stir things up that needed to be laid to rest. Unfortunately, he never let anything go and harboured a grudge you wouldn't believe."

"How many times did you say no," Jane Collins asked, "I did say 5 or 6," replied Marie. "No sorry, not at the parties, last night when he allegedly attacked you." She enquired. Marie's head dropped, feeling ashamed she replied. "None I don't think so, anyway. It all happened so quickly it was just a blur, and I was too scared to say a word. He had a knife which he pressed into my throat, he told me not to scream and if I didn't, I may just live. Funny thing is, at that point, all I wanted to do was die. If God had decided that it was my turn and came for me then I would have gone willingly."

"The knife, can you tell me anything about it, Marie. How big was it? what colour was the handle? Did it have any distinguishing marking on it?" The detective asked." Anything at all that may help us make sure it is the right one if we find it?" "Yes", Marie replied, "From the top of the handle to the end of the blade it was about this long, Marie held out her two index fingers about 12 inches apart. The handle was black, it had a small picture on it that looked like an animal, possibly a horse, but I could be mistaken as his hand was covering it for most of the time. I only got slight glimpses here and there and the rest of the time I had my eyes closed. I am sorry but I really can't remember it all, maybe it will come back to me. I still feel like I am talking about something that has happened to someone else, these things just don't happen, and certainly not to me." Marie said with a lump forming in her throat, why me? Why now?" She asked. Jane held off a couple of minutes before responding. Taking in and digesting all that Marie had just told her, for some reason and she never liked to take sides, but she believed her. There was just something about her that spoke truth, genuine. Obviously, she would need a lot more proof than someone saying I didn't do it, but she did believe what she was hearing, what she had heard.

"Not at all, it's absolutely fine, Marie" Jane Collins eventually replied leaving Marie hanging for an answer no more. "You are doing good considering what you have been through, you would be surprised but some people can't talk for days, weeks or sometimes even months afterwards. The witnesses we have normally we can't get anything out of them. I know they can't help it, but we need to catch these people and by the time they are ready to talk, any evidence has long since disappeared, faded, or washed away by the rain. So, anything no matter how small it may seem, believe me is a blessing. If we can get onto it now instead of holding back it could be of great importance in our enquiries further down the line." Jane said, "Just try to remember, I know it is hard, but anything at all" she added.

"If we get as much information now as possible then when it comes to piecing things together down the line it makes it so much easier to make things link. One missing detail can hinder our enquiries and turn an open and shut case into a cold one, and none of us want that." Jane explained.

Chapter 10: There's more than one way to skin a cat, Mr Stevens.

I never killed the cat, I only found it, but it did often go through my mind," What if?" And that what if? Kept getting bigger and bigger until I knew I had to sate my appetite. It did take a few years, and then some but when the time came, I knew only too well that I was ready. Maybe if I had found the fox that probably killed the cat then things would have turned out differently and I would have killed earlier, but I didn't and, I didn't.

Seven-year-old Colin Stevens was standing in the garden of the house he shared with his adopted mum and dad, in his hand he held the black-handled assault knife he'd had since he was three. The one he found on the street in Sarajevo and was lost by a Bosnian soldier all those years ago, the one with the black horse on the handle. The one he had done so well to hide from everyone including family and friends, social workers and more importantly the police, and the one he now only brought out for special occasions.

Today was most definitely one of those special occasions and Colin couldn't hide his excitement. He was beaming from ear-to-ear, looking down at the body of the dead cat that he had found in a bush behind the house last week. It had been partially eaten by a dog or maybe a fox but there was certainly enough left for his experiment.

He had carefully wrapped what was left in a plastic bag and hidden it until he knew his parents would be out and that was now, they were not due back for a good while, so he had plenty of time to do whatever he wanted with no disturbances. The plan was to see how easy it was to skin it and if needs be, cut it up, dissect it. This was something he had learned as a very young boy from somebody, somewhere but that was all he could recall, just somebody, not who or why. What he was going to do with the pieces after was anybody's guess. He hadn't thought that far ahead but at least by skinning it, he would have an insight as to what he could do, what he was truly capable of. Colin was changing but not for the better. Even he was starting to realise that some of the things he was doing were not normal for anyone but especially someone of his young tender years.

Back at the prison Connie wanted to find out why Colin turned so quickly from Doctor Jekyll into Mr. Hyde and what it was that pushed his buttons, so enquired about Jack Williams and Martin Jackson.

C.J.   "You said you didn't like the detectives, the ones working on the case, what was it about them, anything in particular?"

C.S.   "Not detectives, just one of them, Jack Williams. He was a total prick. I could tell from the second I met him, and by his attitude I could see he felt the same towards me. The other two were fine, Martin Jackson and Jane Collins, just police doing their job if a little unorthodox and amateurish at times. They were a fuck-up waiting to happen them two and quite often did, it was laughable and kept me entertained if nothing else. It was probably down to them and their ineptitude I escaped from the lock-up when they didn't cover all the bases. They thought they had but I found the only one they hadn't contemplated."

C.J.   "So, tell me about Jack Williams then, why did you both hate each other so quickly, so much? what telling factor made you think he was a prick, as you called him."

C.S.   "He spoke down to me from the second I met him. He may have thought he was being clever by pretending to be nice at times, but I could tell. With people like that you just know, little things like; the tone of their voice or the look up to heaven in disgust every now and then, as I said, you can just tell. He had that unbecoming swallow-my-knob attitude as if he was God, and everyone else should be his followers or disciples."

C.J.   "Was he not just doing his job too? How can you distinguish between them?"

C.S.   "It was all in the tone of his voice or at least how he spoke, with some people you can just tell, it's hard to explain to someone but believe me I could tell, I knew only too well, and I am damn sure he knew I knew and vice-versa."

C.J.   "Oh, I don't doubt for a second that you had your reasons Colin and, who am I to tell you otherwise? I never met him so I can't comment but it's hard for me to understand when all you say is I could tell without a proper explanation. You are sat here telling me he was a bad man when you killed people, what right do you have to distinguish between good and bad. Is that not hypocritical."

C.S.   "No, I don't think so, just because he was a policeman doesn't mean he was good through and through. Same as all criminals are not bad people, it's down to the situation you are in at any given time. It's the same as going for a job interview, you can usually tell in the first 2 minutes if they like you and you stand a chance, or they don't like you and you haven't got a hope in hell of getting it. If they ask you to sit down so they can get it over with then you may as well get out of there because you didn't make enough of an impression, you haven't made the grade. Whereas if they say come in, sit down, can I offer you a cup of tea or coffee then you have a fighting chance, and the rest is up to you. That too is all in the tone of their voice or their attitude towards you, if you can read it that is, and I seem able to."

C.J.   "Now that explanation I do get. It's happened to me, I felt I wasn't given the opportunity to prove myself and their mind was already made up and wondered why they even called me in at all, I guess I made up the numbers that was all."

C.S.   "Now you are with me, he was just like that. He was the boss that wouldn't give me the job but would still revel in making me travel the 40 minutes to the interview just so he could reject me, and no doubt had a damn good laugh at my expense too. As I said, he was a complete prick."

C.J.   "I guess some people don't have the people skills that others are blessed with whether they mean to come across that way or not."

C.S.   "I would say that is a fair assessment, anyway back onto him, he was a moron of the highest order, I could tell from the day he turned up at my door......"

Chapter 11: Question time for Colin.

Nobody likes to be woken from a deep slumber and when it's two cops that are banging on your door then it just gets one-hundred percent worse. I certainly had that bitch to thank for that, her and that fucking gob of hers' that she couldn't keep shut. I thought for a while that I was done for, but things had a habit of working out for me so why should this time turn out any different? Luckily enough she shot herself in the foot a couple of times and just as I had planned meticulously, no matter how innocent she was. she looked guilty as hell.

Colin Stevens was woken from a deep sleep by the constant ringing of his front doorbell, he rolled over and pulled the pillow over his ears, but it wasn't going away. It was almost as if someone was leaning on it and wouldn't stop. After five minutes of what seemed an eternity he went over to the window, opened it, and pushed his head through. Looking down he saw two men both dressed in suits and ties standing at his door. "Can I help you gentlemen" he asked them. "Whatever it is you are selling I don't want any, so just fuck off will you, and don't come back." he shouted down to them. "Mr Stevens, Mr Colin Stevens" came the reply. "Yes, that is me and you are?" he enquired." I am Detective Jack Williams, and this is my partner Detective Martin Jackson we would like to speak to you about last night if that is possible." the detective said. "Last night," Colin replied, "what about it, I don't remember anything happening that should involve the police." He replied. "I think it's best we come in and discuss it sir, we wouldn't want any dirty laundry to become the topic of conversation now would we." As he said this Jack Williams ushered Colin to look at the twitching curtains of one of his neighbours.

"That's probably a wise idea Mr Williams they like their gossip around here and I don't want to be part of it." Colin answered. "It's not Mr Williams," Jack responded, "It's Detective Williams, Mr Stevens." He said but Jack just felt there was something about this guy, something he didn't like, and his hunches were usually spot on most of the time. Of course, he had been wrong on the odd occasion here and there but as a rule he was usually right on the nose.

Colin, realising he had touched a nerve apologised to Detective Williams, although he didn't mean a word of it and said he would be right down. He dawdled for as long as he felt he could get away with and then about five minutes later he opened the door and invited the two officers in, they obliged, and he took them through to the sitting room where they positioned themselves one on the sofa and the other standing by the fireplace. Funny thing about cops, ninety-nine percent of the time, at least one but maybe both stand up, they never seem to want to sit down.

"So, about last night," Colin Stevens began, "What would you like to know, although again I can't really see anything that occurred last night would need the police to be involved." he continued. "Do you know a Miss Marie Calvin Mr Stevens," asked Detective Jackson. "Of course." he replied, "She is one of the office staff at Allen and Co, the company I work for, is she ok, what's happened?" he asked. Jack seemed to think he knew more than he was letting on but went along with the charade, just for amusements' sake. If he was given even half an opportunity he would be on Colin Stevens like a rash on a hooker's privates." Just give me the fucking opportunity, go on just do it, give me a reason he thought to himself.

"Miss Calvin came into the station this morning and said that she had been attacked last night, she alleged her attacker had raped her and left her shaken with a few cuts and bruises when he held her down." Jack explained. "Oh my god that is awful," Colin said in an almost blasé tone. "How is she, is she hurt, and if so, how bad." Colin asked but already knew darned well what the answer was. "You tell me Mr Stevens, if you can" came the reply, "You are the one she has accused of raping her. Now if you would care to accompany us down to the station and answer a few important questions then we would be most grateful." There was a sarcastic tone to Detective Williams' voice that Colin didn't like, he didn't like it one little bit. Ten minutes he had known him, and he knew he didn't like him. With some people you get to love or hate them over time but this one, he was straight into the hate file.

When they arrived at the police station, Colin Stevens was rushed through to interview room 4, the same one coincidentally that Marie had been in earlier on in the day. He took a seat at the desk in the middle of the room and the two detectives stood and looked at him. "So, Mr Stevens I am guessing your idea of events from last night are going to be somewhat different than Miss Calvin's. Would you care to divulge what happened, in your humble opinion, and please Mr Stevens don't leave anything at all out." Jack said to him in a very officious way almost as if he was treating him like a naughty little schoolboy, although things were far more sinister than that. Jack already had him down as guilty, and Martin could tell so kicked him under the table and when Jack looked at him inquisitively, he just rolled his eyes as if to say get a grip.

Colin began a tale that would have felt more at home in a romantic novel by Barbara Cartland or Mills and Boon than where it was, on a very serious police report. "Rape is such an over-used word, and she wasn't raped. It's a darned site easier to cry rape than it is to prove your innocent and yet somehow the shit always sticks, it's part of life's course. What occurred last night was consensual sex between two grown-ups, me, and Marie. She made a play for me and not for the first time I must admit and there was no way I was going to say no. I have been into her for years and she even sucked me off once at a Christmas party about 3 years ago. I bet she never mentioned that to you, did she."

The lying bitch was gagging for it and got exactly what she wanted, rape my arse, she lay back and took what I gave her, and she took it willing with a big smile on her face. If you are telling me that she has found her morals then I will tell you this, she has fucking none. No morals what so fucking ever. Last night she was screaming like the whore she really is, and you can put that down on tape. I am not going down for this, fucking bollocks, no way, I am not going back to jail on some bitches' say-so." He bawled out in a very angry outburst, it was a tirade that just went on and on and on.

Jack or Martin couldn't get a word in, so decided to leave him to it and wait until he had finished. It took a good while, but Colin eventually calmed down and went quiet. It was at that point that Jack asked him, "Is that it, anything else you would like to add? Colin just shut up and shook his head, he knew he had done himself no favours by blowing up like he did, but quite simply didn't care.

Jack Williams could sense the anger in Colin Stevens' voice, he knew he had hit a nerve and played on it. He didn't have to look hard to see what he already knew and could sense the hatred and a viciousness that came with killers, rapists, and abusers. He had seen it countless times in so many others and Colin had it in abundance. It was always someone else, always someone else' fault, a different person to blame each time and never their own doing. Some of the time it was someone else's fault, and that someone else was another side to themselves like an alter-ego or a schizophrenic doppelganger, but proving it was the hard part if not impossible. Jack could see Colin was getting irate and said to him, "Can you calm down please Mr Stevens, I am not judging you, not yet anyway, that may come at a later date, who knows?" He said it with a sly grin on his fat face, relishing the fact that he could see Colin getting even more aerated as he did. "Although, I am beginning to see you may have anger issues that need addressing. I need to get all the facts on the case before I can do that." He continued. Colin knew by the tone in Detective Williams voice that he had already made up his mind and felt he had lost the upper hand, which was a bitter blow, a very bitter blow indeed.

Although she had covered plenty of ground in the interview, Connie wanted to know how an average man became a rapist, a rapist became a killer and on the top of that, how that killer became a serial killer. And if anything, what was next on the agenda, where else was there for him to go before he was caught or handed himself in.

C.J.   "When did the fascination of raping and killing kick in? At what point in your life did you think, yes that's my future, I want to do that? It is not exactly what any normal person decides one day, yes that is what I want to do"

C.S.   "As we have found out already, I am not any normal person. I have been reading up or studying about serial killers since I was about 12 maybe, it's always been a morbid fascination of mine. It's sort of like when you hear there has been a car crash and you feel you must go and have a look at the resulting damage, we all do it, it's just a part of who we are. After a few years of reading about them I wondered could I ever be one myself. Never actually thought I would be but look what happened."

C.J.   "Which serial killers, would I have heard of them?"

C.S.   "It didn't really matter which ones, if they were serial killers then I wanted to know about them. Firstly, it was Bundy, then Gacy, Dahmer, Nilsen, and the likes, you know the main ones then there were others like Ridgeway, Rader, Stayner, and well the list is endless. Have you ever heard of Samuel Little, Connie?"

C.J.   "I can't honestly say I have, no, why? But I have heard of Bundy, Dahmer and Gacy, was he the clown guy, right?"

C.S.	"He was, but Samuel Little is by far Americas worst serial killer. If you add up the victims of Bundy, Gacy and Dahmer they don't reach the total that Samuel Little killed and yet his name remains unheard of in so many circles of life. By reading about them it keeps my fascination up and in doing so is keeping their names alive and my own of course."

C.J.	"I am not familiar with Rader or the other one, sorry what was his name again?"

C.S.	"Stayner, Cary Stayner."

C.J.	"And what was it that he did?"

C.S.	"He murdered 4 women in a five-month spell. A lady and her daughter, and her daughters' friend who were both teenagers, and a park naturalist who he decapitated."

C.J.	"That couldn't have been nice for whoever found her."

C.S.	"Is it ever? although I can't exactly say much can I, leaving them to be found the way I did; I think it would be hypocritical of me. The strange thing about Cary Stayner is his younger brother was involved in a high-profile abduction case when he disappeared for 7 years when he was only 7, being imprisoned and abused all that time until he managed to escape when he was 14 with another young lad that had also been abducted."

C.J.	"The poor lad, abducted and abused and then his brother turns out to be a serial killer, that must have affected him all his life and probably still does today."

C.S.	"No, not really, he is dead, he died in a motorcycle accident about 10 years after his escape, their uncle was also shot and killed at home, not a nice time for the whole family. Some people just have no fucking luck whatsoever, do they." Colin said chuckling "Sorry to laugh but the irony of having so much bad luck just tickles me, it really does. Kind of like it is a punishment."

C.J.   "That is so true Colin, no luck at all but I don't see anything funny about it. What about Cary, was it? the older brother! what happened to him?"

C.S.   "He is still on death row, has been ever since, just a matter of time really before the big day."

C.J.   "And the other one, Denis Rader? Another new name to me."

C.S.   "The B.T.K. killer, self-titled. That is why I hated being called The Cotton Mill Rapist, all these guys with cool sounding names and that was all I got called. That was the reason I came up with The Button Murderer, there was more thought in it, rather than just raping by a mill, any old Tom, Dick, or Harry could do that, well if they are sick in the head and willing to, that is."

C.J.   "B.T.K., what did that stand for?"

C.S.   "Bind, Torture, Kill. That was his M.O. or Modus operandi, how he did things and in that order. He was a family man with two children too."

C.J.   "Doesn't sound like a nice person if he is willing to treat people like that. I wonder why they don't seem to hurt their loved ones."

C.S.   "Bundy was the same, I guess love is a strange old thing. But in the end, they are all serial killers, me included, we are not nice people, none of us. He (Denis Rader) killed at least 10 people and sent letters to the press, teasing, and tormenting the police until one day the letters just stopped. Then after 11 years, just as the police were about to call it a day on their investigations the letters started again. He was a right daft cunt, the prick."

C.J.   "Why was he a daft cunt? explain if you may."

C.S.   "The police found out the type of paper he was typing on was only sold in one place and the typewriter he used was from the church centre he looked after, so they just went round and picked him up. And all this after he had eluded them for 17 years as well."

C.J.   "Bet he felt like a complete idiot, making it so easy for them in the end."

C.S.   "Apparently, he was ready for his fate, a bit like me when I gave myself in, it was time and I knew it, as did he. When the police came to pick him up, they asked him if he knew why they were there and he calmly answered, "I think I can have a good guess."

C.J.   "He could have got away scot-free if he didn't get a thrill out of teasing them, or bigging up his ego. If he didn't torment them about his killings he may never have been caught, he was the biggest factor in his own downfall, therefore, as I said a daft cunt."

C.S.   "No, that would never have happened, he would have been caught eventually as when they caught him, he told them he was ready to kill again, and he would probably have kept killing for as long as he remained free. Once the thrill is there it never leaves, it may lie dormant for weeks, months or even years but it will be back one day. I would have killed again one day but I felt I'd had enough of that and was getting bored with it all. If I had stayed free then I would have killed again, eventually, I have no doubt about that, whatsoever."

C.J.   "So, let's get this straight, what you are saying is once a serial killer, always a serial killer."

C.S.   "I guess I must be, yes. I think that is exactly what I am saying."

Nodding his head in agreement Colin stopped for a second and then continued with the story of Marie, Jack, and the police station interview……

"Everyone was leaving to go home for the weekend and Marie came to me and asked if she could see me in my office. I asked what it was about, and she said she would rather tell me in private, where there were no prying eyes, or listening ears. She arrived at my office about 5 minutes later, I invited her in, and she brushed up against me pressing her breasts against my chest and squeezing through the doorway. I felt aroused immediately, and as she went past, I heard her whisper, well are you coming or not, I hope you are, because I am wet for you. Not believing my ears I followed her into the office where she pulled a bucket of champagne on ice and two glasses from under my desk and began to pour. How they got there or where they came from, I have no idea. It was probably while I went to see Mr Allen, he called me and asked me to pop in to see him before I left. I didn't really care where they came from as I was just away with the moment and couldn't believe my luck." Colin told them.

"Before I knew what her full plans were, she lay on my desk, opened her legs, and said come on then fuck me, I've kept you waiting long enough, you should be well ready to fill me now. I really couldn't believe what was happening or what I was hearing, I had been ready for years and tried everything and yet now she was coming on to me. I did what I had to do, couldn't have taken more than a few seconds, I was fully aroused and came quicker than I wanted to. In fact, I was pissed off that I was done as I wanted it to last longer. When I was done, she pushed me off, said is that it and laughed. From the ecstasy to the agony all in a couple of seconds and I felt like my world was over. Marie walked out the door, said thanks for nothing and I didn't see her again." He finished.

"You said she brought out the champagne and glasses, that's odd because she said you supplied them, why would she say that Mr Stevens?" asked detective Williams. "I have no idea maybe you should ask her that question," came the reply, "All I know is when I went to see Mr Allen there was no champagne but when I returned, there was." he lied. The two detectives decided it was time for a break and needed to discuss a few things anyway, so they excused themselves before leaving the room. Colin was left sitting at the desk in interview room 4 for about 10 minutes, before being taken to the cells by a policeman in uniform that he hadn't seen before.

Knowing they had nothing and would be unable to get any form of conviction they were left with no choice but to bail out Mr Stevens and send him on his way, but not before warning him not to go far as he would more than likely be required for further questioning as and when they needed him. "Of course, Mr Williams, wouldn't dream of it," Colin answered knowing how much it would annoy Jack. Jack failed to respond, he'd had more than enough for one day and was glad to see the back of Colin Stevens, for now but even then, knew he would be seeing this prick again and soon, although never would be too soon in Jacks' eyes. He really detested everything about this fucking cunt and made no secret about it.

Chapter 12: Jack's demise.

When things fall right for you then they fall right. Jack Williams was an interfering, no-good busy body that had nothing better to do than piss people off that didn't share his beliefs. I was one of them people and when I was at Marie's, which I had got in by using her key to open the door and simply walk in, and he walked in with her I was shocked. Seeing them doing it from behind the door was something I never expected. I was just standing and watching, they were too engrossed in each other to even realise I was there. I never actually planned to kill him but when I did, it helped my case no end. This guy who hated me and would have found me guilty of anything if he could, was now dead, perfect situation, for me.

About a week into the investigation of the alleged rape of Marie Calvin by Colin Stevens, the police had nothing to go on except Miss Calvin's word, and unfortunately for them, but especially unfortunate for her that has never been enough for a conviction, ever. Jack Williams decided to bring in Marie one more time, just to see if anything had been left out. Maybe a spark in her brain could bring new information forward, anything no matter how small it may appear, the case could just hinge on it being made known to them. Alas, it was to no avail, Marie could add nothing and so was told that Colin wouldn't be charged due to lack of physical evidence. The results taken of the semen samples had come back as being Colins but that did not necessarily mean that he had in fact raped her. And with two conflicting stories from two people that have a history, albeit a turbulent fly-by-night history, it could not genuinely be determined who was guilty or who was innocent.

She was told it would be virtually impossible to get a conviction and if it did indeed make it to court then the judge would more than likely throw it out through lack of evidence anyway. Also, they would have to look at both sides and fully investigate Colin's claims too. The glasses and Champagne came from somewhere and there was more evidence against her than in her favour. What a complete mess she thought to herself, how had she been so gullible and fallen right into his plans. He had set her up like a kipper and she had just swum right into it believing everything he was saying, why would he lie. The thought never even crossed her mind.

Marie had come to the station on the bus and was a little agitated over the outcome of how it had all panned out, so Jack said he would drive her home in his car when they were done. Being stuck on a bus, on her own and losing herself in her thoughts was probably the last place she wanted to be after the bad news she had just received. She accepted gracefully and they both headed down to the car park. On the way home Marie asked Jack if it was at all possible to stop at the supermarket on the way home to pick up some wine. She said she felt she needed something a little stronger than tea and that she would settle down better with a good book and a glass of wine. Something just strong enough to relax her and bring her down from the roller coaster of a ride she had been on for the last week or so.

Not even a roller-coaster really, more like a helter-skelter through the shittiest few days of her life so far and if Colin had anything to do with it, he may not be finished yet. Although they are both rightly classified as thrill rides at least the roller-coaster has its' fair share of ups and downs. Whereas the helter-skelter is just a complete downward spiral, like the one she felt she was on now, riding into oblivion and unable to do a damn thing to stop herself from landing in the pit of snakes that no doubt waited for her at the bottom.

The difference between a Roller Coaster and a Helter-Skelter is quite simple, the Roller coaster has highs and lows or ups and downs whereas the Helter-skelter is a one way downward spiral and there is no escape from it.

Just how appropriate the lyrics are from the Beatles song 'Helter-Skelter were in her life at this exact moment in time Messieurs McCartney, Lennon, Harrison & Starr will never know, but Marie is quite convinced that they were written just for her. Written nearly 50 years ago, but for this exact moment. Charles Manson may have disagreed but then that is his prerogative.

When they reached the supermarket, Jack remained in the car and watched as Marie disappeared through the automatic sliding doors into the Gateway store. Unbeknown to him she was on a quest to find the best bottle of wine she could muster for the £10 she had in her purse. She picked a lovely looking bottle of Pinot Grigio described as a 'crisp, lighter-bodied wine full of fresh and vibrant floral aromas' from the chiller cabinet and costing just £6.99, meaning she even had some change. As she turned to head for the counter, she was stopped dead in her tracks by something she never expected. Or rather someone that was the last person she expected to see.

 Colin was standing directly in front of her, smiling almost in a mocking way and wouldn't move. Then as she moved to the side, he followed, blocking her path and every time she tried to move past him, he would move ever so slightly but only back into her path and so blocking her exit, again and again and again. He did this a few times until she'd had enough and screamed at him, "What do you want now? haven't you done enough fucking damage to me, you have ruined my life."

Colin wasn't in the mood to back away and just replied to her, "You think I have done enough damage and ruined your life I haven't even got started yet, just you wait, when you settle down and least expect it, that's when you should worry. I can get to you anytime, anyplace as I see fit and then and only then, you'll see what I gave you was just a taster for what's to come." A petrified Marie turned to run, and in a bid to escape she ran straight into the arms of Detective Jack Williams who had come into the shop to see what was keeping her and had heard just about everything Colin Stevens had said.

 Jack reached out to grab Colin but was sucker-punched square in the jaw causing him to fall the floor with a bloodied lip and bruised pride. If he wasn't expecting that he certainly wasn't expecting Colin to carry on the assault. But Colin wasn't finished and jumped onto Jack, pummelling him with punch after punch in such a vicious attack that Jack was unconscious in no time at all, before he had even recovered from the first strike. When the red haze dimmed, and colin had realised what he had just done, he hotfooted it fast as he could out of the supermarket in a bid to get away. He made it to his car and jumping in, sped off with a couple of wheel spins thrown in for good measure. Everyone that had heard it, turned to look at who was making such a racket but just put it down to idiotic and adolescent youths' and carried on with their own business or shopping duties.

Inside the supermarket, Jack, after just coming round was still a little groggy and puffed out his cheeks as he tried to adjust his sight which was still a little blurred. When he regained total vision, he saw Marie was alright, looked at her, smiled and said, "Thank fuck for that, thought he had got you." "I am fine, how about you, are you ok," Marie responded, "You look like shit." She then said. "Not surprising really, is it?" Jack asked, "Anyone would with a beating like that. I would have had him if I saw it coming. Come on, let's get you home." Jack said to her. Marie was tempted to forget the wine but decided she probably needed it more than ever now and headed off to the counter to pay. Marie and Jack with his bruised ego following, then headed off to Jacks' car and from there on to Marie's apartment.

When they arrived at her apartment Jack went in with her to make sure it was clear, and she was fine. Who knows what that psychopath is capable of after that he thought to himself? Although Marie had said she would be fine he wanted to check for himself just to be sure. He asked if he could wash his face to try and make himself look respectable as he didn't want to be the topic of conversation on everyone's lips when he left hers and she pointed him in the direction of the bathroom. After a short while he came out of the bathroom and looked so much cleaner. Most of the blood had been mopped up and there were just a few scratch marks and bruises especially around the parts of his face where he had taken a good kicking from Colin. The blood may have dried up a little, but the aches and pains were still there though, and just reminded Jack that he was not getting any younger.

Marie had found some ointment and began putting some on a cloth to treat his wounds. She told him to sit in a friendly but bossy way, which he did, and she went about dabbing the wounds to ease a little of the pain and stinging. He winced the first time she touched one and then again, every time she touched another then another and another. There were plenty of wounds so he winced a fair bit for the next five minutes of treatment and yet he felt so relaxed with her at the same time. She told him to stop being such a baby and as she was close-up to him and while she was tending his wounds there was an awkward moment or two where their eyes met, and they found themselves staring at each other intensely. He took a deep breath and tried to pull away, but the magnetism was too strong. He was putty and she was the mould, she could have bent him and shaped him in any direction, and he wouldn't have cared.

 Before either of them knew what was about to happen, and certainly before they had time to stop themselves, their lips had met, and they were engaged in a passionate kiss. The kiss led to pure lust, and it wasn't long before their clothes were shed and lying on the floor as they made love in a hot, passionate, steamy embrace. In no way planned but gratefully accepted in equal measures by both Jack and Marie.

Jack was trembling with excitement, it had been a while, an eternity in fact and he had forgotten most of what he had learned over the years, but Marie helped him through it by placing his hand in the right places at the right times and moving her body in time to his awkwardness to make it more intimate, at least for her anyway.

It wasn't planned, it certainly wasn't expected, it was just a passionate lust filled moment and it came as quite a shock to them, just how easily they had dropped their guard. Little did they know, either Marie or Jack as they were both so engrossed in each other to notice that standing behind the door to the bedroom, watching through the gap made by the slightly ajar door was Colin Stevens. Watching like a stalker, hiding just out of view, liking what he was seeing and in his own way kind of getting off on it.

Colin waited till they had finished, he felt it would be unfair of him to stop them in their moment of climax and to rob them of the sensation, but he himself was also tingling, maybe he could have Marie again now she had been warmed up and ready. At that point Colin walked into the bedroom and said, "Well who would have seen this coming, the cop and the so-called victim fucking for fun while the investigation is ongoing. Wouldn't they just love to hear about this down the station." Jack went to move off the bed but Colin, pointing a gun in his direction simply said, "Don't even think about it lover boy, unless you want me to splatter your brains over the wall, go on, just give me a reason, sound familiar, does it? Funny how fate comes back to bite you on the arse, isn't i?"

Once Colin had started, he just couldn't stop himself and having spoken for quite a while, just whittering on about nothing really, he tried to pass the buck and blame Jack for his own injuries by saying, "If you hadn't come into the store none of this would have happened,". (Once again, someone else's fault and not his own). "But you had to be the big man and try to protect the hapless and apparently helpless little whore didn't you. So, what are we going to do now?" asked Colin. Jack going for the air of surprise, jumped off the bed and lunged at him but Colin was ready for it and got away two shots, both of which hit Jack in the chest, knocking him to the floor.

"What did you do that for you crazy son-of-a-bitc?" Colin screamed at Jack. "Did you not think I would do you because you are a cop, serious miscalculation on your part, and you call yourself a detective. Never underestimate the will for survival. Man has lasted for millions of years, and I have no interest in stopping the trend."

Lying in a pool of his own blood Jack's breathing quickly became rapid and shallow, everything went as cold as the chilliest of winter breezes. The damage to his body from the bullets was irreparable. It was the end, and he damn well knew it. The pain had increased beyond measure, and he had lost enough blood to fill a bucket, maybe even two, his time was very close. He looked at Colin in a demeaning way and then at Marie and shook his head as if to say sorry if I have let you down. She shook her head and then nodded in return as if to say, you didn't. although no words were exchanged they both knew.

Colin had seen enough and decided to put him out of his misery and just to make sure fired one more shot into the temple of Jacks head, killing him instantly. Marie screamed uncontrollably until Colin pointed the gun at her and bluntly told her to shut the fuck up or she would be next. She stopped immediately. It's amazing how much power the one pulling the strings has in situations like this, they can make anyone do anything they choose and when they choose. Marie was obviously still a complete wreck but just had to learn how to control it, she didn't want to give Colin any excuse, Jack had, and he had failed miserably, she had seen him killed and she didn't want the same fate.

Colin leaned over Jacks body for a second, Marie thought he was checking for a pulse to make sure he really was dead, but he was as a matter of fact inserting a receipt for a bottle of champagne into Jacks top pocket. The very same champagne that Colin and Marie had been drinking in Colin's office a week ago at their secret little meeting last Friday. Knowing Marie had no idea, Colin happy with his days' work stood up and casually walked out of the bedroom down the hallway and out through the front door to Marie's apartment. It was almost as if he hadn't just murdered a police officer in cold blood, but he had and he felt empowered by it. He felt good, the sensation he felt as he pulled the trigger to finish Jack was like nothing he had ever felt before. It was like he had been plucked off his sofa and placed by the hand of God onto his very own cloud nine.

He hadn't even felt this good when he killed that tart on the green, but then that had been an accident, apparently if you believe what the media reported. She tried fighting back and paid with her life. He grabbed a rock that was at hand and used it to smash her skull. They can call it an accident if they want but Colin knew different, so what did it matter what them unbelieving morons thought, he was there and he knew the truth.

He was willing to share the truth with anyone that wanted to listen but had not had any takers thus far, until Connie Jones that is. In her he saw his chance and would keep talking as long as she wanted to listen.

C.J.   "There always has been some doubt as to who was the first of your victims. Sorry, I don't mean victim as we know that was years before. I mean the first one to be murdered, not attacked. Was it the girl by the cotton mill or the girl they found in the lake? When they found her, she had been dead some time and the timing between them was estimated as being very close."

C.S.   "The girl by the cotton mill was first but only by a day and because the papers made me out to be some sort of amateur, I had to prove them wrong. If it hadn't been for the papers the other girl would still be alive, I wouldn't have had to have done her."

C.J.   "There you go again Colin, not your fault. Two women dead by your hand and you try to make out you are blameless or at least pushed into it by someone else."

C.S.   "There you go again putting words in my mouth. I have never claimed to be innocent, the exact opposite in fact. I knew I was guilty but to be scoffed at by a bunch of fucking retards that are making up stories just to sell more newspapers, only this time at my expense. I wasn't having it and that is why I planned it and carried it out to perfection to prove they were the amateurs, not me. They were that amateur they didn't even know it was me that killed them both, but I did and was laughing my tits off at them, mocking them."

C.J.   "So, what you are saying is you killed an innocent woman just to prove to the media that you could do it and for no other reason."

C.S.   "That sounds about right, and I don't mean to come across as all nonchalant or anything, but I did find it easier to kill her as I felt I had to do it because of what they said as opposed to wanting to do it just for fun."

C.J.   "It seems a bit of a lame excuse if you ask me."

C.S.   "Well, it's a fucking good job I didn't ask you then isn't it."

Colin regretted saying it as soon as the words had left his mouth and tried to apologise. Connie went quiet and dipped her head, he could tell she was hurt by the comment and tried to make amends……..

C.S.   "Sorry, that was uncalled for…."

C.J.   "You seem to be forgetting that you wanted me here to tell your story, I didn't volunteer although, don't get me wrong on that I was more than happy to come. This article is either going to make me or break me and I am not willing to suffer abuse at your hands Colin. You wanted me here because I am a professional and good at what I do, so either treat me with the respect I am due, or we can forget the whole thing and I will walk out the fucking door right now, the choice is yours."

C.S.   "You are right and again I am sorry I didn't mean to lose it but sometimes shit just happens. That is how I am and no matter how much I try to be nice: the truth is I am just not a nice person at all. The nasty streak is waiting dormant in me and when I least expect it to, it erupts like a volcano and I have no way of stopping it, I just have to try and please it to calm it as much as I can. I don't normally apologise for anything, but to you I say I am sorry, and I genuinely mean it"

C.J.   "OK, so long as we are straight, the next outburst and I walk, that's me done.Did you even know the names of any of your victims or was it all just thrill-seeking exercise for you and a chance to get your rocks off cheaply."

C.S.   "That's a mighty blunt way of putting it and yet also cutting at the same time, but yes, I guess it was a cheap and nasty way of pleasing myself while making someone else suffer and to be honest I pleased myself again when I got home, if you know what I mean. But in answer to your question the only name I knew was Marie Calvin, and that was because I worked with her, the rest I learned at the trial, but I wouldn't remember any of them now. I wasn't in it to get to know them personally, it was a quick fix to an addiction I had."

C.J.   "Had? you just said an addiction you had, are you cured now?"

C.S.   "No, I wouldn't put it down as cured, I wouldn't say it was possible to cure me as things go but while I am in here there isn't much chance of doing anything is there. I would say more waiting idly in the wings just in case, I mean you never know."

C.J.   "I know you don't care or probably won't want to know but their names were Colleen Myerscough and Sandra Davies not that it means anything to you, but just so you know someone did care about them. So, I don't think it's fair to refer to them as just number 1 and number 2."

C.S.   "Thanks for letting me know, unfortunately though I have already forgotten them. I have mental images of them in my head and that is all I need."

Chapter 13: Accident or murder.

As I have said, they can believe what they want, I knew the truth. I saw her, I followed her, I caught up with her and I killed her. No, it wasn't planned but it happened, and it happened because we were both there in that same place at the same time. It was murder and it really ticked me off that they said it was an accidental death, not likely. So, I had no other choice but to prove them wrong. I knew I could do it again and felt it was necessary to prove the doubters wrong, and so I did with devastating consequences.

When Collette Myerscough was found murdered a mere 50 yards off the gravel path that runs the length of the village green, nobody thought for one moment that she was a victim in the cotton mill case, although there were slight similarities, i.e., the fact she had been raped. Nobody had yet been murdered by this monster. It was only weeks later when another victim was killed that the police felt she could in fact be linked to the Cotton Mill Rapist and after analysis of the sperm deposited turned out to be an exact match. Then and only then did they know for sure that they were dealing with the same man. A scary sick motherfucker that seemed to know no bounds but, just one man all the same which in turn was a little blessing that there weren't two sadistic morons wandering around at the same time.

Her skull had been hit so hard by a rock that it had fractured in two places, and she was more than likely dead before she was raped. Such a horrible thought although for her it may well have turned out to be a blessing as she only knowingly underwent one horror that night when if she had survived the initial blow, it would have been two. The rock that was used to hit her was casually tossed and found about 3 feet away from her body still covered in her congealed blood.

The police themselves believe it wasn't a planned killing and possibly a mistake or accident. Their thinking was that Collette may possibly have fought back and her killer may have reached out and grabbed the first thing that he could get hold of, which in this case turned out to be the rock. Then when he had finished and realised that she was dead, ditched the rock by simply tossing it away. This was all pure speculation but appears to be one version of the truth that would make sense with the evidence that was available. Their liberal use of the words simply and accident would later come back and bite them in the butt, that however they had no idea at the time. They had made someone very angry, and that someone now felt he had a point to prove.

Whatever happened or didn't happen on that night, only two people know for sure and one of them is dead so can't tell. One thing that is clear, and the facts can't change it is that Collette Myerscough became the first murder victim of the man who would eventually be dubbed by the press as the Cotton Mill Rapist.

Looking at the photographs hanging on the wall of the operations room one thing struck Martin, every one of the women were similar in looks and height and near enough all of them had shoulder length blond hair or longer. Marie too had blond hair, he asked himself was that why she had been targeted also? But what they needed to find out is why did this guy have a fascination or hatred for blondes and where had it come from. At what possible juncture in his life had he turned that much he was willing to kill for no reason but the name of what can only be described as pure detestation of a certain hair colour.

Seven-year-old Colin Stevens cowered in fear at the sight of his mother walking up the garden path. She had been out all day and he had been left alone, he hadn't meant to do it and you can bet she was sure to notice. The black ink stain on the wall in the hallway, the one he had made by accident coming down the stairs when he slipped, and the pen he was holding in his hand had scraped along the wallpaper leaving a mark around five inches long. He had tried to clean it by scrubbing it but that had only made it worse and now there was a big blurry patch.

When his mum walked in the door and saw the mess he had made, she called him and waited. He arrived like a lost and lonely lamb with his head bowed in shame, knowing what was coming and expecting the worst. She wasted no time in waiting for an explanation and launched into a beating that would put a professional boxer to shame, he knew it was coming, it always came. There was nothing else for him to do but stand there and take it as he was weak and powerless to stop it. He also knew it was going to be bad but even Colin was surprised at just how bad it was this time. It made some of the other beatings feel more like a tickle fight.

He had taken many beatings from his mum over the years and was petrified of her. So, at that exact point in his life, he vowed to work hard and make himself stronger and believe in himself more. He would never again take a battering from her. She may well have been a small, slender blonde lady but she could certainly pack a punch and hurt him, and she seemed to take pleasure in it too, almost as if she was torturing him for fun because she felt she could get away with it. Colin was adamant that she could give a professional boxer a run for his money, she was that strong. It never used to be like this.

Whatever happened to the loving mother that she used to be? Before the alcohol, before the drugs. He knew there was no chance of ever getting her back, but it didn't stop him dreaming, he just wished and prayed that she would return as he started on a fitness campaign that was going to change him completely.

C.J.   "When you took a beating from your parents, did they know when to stop or did they just carry on until you were unable to move."

C.S.   "Most of the time they were so drugged up or drunk that I don't think they knew what they were doing, so they just carried on. I begged them to stop but my pleas fell on deaf ears, they didn't care."

C.J.   "What made them start, why did they attack you when as you said things were going great."

C.S.   "It was the cocktail of drink and drugs, the more they had the worse it got. They'd start on each other and when I tried to stop them it all became my fault and they both turned on me. Eventually they teamed up and turned on me, venting all their anger and hatred in my direction every time."

C.J.   "Did you ever fight back and hurt them?"

C.S.   "Why, when it was pointless, I was small and between them they had the strength of an army, if I fought it would probably have been the end for me. I did think about it from time-to-time but never acted on my impulses"

C.J.   "So basically, you saw no other way out, you took their problems as your own and soaked up the consequences they were due in order to keep them together, you have to be commended for that."

C.S.   "I know I was adopted but they were my parents, I loved them, at first anyway. Sober they were great, we were just like a normal family, very loving, just like a mum and dad should be. I tried my best to stop them drinking by hiding it for them, that again made me enemy number one and a target for their abuse. Once they had found it, they took no time in polishing it off and that's when their revenge, as they called it would start."

C.J.   "You had a tough upbringing in Sarajevo and then these people who are there to protect you turn you into a human punchbag, it was a hard lesson in life before you even reach 8. Other 7-year-olds were watching cartoons while you were forced to fight just to survive, it hardly seems fair."

C.S.   "At first, I looked for sympathy, but I cottoned-on pretty quick that none was coming. Funny really, well not at all really but you must laugh at the irony, the only people that it could come from were also the very same people causing it. So, I just sat back, and I soaked up their shit and toughened up, it was all I could do. If I didn't, I can guarantee I would not be here now, or they wouldn't be."

C.J.   "So, what choice did you make to toughen up, how did you push aside the fact you were only a kid."

C.S.   "By using the only thing, I knew how to use, my knife and taking all the strength I needed from it...."

Seven-year- old Colin Stevens stood in the garden of the home he shared with his adoptive parents. Both his mum and his dad were out in town and not due back for a while so he intended to use the time as good as he possibly could. In front of him lay the lifeless body of the dead cat he had found in the bushes behind the house a week earlier. In his hand he held the army assault knife he was going to use to skin it. A little squeamish after the first cut he soon got over that and settled into it, completely decapitating it before moving on to the full skinning. He wretched a few times and small droplets of vomit landed on the floor by his side and the smell made him wretch even more. It took a while for his stomach to settle down enough for him to start enjoying it but once he was in full swing there was no stopping him.

After the initial shock of seeing the insides spilling out, and the enforced retching due to the hideous odour which eventually died down it turned out to be an easier job than Colin ever thought it could be. How crazy that a seven-year-old could even think about skinning a cat let alone go ahead and do it for real. But it seemed to come naturally to him. The only saving grace in how psychotic Colin was beginning to turn was the fact he had stumbled upon the dead cat and not taken and killed it himself although, who knew how long it would be before that was the case. How many ways are there to skin a cat? There were many and he was only on number one. Would he do it again? Possibly, if the chance was there then he could see no reason why not.

When he had finished, he looked down at the mess that he had made on the floor and knew it would have to be cleaned up before his parents were home, or once again there would be hell to pay. So, he did the only thing he could think of to hide the evidence, he packed it all up in a plastic bin liner and placed it in the rubbish bin. He dug down to the bottom and hid it under the rubbish that was already in it and covered it over, so it was not as noticeable or at least no longer visible when the bin was open. There was still a little stench emanating from the bag, but the smell of the other trash would soon drown that out, so he felt good and kind of proud of himself with what he had achieved. Now the only job he needed to do was clean up the puddle of blood on the patio which he set about doing by getting a bucket of water and plenty of bleach.

He got himself a scrubbing brush from the cupboard underneath the sink in the kitchen and when he got back out into the yard he dropped to his knees and started scrubbing as hard as he could. He had to hide all traces of what he had done and when he had finished knew he had done a good job. The yard was spotless and just as it was before he started. Them dumb fools are never going to know he thought to himself, meaning of course his mum and dad with whom he had lost all love and respect. This is where the real deviousness in Colin began, because once he realised what he could get away with he felt he couldn't be stopped not by them and not by anyone and God help anyone that tried or even got in his way.

Nobody could ever have imagined how far he could or would take it. If you asked him, he would surely have been unaware himself just how far he could go or would be willing to go.

Time quickly passed, and Colin now a fully grown man was standing in a crowd of people watching the police as they were coming and going like an army of busy ants, into and out of from an apartment in which he had not long ago murdered a policeman in cold blood.

Chapter 14: Marie's apartment.

Once I'd had her key cut, I could come and go as I pleased and the dumb bitch never suspected a thing, it was easy as ABC. I went during the day when she wasn't there, sometimes at night when she was. Occasionally I felt she knew, but how could she. So long as I was careful enough the world could be my oyster, and she (Marie) could be my plaything, fucking with her mind was just as good as actually fucking her.

The police and forensics were all over Marie's apartment looking for clues, even the smallest or minor of details was not overlooked. The death of one of their own is something that doesn't happen very often and when it does the shockwaves spread through the entire police community, everyone mucks in to help the investigation. Jack covered only partially with a thin sheet lay dead on the floor of the bedroom, the bedroom in which he and Marie had made love in a mere few hours ago. Marie, still in denial and shock was in the lounge with Detective Martin Jackson, Jacks' partner, telling him about what happened and how Colin must have followed them from the supermarket, broken into the house and lay in wait for them.

Martin was a little confused as to how Colin could've followed them home, then break in, and then lie in wait for them when they would have been in the house already. "What was Jack even doing here?" Martin asked Marie. "He gave me a lift home from the station, and he was making sure I got in safely after the encounter with Colin at the superstore. He was badly beaten, the CCTV from the supermarket will show that Colin attacked him and left him for dead." She replied. "Only one thing about that, the CCTV at the supermarket wasn't working last night, in fact it hasn't been working for weeks, they've been having technical problems and not got round to having it repaired." Martin said to Marie.

"Play fair with me here Marie, my partner is dead, he was found on your bedroom floor with three bullet wounds, two to the chest and one in his head. And not only that he was found stark naked, so something occurred before he died. It really doesn't take a genius to work out what was happening before he was shot. Did you fuck him Marie, I need to ask, and you need to answer? You need to be honest with me from now on or else I may have severe doubts as to the truth of rest of your story." Martin said accusingly. "Did you fuck him?"

"No, I didn't fuck him, but yes, we made love, and it was wonderful, is that what you wanted to hear. I was tending to his wounds which he received protecting me, making sure I was ok. I felt responsible and I was helping him nurse them when we just, well we just, you know. It wasn't planned, it just happened. After we had finished but before we had a chance to get dressed, Colin walked in and held us both at gunpoint before shooting Jack twice in the chest and after tormenting him for a while shot him in the head to finish him off. That's what Colin is, and that's what he does. He is a psychotic and completely unstable man. I have said this on numerous occasions, but nobody will believe me. They all just look at me and say I am crying wolf again. But one day you'll see, you'll eventually see his true colours. He can't help himself and finds it impossible to keep them hidden for too long." she replied." Why the hell does everyone look at this bastard as a hero, he is fucked up in the mind and very dangerous, not one person can see it but me."

"Think about how it sounds Marie, you are trying to get us to believe that a man you willingly performed oral sex on, then said you hated, got you alone in his office and raped you. He then attacked a detective in a busy supermarket with people around, followed you home and watched you having sex and then shot Jack three times. How plausible does that sound to you, not very hey. I am trying my best to help you, but I am getting nothing in return. You need to help me for me to be able to help you, Marie." He answered.

"This man by the way, this so-called maniac also says the exact opposite of what you say and that you are the maniac and that you instigated the meeting, you bought the champagne and glasses and that you willingly had sex with him in the hope of a promotion at work." Martin continued. "That's it." Marie said having a eureka moment, "That's the reason he called me into his office in the first place, he told me that Mr Allen was pleased with the work I was producing, and I was up for a promotion. I forgot to mention that with all that has gone on." She spoke.

"Or was it the fact that I mentioned it and you are now changing your story to suit, that's what it appears to me. You seem to be making it up as you go along Marie. Colin said you were seducing him to try and get a promotion and now you are turning it around again to be in your favour and expect me to just believe you." Martin replied frustrated as anything. "Jack believed me" Marie said, "Well Jack is dead." Martin shouted bluntly at her, "And as far as I am concerned it could be because he, as you say believed you or trusted you, so I don't want to make the same mistake and end up like him" Martin responded. "I won't be letting my guard down Marie so don't be getting any ideas. Jack is dead and I won't be. How can I be sure you didn't seduce Jack to get him off your case and then shoot him.? None of it makes any sense at all."

An officer came in with a slip of paper and handed it to Martin, he leant over and whispered something in his ear and then just as he had come in, he walked back out again and back towards the bedroom. "This is a receipt found in Jacks' pocket, it's a receipt for a bottle of champagne, the same type you were drinking in Colin's office last week. Did you buy the champagne Marie, did you take the glasses into Colin's office, did you seduce him? Did you kill Jack, did you kill Jack?" He screamed at her.

He was going for shock tactics in a bid to make her crack but ended up shocking himself more, he stopped the onslaught but not before Marie replied sobbing uncontrollably, "No, no I wouldn't, I couldn't, I didn't." Martin spoke in a soft but firm voice," Marie Calvin I am arresting you on the suspicion of the murder of Detective Jack Williams, you do not have to say anything. But it may harm your defence if you do not mention when questioned something which you later rely on in court. Anything you do say may be given in evidence." "Are we clear Marie do you understand the charges. He finished. "Yes, I do," she answered sobbingly, "I didn't do it, I didn't kill him, I haven't killed anyone, I am not a murderer."

Colin broke off talking to tell Connie that he didn't always hate Marie, and to make it known that he was at one point in love with her. Maybe he fell a little bit too easy and could have been a little more demanding than he should have been but was that a reason for her to mock him in the way she did, especially in front of workmates.

C.S.   "And do you know what, she was completely correct in what she said. She wouldn't have hurt a fly, she was one of the sweetest, nicest women you could meet, at first anyway."

C.J.   "At first?"

C.S.   "Yes, or up until the time she made me out to be a cunt in front of everyone. I was really into her and thought she felt the same, but it turned out it was just a game to her. She used me for a quickie that she initiated and then basically left me with my pants down, and I do mean that literally. She left me on show to everyone, the bitch."

C.J.   "Probably a stupid question but, how did it make you feel?"

C.S.   "I lost face and the respect of other workmates all due to her, so what I did was payback and deserved, well some of it anyway. Maybe I did take it a bit far with her kidnapping and murder but by then I had lost the plot and had no control over my own emotions or actions. Rightfully or wrongfully, she was the recipient of my actions or revenge as I call it."

C.J.   "Did that happen very often to you, the losing control because so many women were attacked and yet you killed only 4 of them. And by saying only 4, I am not trying to make light of it or put you down in any way, 4 is still 4 too many in a normal person's eyes."

C.S.   "On a few occasions I would get home and wonder where I had been or what I had done because I would have no recall whatsoever. If I had attacked someone, I would only find out about it in the news and then I wasn't sure it was me, I just accepted that it was because all the attacks seemed the same, I was in a daze when it happened, kind of high on the feeling of it all."

C.J.   "That could possibly be why you didn't know how many victims there had been, they had been deliberately blanked out of your mind, or forgotten."

C.S.   "Maybe so, either that or the pot I was smoking, I did have a few blanks because of that, I won't lie to you."

C.J.   "But the pot wouldn't have made you kill, it is more of a stimulant and kept you calm, so that must have been you all along."

C.S.   "I was very stimulated if that is even a word, but I don't think it is now to be honest. Yes, the killing was just me and my experiment on seeing how far I would or could go. A step more or further each time, just a typical serial killer and all the traits that go with it."

C.J.   "Further than you originally thought you would, I would guess or more than you felt you were capable of at least, did you ever imagine you could do what you did?"

C.S.   "A lot further but then again not as far, depends on how you look at it. I have a split personality and therefore two choices or outcomes, that makes it hard to know what is right and what is wrong. All the right things happened to one side of me while all the wrong things were contrived by the psycho in me, I knew I was capable but to follow it through I'm not so sure, until the first time that is, then I knew and there was no stopping me."

C.J.   "That is something only someone that is wrong would say, as if to try and justify their actions. Why did the good you not try to stop the bad you, or at least try and talk him down?"

C.S.   "Who said I didn't? I had plenty of mirror talks with myself. I have no justifications of my actions at all, I would love to know the answers myself, but to get answers firstly you must listen to questions, and I didn't, I don't. My attention span is not that great. If I wanted to listen, then I would have but chose not to. When the good me tried to talk the bad me down, then I just blanked him out or at least tried my best to, but it wasn't always possible."

C.J.   "You have to fight the demons and not give in to them when they surface, that is what most normal people do."

C.S.   "Normal is not a word that I would label myself with, or anyone for that matter. Who is to judge what is normal and what is not, the threshold is different for everyone after all? Something you find normal I may see as crazy and vice versa, it comes down to personal choice or taste in the end."

C.J.   "Some of the craziest people have had some the most powerful jobs and completely screwed them up whereas some of the sanest people are overlooked for everything, that is how life works."

C.S.   Then I should be prime minister one day. Although I do believe my chance has come and gone."

They both laughed for a short while and then Colin continued with his story....

Chapter 15: Necrophilia.

I had read about necrophilia in books about serial killers and heard about it in all the documentaries, and I won't lie, I was curious. I wasn't so sure it would be for me per say, but thought I would give it a try, nonetheless. The only way I could describe it would be, like a quick cheap fuck but with none of the hassle.

Colin Stevens was in jubilant mood, high on emotion and the buzz success brings and nothing was going to bring him down from the dizzy heights he had reached today. He was prancing around the bathroom miming 'Hot Stuff' by Donna Summer into the toothbrush he was pretending was a microphone and he had grasped tightly in his clenched fist. He was preparing himself for a night on the town, the party bus was on its way and Colin was making sure he was getting on board. He was in fact so high that nothing could bring him down, and he didn't want it too.

Even by his own standards he admitted he had been very lucky today. You make your own luck in this world is something he had always said and seriously believed it to be true, but today two birds had been killed with what appeared to be just one stone, thrown. Not only had he managed to get rid of the threat to himself posed by that know-it-all prick of a detective, Jack Williams by executing him, mafioso style, but he had also managed to pass the buck and put the blame entirely at Marie Calvin's feet. If that wasn't enough for a celebration then the fact that the police were now having doubts about the rape allegations made by Marie against him, then all in all it has been the most productive of days. A very productive day indeed and he was in the mood for a celebratory drink or two.

Towel drying himself after what was a very refreshing shower he walked into the bedroom and looked at the clothes he had already chosen and laid out on the bed ready for his night out. Very dapper he thought to himself, what ladies could refuse, and so fucking what if they do, that had never stopped him in the past, so why would it now. Hahahahahaha, he laughed quietly to himself and yet it felt piercingly loud in a villainess, evil kind of way. All he needed to be doing was stroking a fluffy White cat and he could have passed himself off as a Bond villain, like a Blofeld or a Scaramanga or any of them really.

Once he was dressed and ready for the off, he moved over to the cupboard in the corner, the one with the false bottom. Underneath which he stores the things he values most in life, hidden from the view of any ordinary person. To see these special possessions, you must know Colin well. Really well in fact and of course be a psychotic narcissist, just like him. Either that or one of his victims, just like the lady in the lake had turned out to be.

He had only ever shown the contents of the cupboard to one person before and that was her, and that after he had abducted or kidnapped her at knife point. He needed to prove to the press and cops that he wasn't the amateur they had stressed he was, and it was no fucking accident, but they will soon know, he was sure of that. He wanted to prove to them and himself that he was professional and very thorough in all he does. Maybe after this they would take him seriously. He had then taken her back to his apartment after abducting her from the street and throwing her into the boot of his car. He then bound her hands and let her know that he had every intention of raping and murdering her. He felt her fear was his strength and he was getting off on it big time, getting stronger with every tear she cried. After all she had now seen the inside of his gaffe and was in the position to spoil his party and let out his big secret.

Immediately prior to cutting her throat with his trusty blade, he showed her his collection of buttons that he had taken from previous victims and even cut one from her blouse, placing it in with the others so she knew she was next and the fear he saw in her eyes gave him a buzz, the thrill he had been waiting for. He closed his eyes, breathed in her fear, its' strength was empowering. He was feeling so high on the emotion that it was going to take an eternity to come back down, and he didn't want to in any case. He was happy being high, the higher the better.

She pleaded with him for her life, but he didn't listen, and he cut her throat with one quick slice as if it were a knife gliding through butter and then watching the blood spurt out everywhere. He also tasted a little, the first time he had ever done that but realised this was a big mistake, a step too far for even him. It tasted disgusting and nearly made him puke so he vowed never to try it again. He was a murderer, but he was not a cannibal. They say you learn from mistakes, and this was a big mistake he needed to learn from to know what he was prepared to do and what he was incapable of doing. If it were possible for someone like him to have morals, no matter how small they were, then surely this was the time.

He kept the body in his apartment for three days and performed sex acts on it, or necrophilia if you will, the art if you can call it an art of having sex with a dead lifeless corpse. This is the point that his entire idea of having any form of morals broke down and disappeared.

After cutting her throat he remembered back to the cat he had skinned and even thought about doing that to her, but she looked so placid and calm, and he didn't want to disturb her newfound peace and degrade her any more than he already had. So, he shagged her instead, not degrading in any way, right. He threw her in the boot of his car and took her to the park where he dumped her in the lake.

Connie was aghast at what she had just heard, asked him to repeat it. "Say that again."

C.S.   "Say what again, which part?"

C.J.   "Necrophilia?"

C.S.   "Yes, but only for a couple of days, after that she started looking bad and it put me off."

C.J.   "And have you tried necrophilia with any other victims?"

C.S.   "No, it was just her. At first, she looked fine and at peace like she was asleep and not dead. If I went off that memory then I probably would have, but she started turning a bluey-purple colour, she both looked and smelled awful and that put me right off."

C.J.   "So, what made you think of trying it, only the most depraved of people would even consider it as an option."

C.S.   "Progression, I guess. You try something new and if you like it then you do it again but if you don't then you don't. Eventually you try something completely different, and you can't really get any different than that."

C.J.	"You are talking about it like you were giving up drinking or smoking, having sex with dead bodies is neither of them, it's out there with the worst of the worst."

C.S.	"Probably about as far away from them as you can get but I suppose it can be an addiction just like smoking and drinking can. Ed Gein, Edmund Kemper, Jeffrey Dahmer, Garry Ridgeway and even the most famous of all Ted Bundy were all necrophiles. Some of them even re-visited the bodies after weeks or months to do more to them. On that count maybe it is a good thing that I was appalled by how she looked."

C.J.	"She only looked like that because of you and nobody else. So, to blame her for looking bad when you caused it is incredulous to me."

C.S.	"When did I ever blame her for looking bad? I didn't know she would turn so quick and that was down to me entirely. But I just said I didn't like it not that I blamed her for it. The way I look at it is I would never shag an ugly tart so why would I shag an ugly corpse. She was one ugly corpse and that's why I disposed of her body by throwing her in the lake."

C.J.	"Woah there, unbelievable how can you say such a thing and look serious while you are actually saying it."

C.S.	"What can I say, I told you that you may not like some of the truths that I will reveal and your words to me were 'I'm a woman of the world, try me'. So, consider yourself well and truly tried. If you don't like it then there is the door, and we can forget the whole thing."

C.J.	"You were right, some of it is hard to hear Colin, but I am not going anywhere, I said I would do the story and that is what I am going to do, I am here till the end. It's not about me or my tastes, it's about you and getting your story printed, no matter how fucked up it may be or how fucked up you were at the time."

C.S.   "Ok then, if you are sure then I will continue......."

After three days she was starting to smell and was turning a bluey-purple colour and she was starting to freak me out, so I decided to discard of her body. In the early hours of the third day, I smuggled her into the boot of my car and drove her to the park where I dumped her in the lake. I was not sure at the time if anyone knew she was a victim of the Cotton Mill Rapist, but I did and to me that was all that mattered. Why should I care what they want to believe or what shit they are willing to print when I knew the truth because I was present, and they weren't?

Colin Sprayed himself with deodorant and feeling refreshed, picked up the knife from the cupboard base and put it into the pocket on the inside of his jacket, he was now ready and certainly prepared for a night to remember. Just a shame for someone else tonight it was most definitely going to be a night they would want to forget but would never be able to. On leaving the house, Colin walked down the street to the taxi rank and got a black cab into town, watch out ladies Colin Stevens is happy as Larry, whoever that is and on the prowl.

After a few hours of doing the rounds and visiting all four of the main pubs in town Colin decided to call it quits. It was now a quarter to midnight, and he'd had four pints of lager and three double Drambuie and Cokes. It was far more than he would usually have, and he was feeling a little worse for wear. He didn't normally drink this much in fact he rarely drunk out at all but tonight was a celebration and one that doesn't come along very often.

It took him about fifteen minutes to reach the High Street, zigging and zagging slightly with the alcohol proving efficient enough to take effect. He thought it would probably take him another 20 minutes or so to get all the way home if he was lucky enough that it didn't rain and make him hide under shelter until it subsided. Although rain wasn't forecast it had been known to happen at the most inopportune times. While walking down High Street he noticed someone moving on the other side of the road and on closer inspection he saw it was a woman and she seemed to be alone, just as he liked them. Had fate dropped another one right into his lap he asked himself. She stopped at the shoe shop for a short while and appeared to be admiring the shoes in the window. While she was pre-occupied with the shoes she hadn't noticed when exactly, but the man she had seen on the other side of the road a few minutes earlier had disappeared and her heart was pounding with fear.

She was quite relieved and started to calm down a little as she was starting to get a little worried about him, especially after reading all the stories in the papers and hearing the news reports about a rapist being loose around town. She carried on walking down the road while keeping herself alert and indeed she should have been worried, indeed there was a rapist on the loose and thrice indeed he was the man she had seen. What she had failed to notice was that the man that she had seen and got a good view of had darted across the road when she wasn't looking and headed down the alleyway that leads behind the row of shops which included 'Clarks', the shoe shop she had been looking in and was now ahead of her at the point where the entry re-emerges onto the high street and was lying in wait for her to pass.

Fifteen minutes earlier.........

It was 11.55 p.m., just a few short minutes from midnight and Jane Felson was finishing her shift at Castalia D'Itonia, the Italian restaurant at the top end of Sutton Road. It had been a good shift and they were busier than usual. Time had flown and the tips were good. If things carried on like this then before too long, she would be able to treat herself to the new boots she had been admiring in Clarks the shoe shop window. In fact, she will be passing by Clarks on her walk home so may just stop for a moment or two to admire them a little more and say hello. A bit of self-induced torture she knows when you want something that bad then maybe a little reverse psychology will work and just seeing them will help her urge to buy them stop before she can fully afford them at least.

It was a walk she had made each night for the last three weeks since she had been given the job at Castalia D'Itonia. She loved it and was getting on well with fellow staff members and customers alike. Jane bade her farewell to Paulo, the chef and exited through the big glass double doors out onto Sutton Road before turning left at the top into Wilson Square which in turn led onto the High Street. She only lived about a 10-minute walk away and had never been afraid to walk anywhere in her hometown, ever. Even with all the stories of a rapist on the loose she still felt safe as these things in her own words, never happen to you, it's always someone else. Although she was a little more cautious than she had been, she still wanted to live her own life and not be dictated, as to when and where she could or couldn't go. Ignorance is a damning thing, God help her.

While she was walking down the High Street, she noticed someone moving on the other side of the road, the person was walking parallel to her but about 20 feet back. A little nervous, she stopped at Clarks shoe shop as she had said she would to admire the boots in the window, the ones she had been saving up her tips for. It wouldn't be long now before she could buy them and feel she had really earned them. While looking at them she caught a reflection in the window. She could clearly see it was the figure of a man and he had also stopped walking on the other side of the road. What was odd was that he was looking in her direction, directly at her and she could see his face clearly. He had no idea she could make him out and so just kept staring as she was facing the other way and unaware as far as he was concerned that she even knew he was there.

She didn't recognise him, so he obviously wasn't anyone she knew, so why had he stopped at the same time and why was he looking over. Possibly, he felt he recognised her or else he had ulterior motives which was more likely the case and she was starting to worry. She built up a mental image of his face in her mind, trying not to leave anything off. Knowing she was on her own she tried not to let her fear get to her too much and looked once more at the boots in the window before deciding to head off home.

Not wanting to let on that she knew he was there she had a quick glance back out of the corner of her eye but saw nothing, no-one at all, he seemed to have disappeared. She looked everywhere, both up and down the road but there was no sign. Relieved, she walked on along the High Street and was just passing the alleyway at the end of the road when her initial fears were realised. One hand reached over and covered her mouth as the other was wrapped around her torso dragging her into the alleyway. Trying to scream but only letting out a muffled groan and obviously petrified beyond belief she heard a voice say 'scream again and you die' as she felt the cold steel touch her throat, the cold steel of a knife.

Fighting appeared futile as she was only slight, and he was six feet plus and she had no answer to his brutish strength. The paralysing fear she felt left Jane feeling she was about to pass out but unfortunately for her she didn't and was conscious enough to remember every sordid horrible detail, from the removal of her underwear to the rough treatment her vagina took from the dryness of his unprotected cock. She will never forget the grunting, the panting and the seemingly never-ending of the rocking back-and-forth thrusting until he had finished and emptied himself into her. A feeling she will take with her to her grave, the worst moment she has ever had to experience by far and one she never wants to experience ever again.

She was no stranger to men being rough with her and in fact at times craved it and quite enjoyed the feeling. She didn't ever think she was a prude and was open to new experiences, but this was different. This was far from one of those love experiences to sit back and enjoy. This was someone that had no right or invite to be there, violating her space both inside and out and all for his own perverted pleasure. Too late now she knows but she wished she had listened to people and ordered herself a taxi.

When he had finished and after what seemed an eternity to her, he pulled out, still dripping and ran off down the High Street. Happy at his latest conquest, pleased with the souvenir button that had been ripped off her blouse and excited another victim was going to be added to his ever-growing list. Only oblivious and totally unaware to the fact she had seen his face and was already plotting her next move, she was going to go straight to the police station before the image faded and she wouldn't be able to recall him at all. But for the next few minutes she just sat in a heap in the alley crying to herself, funny thing is she wasn't scared any more, just angry, and full of hatred and contempt. She was under no illusion or threat that he may return, she knew he had gone and wouldn't be back. How? She had no idea, but she just felt it was so, he was a coward and cowards don't deal with confrontation and if he returned that is what he would get and he knew it.

If she went home right away, she knew her memory would fade and she would not be able to recall what he looked like, let alone be able to describe him in full detail so she made the decision to head to the police station, post haste. So that is what she did for her sake and the sake of all the possible future and past victims of this animal.

Chapter 16: At work with Detective Jackson.

The only dealings I had with Detective Martin Stevens were during interviews or when I handed myself in, I can't really comment on him as I didn't know him, really. But he seemed honest enough and just doing his job, I can't hate him for that. Maybe other things, but not that. .If there was any reason then it would have been the amateurish way he went about certain tasks but that may be my problem and not his

Martin Jackson was a good cop, no scratch that, he was an excellent cop with 24 years' solid experience and a keen eye for detail. Starting out as an 18-year-old-rookie he had worked his way up from walking the beat to the dizzy heights of Detective Inspector. It had cost him one marriage and countless sleepless nights, but at this juncture in his life and at this time it all seemed worth the sacrifices he had made at least that is what he kept telling himself to justify his actions and choices.

It had taken a lot of hard work and determination mixed in with more than just a few slices of luck and added to a small amount of ass-kissing. He wasn't one to roll over and have his tummy tickled in any way, but he felt a well-timed compliment here and there to possibly enhance his promotion prospects were a chance worth taking and it had worked when he looked at just how far he had come.

He didn't even mind that most people saw him as Jack Williams' sidekick or understudy even though he had been in the force two years less than Jack and was at the exact same level. The two most telling factors in it were one; he knew himself that he wasn't, and two; Jack never made him feel even the slightest bit inferior. In fact, to a degree, it really worked in his favour as most people would go straight to Jack for something believing he was in charge and in doing so leave him in peace to just get on with his work and he always had more time for his paperwork than Jack did. Quite often Jack would have a good moan about how far behind he was with his work, but Martin never rubbed it in that he was up to date, even occasionally ahead of schedule. Swings and roundabouts he thought to himself because it wouldn't be fair to Jack and if the shoe was on the other foot Jack would never make him feel inadequate.

Martin loved the job, and he loved the people he worked alongside. He hadn't once even come close to losing the buzz or feeling of excitement he got when he secured his first conviction. Seeing a no-good underbelly of existence paying for their crime and knowing he had a great deal to with it made him feel like he was doing his own personal bit to help society. He was doing it for all the law-abiding citizens, all the Joe and Jane Bloggs that stay on the right pathway and wouldn't consider for a moment the illegal route to fame and riches. He often wondered exactly what made people turn from where they were to where they are, but everybody is different. The main difference is when to say yes and when to say no. Get it wrong you will be a criminal but get it right and you won't.

Everything pointed to Marie being one and also to Colin being innocent, yet for some reason he felt the roles should be reversed, that Marie was innocent and there was something not quite right about Colin Stevens. Why he had no idea, that was always Jack's domain, but now with Jack gone maybe it was time for him to step up and try to listen to his own ideas.

So where had these doubts about Marie stemmed from, he needed to sit back and look again but this time with an open mind. He found it hard to get away from the fact that all the evidence was pointing in the direction of her being guilty. Maybe it was too easy, possibly the evidence was so well manufactured that it was made to slot together just like a jigsaw that he had fell hook line and sinker and put it together to get the result that Colin wanted and in so doing deflected any blame away from himself. Martin was a big fan when he could find the time to watch her, of Judge Judy, and as she said on numerous occasions, "If something looks wrong then chances are it is not going to be right" and that certainly looked the case now. It was all too perfect. But the biggest clue, and one he couldn't refute in the slightest was the evidence he held in his hand. It was a photofit of the attacker in the Jane Felson case as described by Jane herself that had more than just a close resemblance to someone he knew. Someone he had encountered quite a few times lately one tricky son-of-a-bitch called Colin Stevens. Could it be possible that the cotton mill rapist had been under their very noses and closer at hand than they ever could have imagined, was Colin Stevens the one person that had eluded them for so long.

Things had been going mental lately and although for so long he had kept on top of it all for the most part, since the murder of Jack the backlog of work was building and growing by the day. Today however appeared to be heading towards a quiet one and he may be able to clear a fair bit of it, so long as there were no unexpected intrusions. Martin only had two scheduled appointments although that could change at the drop of a hat in this line of business and often did. He was pencilled in to speak with Brian Allen, head CEO and founder of Allen and Co. where both Colin and Marie work this morning at 10 a.m. and then at 2 p.m. he had a meeting with Grant Spectre, the editor of the local Gazette to discuss when would be the correct moment to release the photofit in the paper.

He didn't want to release it too soon and give a heads-up to the attacker and a give him a chance to flee, but he also didn't want to risk the wrath he would receive if someone else was hurt in the meantime and the facts became known that he knew who it could have been without giving warning. Tight calls mean big falls he thought to himself, he hated the saying with a passion but at this exact moment it made more sense to him than anything else did. He had made some tight calls lately and some had paid off, but others had gone completely tits-up for him and the higher you are the further you will fall. Boy had he hit the ground hard couple of times lately with his pride taking the brunt of it all.

One more mistake and the shit could possibly hit the fan and what a knock-on effect that could prove to have. He was getting fed up with being called into the bosses' office to explain himself, he was starting to run out of believable excuses and his chief was certainly no idiot, even though he tried it on more often than not.

Marie was taken from her cell to interview room 4, a room to which she had become quite accustomed. She sat back in her chair and was asked if she fancied a cup of tea or coffee, she chose the latter. She had her coffee white with one sugar and was really excited in anticipation of the sugar rush as things were that dull and boring in the cells that even this was something major, small things and minds hey, a little buzz can be a major event, but just for a few minutes until reality strikes. Detective Jane Collins walked in and sat opposite to her and smiled, "Hi Marie, how are you today," she asked. "As good as I can be in the circumstances," came the reply. "Tired a little as I didn't sleep, and I could do with a shower and my own bed but apart from that I want all this to just be over..." she stopped talking as she was sobbing uncontrollably. "Why is he doing this to me," she enquired.

"That's what we are here to find out Marie, and to work out if any crime has been committed at all. We only have your word against his, all the evidence points in the direction that you were the aggressor, and that you planned it, you initiated it and you finished it." Jane said. "I didn't, I couldn't, I wouldn't hurt anyone and never have in my life, ever honestly." Marie sobbed.

"We can't rightly arrest him and send him to prison because you say you honestly didn't do it Marie, otherwise the prisons would be full to overflowing and just on somebody's say so. It is our job to look at all the evidence and make up our own minds so let's have a quick recap of the things we know or that have been alleged. You say Mr Stevens called you into his office on the Friday to discuss a promotion whereas he says there was no promotion in the pipeline, and you asked to see him. The champagne was bought on your credit card that was in your possession the entire time and the champagne flutes were from your house, taken according to you by Mr Stevens when he must have broken in. Although there had been no break in or to that matter, any form of damage reported previously." Jane continued.

"You also allege that Mr Stevens used his force and strength to hold you down and rape you on his desk while he says you seduced him and had in fact on another occasion performed a sex act on him at an office Christmas party that you wanted to keep a secret. This we know is true as you have admitted to it. It's not looking good Marie, we need something more than speculation or you could be in serious trouble, or rather you are in serious trouble. If we can't find any evidence against him then you are going to be charged Marie, it's that simple, we are left with no choice." She finished.

Although he had no idea and was totally oblivious to his own surroundings, an invisible web was starting to wind its' way around Colin Stevens and there was nothing at all he could do about it. You can't stop what you can see sometimes, so what hope could there be in stopping something that was invisible to the naked eye. Raping Marie no matter how empowered it had made him feel for the few seconds he was in ecstasy, was a big mistake. Because now the police had a sample of his D.N.A. from the sperm and blood samples they took from him the day after the incident. All they would have to do is put two and two together and if the answer was four, then they had caught themselves the Cotton Mill Rapist. It's all ifs and buts for now but just one lucky break at the right time could be all they needed to gain the upper hand. It didn't matter a jot if he felt they were too thick to see what was right in front of them because one day someone would, he was sure of it.

 Colin had no idea and was as far as he was concerned in the clear and was strutting around like he was king of the world. He had no cares or worries and was living the dream he had craved for years. Unfortunately for him, and before too long, Colin Stevens actions in lies and deceit were going to catch up with him and he was in for one almighty fall. The higher you feel you are then the further you fall, and you may well end up hitting the floor with such a thud that you may never recover.

Chapter 17: 2 meetings, 1 day.

Introducing himself to Mr Allen of Allen and Co. as Detective Martin Jackson, he enquired as to whether, Colin had turned up for work at all and of course Mr Allen replied, "No, not for a couple of days now." Although he kind of expected that to be the case it was still a little surprising to him as he felt, why would someone with nothing to hide take themselves out of their comfort zone and not want to be seen and in doing so, possibly risk fanning the flames of conspiracy. A very strange situation and one he struggled to make heads nor tails of. Not exactly the actions of an innocent man, maybe there was more to this than meets the eye, he thought to himself once again.

Why does everything now seem to be pointing to the opposite of what was originally believed. It all seems to be swings and roundabouts as far as Colin and Marie were concerned and struggling to get to grips with who may be guilty, he was happy to have the chance of going along for the ride. And what a ride it was turning out to be. This one could still go either way, he thought to himself.

"One other thing Detective another employee of mine has not turned in either, Marie Calvin. I have tried calling her countless times but to no avail, there has been no reply from her at all." Mr Allen said. "Ah yes Mr Allen, I can help you with that Miss Calvin is another one of the reasons I am here and so desperately needed to talk with you about." Martin Jackson told him

"Miss Calvin claims she was in line for a promotion within the company and was asked by Mr Stevens to come to her office and discuss the matter last Friday. She said that you and Mr Stevens had been very pleased with her work, and that was the reason she went to his office." he added. "We are very pleased with Marie no doubt about that detective, but I can guarantee there was no talk of promotion, not for the foreseeable future anyway. The economy has hit us as hard as it has everyone, and the money is just not there to fund a promotion. I wouldn't rule it out in the future but for now it is certainly not an option. "Mr Allen explained

"Miss Calvin also alleges that while she was in his office, Mr Stevens barred her exit, then attacked and raped her on the desk in his room. Although traces of his semen were extracted from her vagina and surrounding area there was not enough proof that a crime had been committed and so we had to let Mr Stevens go free." Martin said reluctantly, trying to get some sort of reaction. "Oh my goodness, that is awful news, and what about Marie?" asked Mr Allen, "Is she in hospital, is she hurt, why has she not been in." he asked. "Well, that's where things get a little more than just complicated, I am afraid, without giving away too many details. Marie has been placed under arrest for the murder of one of our detectives, in fact he was my partner Detective Jack Williams." Martin explained to a shocked Mr Allen who just stared straight forward in total disbelief.

After a couple minutes of awkward silence which Martin was happy to wait for to be broken, Mr Allen spoke out and said, "Jesus Christ Detective do you expect me to believe Marie was capable of murdering anyone, let alone a detective. She wouldn't even say boo to a ghost." He insisted. "That is what a few people that know her have been saying Mr Allen, and probably one of the reasons I have my doubts about what has been said. Because believe me, if things didn't seem so far from the ordinary as they do then she would have already had the book thrown at her and serving a life stretch. Something really doesn't appear right, and I am determined to work out what it is and who did what to who and most importantly, why." Martin informed him.

"Please keep me informed of the situation Detective, and if Colin shows up here, I will let you know straight away." Mr Allen said. "Thank you, Mr Allen and yes please do. But can you do it quietly and in a way that Mr Stevens doesn't know, I wouldn't want him to worry unduly when there is no evidence to prove he has done anything wrong." He explained. With that Martin bid farewell and headed back to his car, wondering again just why Colin would see fit to hide himself away. The act possibly of a guilty man or else just fearful of what other people may think of him, after all he never had the best of reputations to start with. Once you start off on the wrong foot, the chance of regaining the right step is always an ordeal and probably why so many don't bother trying for fear of losing their step altogether. As most people are aware of, when you are out of step, the effort it takes to get back in step is immense and doesn't always work anyway. You just end up being more and more hopelessly lost and treading water or on eggshells to be honest.

 Looking at the clock on his dashboard, Martin was surprised to see it was 11.52, he had spent far more time with Mr Allen than he had planned, two cups of tea later and now he found himself behind in his plans. He had wanted to pop by the station on the way to pick a few things up before grabbing a bite to eat and then heading off for his appointment with Grant Spectre, but unfortunately things never pan out as you believe they will and now his plans had to change.

What he wanted to pick up from the office was important but not vital or case threatening and could be put off until tomorrow if needs must. He hadn't eaten for at least 16 hours and was famished so he decided to go straight for a small bite to eat before heading to his afternoon meeting.

On the way he would be passing a Tesco superstore, and he knew from experience they had a café, so he drove his car into the car park and stopped in a bay just to the left of the main doors. Today he was being extra careful not to stop in a disabled bay as he had done on a couple of occasions in the past and the hassle just wasn't worth the aggro it caused. For the simple convenience of having your car in view while you eat really was a pointless exercise when these miserable moaning cunts were about to make you feel bad for no reason whatsoever. Almost as if it was their personal goal and the only reason for them existing in the first place. People like that in Martin's eyes were just a waste of their parent's sperm, they may as well just masturbate straight into the toilet to save making a busybody do-gooder like that, it's just a good wank wasted in his opinion.

Once he even tried to pull a fast one by flashing his badge and saying he was on duty and in a hurry, but they wouldn't have it. He just hated these, no-good-do-gooders with a passion. The ones that always seem to be there when you do something even the slightest bit out of the ordinary. Even though what you have done is not illegal and only inconveniences them for a fraction of a second, and if anyone should know it was him working within the law as he did. And then if that wasn't enough, they just won't let it go and keep on at you until you admit you were wrong even though you knew you weren't and you just plead guilty to shut the Motherfuckers up.

Inside the café he picked up a tray and placed a Tuna mayo sandwich on it. £5.49 he thought, wow that's steep, but I guess it does have all this lovely green crap on it and if that is what they refer to as a healthy salad then you can keep it. Salad was something Martin very seldom ate, why should he be forced to eat something usually reserved for rabbits, hamsters, and other household pets. He also got himself a mug and poured himself a frothy Coffee Latte from the machine and placed that on the tray next to the butty. Once at the till he swapped pleasantries with the girl who then rang up his two items. That'll be £7.28 please but do you realise if you buy a packet of crisps for 99 pence the total cost will be just £6.50 if you want to that is, but you really don't have to. Martin was a little shocked at this revelation and asked how could buying something extra make what he already had cheaper. He was a cop for Christ's sake and he couldn't work it out. We have a meal-deal on today, a sandwich, a drink, and a snack either crisps or a chocolate bar for £6.50. Fine he said and went and got himself a packet of ready salted crisps. Thank you I would never have guessed that even though at that precise moment he saw a giant sign directly in front of him saying "Meal Deal – Sandwich, snack, and drink £6.50…. He just paid and moved away as quickly as he could with his tail tucked between his legs in a retreating kind of manner.

Martin found himself a seat in the window and when he peered out, he found to his surprise he was directly in front of his car. This made him smile and then he chortled a full on, belly laugh to himself. Anyone looking must have wondered what this mad psycho was about and steered clear of him, nobody needs to be lumbered with a psychopath. All the effort he could have gone through to be in this position, close to his car and it just happens by pure accident, typical.

While having his lunch he went over a few facts to do with the case, well actually cases now because the pair of them, Marie and Colin were racking up a few files between them and with Jack no longer there to help he didn't seem to be getting very much done. He was still working just as hard as he ever did, or even harder really but it still didn't seem to be enough to stop the workload building up.

One thing that was really playing on his mind was the gun, where was it, how could it just disappear. Someone must know and they just weren't telling. They had to, possibly even one of Marie and Colin but without it there was not a lot he could do about anything. He had no proof that Marie had pulled the trigger and may well have to let her go, but not before he thought he would give it one more shot to see if she would slip up even in the slightest. But her story hadn't changed at all from the first time she was interviewed. It was constant and he hadn't seen any tell-tale signs that she was lying, the kind that you normally see in people. The nervous twitch, the hand running through the hair or even the foot-tapping nervously on the floor. She didn't even seem to be struggling for words and hadn't said "um" once. She was as cool as a cucumber and showing no signs of deception whatsoever, not even close to it. Either she was one of the most cunning, conniving bitches that he had ever met, or she was innocent just like she had claimed.

After a twenty-minute break at Tesco he headed back to his car, his wild growling stomach had now been tamed and he felt human again. He had left himself with just enough time to drive the 20 miles to the Gazette offices and his meeting with Grant Spectre. He wasn't exactly a big fan of Grant and there had been a few incidents in the past where Grant had approved the printing of articles not yet cleared by the police, thus causing all sorts of problems for them in their investigations and not to mention, at trials. On one occasion the judge had to throw out the entire jury and rule in favour of the accused because 2 jury members had started an affair. Nothing at all to do with the case he had been working on for months Martin argued, but the scandal was enough to put a question mark on it all and acquittal seemed the easiest option for the judge.

Martin still to this day thinks Grant paid either the judge, the jury, or the victim a bribe to drop all charges or else paid the two jury members to start the affair but it was never proved due to lack of evidence. Funny that Martin had seen the accused and Grant sharing a hug and laughing together about a week after the trial when they swore blindly that they had never met before. He also thought that Grant was a stuck-up pompous twat that had only been made editor of the Gazette because his father owned the paper and had in fact said this to Grant in person before today and no doubt would again if and when he got the opportunity.

Grant hated Martin in return, why only he knows, but he says he has his good reasons even though keeps them close to his chest. He only has dealings with him because he has provided him with a lot of good printable stories due to his position in the police force, ones that he would never be able to get hold of if he hadn't known him. Martin had single-handedly earned Grant his position of editor by means of the stories he had passed on, as well as his own hard work of course, or was it his dad pulling strings?

Martin and Grant's father, Brian Spectre had been good mates at one point until Grant grew up to be the prick that he turned out to be. Now they barely even acknowledge each other as they pass on the street which isn't that often and they hadn't been fishing together for years when they used to go at least once a week. Shame how it turned out Martin often thinks but at least he has as little to do with Grant as he possibly can, so swings and roundabouts as they say. Every bad point has a flip side and not seeing Grant is as good a point as Martin could think of right now.

On meeting the pair of them got the awkward unpleasant greeting out of the way, squeezing each other's hands' tighter than they should trying to take a mile without giving an inch and when they were done playing, they settled down to the business at hand.

 Martin started by telling Grant about the description Jane Felton had given and the photofit they had made, and how he wanted it to be printed in the paper but not for a couple of days. Which would be just enough time to give the culprit a chance to rest easy and believe he was in the clear. And it would also give Martin the time he needed to tie up any loose ends he had to get sorted before swooping and not giving him a chance to hide any evidence that he would be able to discard beforehand if he was aware of how the investigation was going so well.

"So, how long do you want me to sit on it then," Grant asked. "Well, it's Wednesday now so I would say if you put it in Thursdays Gazette. He should see it either Thursday night or at the latest Friday morning, that will give me all the time I need to get a warrant sorted and all the back-up I need to muster," Martin replied. "You have someone in mind," Grant enquired. "Yes, but I really couldn't divulge a name. Only to say I believe he is possibly guilty of more than one crime I just need to put the evidence together to prove it. That is why I need the time really, so what do you say." He asked. "I will do it on one condition." Grant propositioned him. "And what is that?" Asked Martin a little pissed with the game Grant was trying to play. "When you get sorted and have everything you need together and then eventually catch this bastard, you come to me and give me the exclusive. We could sell a lot of papers on an exclusive about the Mill Rapist." Grant told him. "What makes you think it's the Cotton Mill case?" asked Martin. "You just answered that for me." Grant replied. "You can have an exclusive, but only if you sit on it for a couple of days." "Thursday it is, thank you Martin." Grant replied appreciatively.

With this interaction, their business was now concluded, and Martin made his excuses to leave. "Don't forget now," Grant called after him, "My exclusive, and mine alone." Martin just nodded his head in return without uttering a word, apart from the names he was calling him under his breath and headed out of the door and back to his car.

Martin drove away quite pleased with himself, not only had he managed to get Grant to agree to holding back printing the photofit until Thursday, but he also didn't have to give him the full details of why he wanted to wait. He had strung Grant along with a little bit of bullshit and the dickhead hadn't even noticed, or if he had then he hid it well. It may have only been a hollow victory but anything he could get over on Grant with or without realising he would take as a victory just the same. Martin was all prepared and ready to go on the search of Colin's house and already had the warrant in place. But wasn't going to let on to Grant and then have to rush in and act on it now as it was Jacks' funeral in the morning, and he had his mind set firmly on that. If he could get the funeral out the way, then he could pick up the warrant in the afternoon and do his surprise raid on

Colins' house. Colin would be none the wiser that they were on their way and so be totally unprepared and have no time to hide or destroy any evidence that may be there, if any at all. Martin had driven away in a cheery mood and very pleased with himself, very pleased indeed.

Chapter 18: Goodbye Jack.

Nobody noticed me hiding behind the oak tree, they call themselves cops but not even one of them knew that their mate's killer was standing only a hundred foot or so away from them and laughing in their faces. They were a country mile away from finding me and yet I was within their grasp.

On his way home Martin stopped off at the off-licence and picked himself up a half bottle of Jameson's Whiskey. He had a feeling he may be too deep in thought tonight to be able to sleep, and therefore maybe the Whisky would help him relax. It seemed to do the trick just as he planned because he started to drink it on an empty stomach and had finished it within two hours. He has no idea what time exactly that he passed out, but it was sometime after 8 as he remembers seeing the end of Only Connect, the Victoria Coren Mitchell quiz show he watches religiously in the hope that one day he will get an answer correct and know why he was right. It could well have been five past eight, or it could have been a little later, but the only thing he knows for sure was it was after that because he remembered seeing the last round where there are no vowels, only consonants.

He woke the next morning with such a hangover as it had been a while since he'd had any form of alcohol, not since his problem days had been addressed and sorted anyway. He had woken up every day telling himself he was better without it and didn't need it and it had worked just fine, until yesterday that is. He needed it and if anyone got in his way, he would have given them hell for. The feeling he had at that moment made him realise why he didn't need it and he was pretty sure it was enough to stop him doing it again in a hurry.

The funeral of Detective Jack Williams was a small solemn affair and passed without incident. Jack hated funerals and was not shy to let it be known, if it wasn't for the fact, he was the guest of honour he would have tried to wriggle out of it in one way or another, that's for sure. There were only a handful of mourners present, he had no immediate family, just a couple of long-lost cousins he never saw and wouldn't have recognised if they were standing next to him in the street or anywhere to be honest. He was dedicated to his work so never had time to make friends and space was limited to the people that worked closest to him. The six people that turned up to say their goodbyes while pretending they knew all the prayers were only fooling themselves as the priest had a pretty good idea. In fact, none of them were religious at all and didn't have a clue, how it showed. They came, they cried their tears, some genuine, some crocodile, then went on their way back to the lives they knew, lives that would be a little emptier from now on. As Martin watched the coffin disappear behind the curtain that closed after it, he dipped his head for a second as if to say goodbye old friend and then made his way out of the chapel.

He knew where he had just been and why but still found it hard to comprehend that Jack was gone, really gone and what was more, he was never coming back. He wasn't off on one of the fishing trips he would occasionally take, but forever and would never be back. For the last 8 years they had been inseparable and had formed a very formidable and yet successful partnership. Jack was a hard man to read but Martin felt he knew him better than anyone and not having him there seemed wrong almost as if one of his own limbs was missing. It was going to take a lot of adapting and getting used to but for his own sake and the memory of Jack he knew he would have to settle in to work as quickly as he could. For this he was going to need the search warrant for Colin Jackson's house. If he could pick it up now then it would one less job to do later and would mean he wouldn't have to be running around like a blue-arsed fly on the day he was going to deploy it, whenever that was but they were getting closer. The fact was they were very close indeed, closer than even they could have imagined.

By now Martin knew he had the upper hand over Colin, purely for the fact the team were ready to move at any given moment and were just waiting for Martin's say-so. Whereas Colin had no idea of any information the police had gathered and so had no idea an investigation into him had even started let alone it being as far down the line as having a search warrant for his property. And yet Martin still wasn't counting his chickens because he had been in far better situations than this in the past and lost out and ended up scratching his head and wondering how, while watching the shit hit the fan once again.

He had only met Colin on a couple of occasions but felt he saw enough in him in those meetings to realise there was something slightly un-hinged about his character. He would be laughing and joking one minute and then suddenly turn vicious or nasty in the blink of eye. Then on realising what he had done and that he had been found out he would try to laugh it off as a bit of a joke. Maybe this was the Colin that could have attacked so many women, a schizophrenic persona perhaps. This was just one of the many questions that needed answering before they would even come close to solving this case.

This was one case that was going to perplex him for a good while to come. All he could do was exactly what he was doing and hope that all the evidence would somehow fall into place.

Chapter 19: 10 years' too long.

If Marie was as she had claimed, just a victim of an elaborate plan to frame her, and Colin had indeed perpetrated the crime himself and planted all the evidence, then he was not only turning out to be one tricky motherfucker, but also a brainy motherfucker. And if they rushed in when they weren't one hundred percent sure then they could blow the case wide open, and potentially, a dangerous man could walk free to kill or rape again. Yes, timing was going to prove crucial on this one, and it was all down to Martin to decide when. Colin he was sure was guilty of something, but what he wasn't sure yet, And Marie, he wasn't that convinced she was 100% innocent, so he was going to have to play it cool on this one and not rush in.

This cautious approach was most definitely the right one in Martin's eyes, although it did come with its' fair share of risks. For example, if the killer struck again possibly in the next few days and it did turn out to be Colin Stevens, the press would have a field day knowing the facts that the police had a name and a warrant but refused to act on them. It could subsequentially mean the end of Martins' career or worse, a torrent of abuse from any potential victims' loved ones.

Martin decided the time had come to play one more ace that he had hidden up his sleeve, something he had been holding close to his chest for a few days now, so he picked up his phone and dialled one of the numbers he had stored in his directory. The voice on the other end of the line said, "Gosh you are one of the last people I expected to hear from, especially this soon, what can I help you with this time". It was Grant Spectre, the editor of the Gazette and Martin enquired, "What makes you so sure I need any help. To which Grant came back with "That is the only reason you ever call. For Christ's sake Martin you are my Godfather and the only time I ever hear from you is when you need a favour." Grant added. Martin wanted to retort but felt he didn't have a leg to stand on and whatever he said would have fallen on deaf ears as Grant was entirely correct in all he had just said.

"You don't do so bad Grant, so please don't play the victim and act all hard done to, it's not becoming of you." At this point Martin forgot any pleasantries that may well have been in mind and just got straight on with what he had called for." I need you to print a story in tonight's evening Gazette, it was Jacks' funeral yesterday and we have a local girl in custody being questioned over his murder. If you could do an article as a kind of tribute to a local hero cop or something like that and casually throw in a mention of a 24-year-old local woman arrested on suspicion of murder, it would help us immensely. It would give our guy a reason to feel home and dry before we spring the warrant on him as he drops his guard. " Martin said.

"I think I already know the answer to this one but, any name on the girl," asked Grant. "No, not at this juncture in the investigation but you will be the first in line when we do release it, I can promise you that." Martin replied giving Grant hope. "Ok then fine, I will run that tonight and then go with the photofit you gave me the next day." replied Grant. "Brilliant, thanks that would be a great help, see you soon Grant, goodbye," and with that Martin hung up the phone hoping this was the last time he had to deal with Grant. Forever would be fantastic but he knew that would never happen because, although they both hated each other, he had to admit that they both needed each other too.

He really didn't need the extra hassle from Grant, not now of all the bad timings. He had just been to his partner's funeral, and he was stuck in the middle of a case that could go tits up at any moment, if he didn't get it right then it could result in a possibly innocent woman going to jail for murder. The last thing he needed right now was a petty squabble with his cry baby Godson, he was past that or at least he thought he was. That is the last thing I need right now, he thought to himself, grow up Grant, you immature wanker, but he didn't say it, only thought it as it probably would have caused more bad blood between them when there was already more than enough.

When he arrived back at the police station Martin went straight into his office and slammed the door shut, he counted to ten to and then punched the wall to vent some of his anger, well not so much anger more like frustration at how things were going, or not going as the case was. After sitting in silence at his desk for about 10 minutes he stood up, moved across the room, and opened the door to his office. On leaving he turned right and headed down the long corridor until he came to another door. This one was ajar, so he walked into the room. He was now in the operations room for the Cotton Mill rapist case. On the wall there were pictures of all 11 victims and a timeline of events, how and when they occurred. He had spent plenty of hours in this room just looking, taking things in, and trying to make heads or tails of all the information in a hope one day to be able to tell the victims of rape or the relatives of victims who had been murdered that they had caught the bastard that had done it and gotten away with it for so long. This shit had been dragging on for far too much time and they needed some form of closure to enable them to get on with what was left of their lives without wondering why the fucker that had done it, hadn't been caught after 10 years.

On a wall to the right and separate from the other pictures was a photograph of Marie Calvin, 'allegedly' the victim of rape and the possibility she was another of his victims but to prove this Martin was firstly going to have to prove that Colin stevens was in fact" The Cotton Mill Rapist." He was getting close he knew, but how close to the truth was he or was this just another wild goose chase that he was on and wasting valuable time that could be better served elsewhere on the investigation or other investigations for that matter.

 All other police work was building up due to the problems in this case and there just wasn't time to do it all, both personnel and resources wouldn't stretch that far and certain sacrifices had to be made. Some of the big decisions on this case had come via hunches, something he didn't usually do but he was willing to go along as Jack believed in it. It was possible that Jacks' legacy had rubbed off on him and he was willing to accept any help he could get, no matter how small it was or even how it was acquired. Maybe hunches were the correct way to go, but he would wait and see what comes of them before he is swung by them and starts to believe in them for himself.

Ten years I have been chasing this cunt and now I am closer than I have ever been to catching him I am more nervous than I ever was, Martin thought to himself, while looking at the picture of Colin Stevens hanging on the board to the right of the victims' pictures. Maybe he was more nervous about fucking up really and having to let him go rather than fearing the guy in question, no matter how nasty he could get. Ten years is a long time, he felt like he had aged about thirty years during it and when he looked in the mirror, he certainly looked like he had. The lines in his face were certainly getting longer and he looked a shadow of the young whippersnapper he used to be, but I guess age gets to us all. He couldn't help but wonder how the first known victim of the Cotton Mill rapist must feel after all this time. If he were her then he would be livid at the lack of progression so he had to solve it , if it turned out to be the last thing he ever did then he would die happy.

Ten years previous……

Rachel Masterson was on her way home after a night out with her friend, they had just been to the Jung-Wah Chinese restaurant and eaten a lovely meal washed down with a couple of glasses of sparkling rose wine. After leaving the restaurant they walked the two hundred yards or so to the bus stop where her friend Sarah Evans was due to board the 11.12 bus home.

The bus was about ten minutes late turning up and after saying their goodbyes and seeing Sarah onto the bus, Rachel thought she could make up the ten minutes by walking across the green by the old cotton mill on the way home. If she walked the long way around and stuck to the streets it would take ages and she had to be up early in the morning so the sooner she was tucked up in her bed the better. It was an easy walk, it was dry, she had just had a wonderful evening out and was feeling on top of the world and nothing could bring her down, or could it.

Although the news reports say keep vigilant as every time you step out there is a one in a million chance of being attacked, the reality is it's only a 50/50 chance, you either will be attacked, or you won't.

If more women thought like this, then the chances are there would be a lot more vigilance around, people would be prepared, they would walk around in groups and the opportunities for psychopaths would be nullified or as near to damnit as could be. But as in all cases of trying to help someone you may as well be talking to a fucking brick wall as nobody ever listens. They just continue taking risks, continue getting attacked, who knows when that will be, then it is always going to remain the case no matter how many people believe it will never happen to them.

When she entered the waste ground by the edge of the green, she had this strange feeling, she had no idea why but just felt someone else was there. Whereabouts on the green she had no idea but just a chilling feeling she was being watched or even followed. On reaching the sandstone wall by the old mill building she heard a small cough, like someone clearing their throat followed by heavy panting or breathing. She was really starting to panic now and had wished she had stuck to the route along the streets instead of taking the short cut. She kept telling herself it was just someone else who had been out for the night and taking the same short-cut home as she was but, deep inside she didn't believe it and was really starting to fear for her life.

She hurried her steps in a bid to exit the green as quickly as she could and get back onto the pathway where there was at least a small amount of street lighting, what she should have done from the start really until her ignorance had gotten the better of her. The breathing she could now hear clearly, and it was coming from behind her and getting closer. No matter how fast she walked, the footsteps from behind her got quicker, not only keeping pace they were in fact gaining on her. Eventually, and in sheer panic she felt it, a hand came around and grabbed her by the mouth as a knife was placed onto her throat. She tried to scream but the gloved hand just made the sound muffled and it was at that point she heard a man's voice say, scream again and you die bitch. You know who I am and what I am capable of so don't mess with me. She had no idea who he was but didn't intend to mess him around and maybe, just maybe she would come out of this situation alive.

She was shaking with the terror and close to shock with the panic when he started to drag her over towards the wall, on reaching it he threw her against it so hard that her head bounced off it and she landed in a heap on the floor. She couldn't move, partially paralysed with the fear but also in pain from the bang her head took on the wall. He used the opportunity to throw himself on top of her and pinning her down he used the knife to cut away her knickers and toss them aside. The mask he wore covered his face and all she could see glistening in the light from the moon were his eyes. Dark, piercing, and full of hatred, she thought she was going to die. In some ways she wished she had because at least then she wouldn't have the nightmares that come about from the memories of something horrific like this. She now knew what was about to happen, there was no way of getting away from the fact and she could do precious little to stop it, just hope and pray it would end before it started, but it didn't.

She felt him going in and was in total disgust at what was happening, why was he doing this to her, what right did he have to violate her in such a vicious horrible way. She had no idea if she truly was going to die but if it was to happen let it be now, please let it be now, before, and not after. At least that way the horror and the fear would go away. She never died that night, he let her live. Although she had no idea at the time, she was one of the lucky ones. Yes, she had the bad memories and suffered constant nightmares, and was scared to walk alone anywhere for years after but she was alive, something that at least three victims couldn't say and possibly more.

Another thing she had no idea of at the time and something she would have easily passed up on if given the chance, was that on that fateful night she became the first known victim of the cotton mill rapist. The first of eleven ladies in the wrong place at the wrong time, all victims of the lust and hatred of a viciously twisted mind. The first known victim that is, who knows how many more?

Martin stared at the photograph of Rachel Masterson hanging on the wall of the operations room. He couldn't help but to wonder how she was doing now, after all these years and with knowing the fact that her attacker was still out there, somewhere doing the same thing to other victims a full ten years later. He felt like he had let her down, let them all down really. He desperately needed this guy to be the one. He had put so much into him, if it turned out he wasn't the one then he had no idea where to go next, he was spent with it all. With a bit of luck and ten years of police work this fucking bastard, Colin Stevens was his killer rapist, he just had to be.

After about ten minutes of just staring at the picture of Rachel Masterson, and not even focusing clearly on anything, just looking in an inquisitive sort of way in the hope a solution might show itself to him. Martin pulled his gaze away and decided to have one more go at Marie before he was forced into having to let her go. He was hoping her story would sway from the original by even a fraction so he could see just one flaw in her interpretation but once again it was as tight a story as ever and she said it exactly as she had the first ten times or more. Either she was the best liar he had ever met, or else she could possibly be innocent and telling the truth. He was swung 60/40 in her favour, but the odds were changing all day, every day, even by the minute.

By now the time had come and Martin had no choice but to let Marie go. Over the countless times she had been questioned about Jacks' murder her story had not altered, not even in minor details and he had just about exhausted every avenue he could think of. Maybe letting her go would help them both to a degree, Marie because she could be in her own place, an environment she knew so well and maybe have a shower and clean up. She could also catch up with the sleep she missed and sleep in her own bed as he knew she hadn't slept well at all in the cells the last two nights. I mean whoever does, and himself so he wouldn't have to keep questioning her when he knew it was such a pointless exercise and yet while she was in his custody he had to press on and keep trying. Letting her go would be a blessing to them both.

Now, just for a few hours or so Martin could concentrate solely on the mountain of paperwork he had to transfer onto the computer system, a job he hated but knew that in this modern day and age of advancement was quite necessary. The computer course for idiots he was forced to undertake certainly stood him in good stead for the way the job had changed so much over the years. With all the new technology, results were now at your fingertips in seconds and without having to go on the hunt for them down in the cellar where they used to be stored in boxes or crates, thus saving on precious and valuable time which otherwise would be all wasted man hours.

Chapter 20: Marie vanishes.

Lady luck had shone her light on me the day they released Marie from the police station. I was outside for no other reason than I just wanted to keep tabs on all the comings and goings, that was when I saw her. There was no way I was going to let her walk away scot-free: her ass was my grass, she was going to pay.

Marie hadn't seen daylight proper, for nearly three days. She had seen the artificial light of the spot lamp positioned constantly on her face in the interview room, and the low-level lighting in the cell that is supposed to be there to enable the guards on duty to see their prisoners clearly, but in fact only serves as a purpose to keep prisoners awake at night. Marie knew all about not sleeping, it had been three days since she'd had any form of acceptable rest or relaxation. As she left the police station the sun was glaring off the white coloured paving stones and bouncing right into her face, so much so that she had to squint a little. To combat the brightness generated she put her hand above her eyes using it as if it were a visor and although it helped, she still had to squint to see but at least she could open her eyes.

She was tired, she felt she stunk of stale sweat, and she was in such a hurry to get home for some well needed rest and a good clean. Partially from being so tired from lack of sleep but also being blinded by the sun she could almost be forgiven for not noticing the car parked up in front of the police station, a black car with tinted windows. The same car that she hadn't noticed being parked outside her house on the night Jack Williams was murdered. The lone occupant watched Marie closely as she walked along the street and at the point when she disappeared around the corner into Aspen Avenue, whoever was driving it started the engine and spun a U-Turn in the road and headed in the same direction, trailing her by about 20 yards.

Standing at the window of his office on the second floor of the building, Martin Jackson looked down at Marie as she walked along the street. He had offered her a lift, but she had declined saying that maybe the walk and the fresh air would do her good, the aroma of the cells although cleaned regularly was one of stale piss and week-old vomit. She needed to get it out of her system to enable her to relax when she got home. Also, the last time she had accepted a lift from a police officer it hadn't turned out too well for anyone involved, and she wasn't ready to risk it. As she walked down the street Martin saw her petite little backside and saw exactly what Jack had seen in her and why he had fallen for her. Not that he was, not in any way but he could see why maybe someone would. She really did have a cute ass.

 He was admiring the view as she minced her way along the street when he noticed something odd, a black car that had been parked outside the police station pulled away not long after Marie had left the building and making a U-Turn in the road followed in the direction she had gone. He watched it until it reached the end of the road and hoped it would turn right, away from the direction in which Marie had turned meaning it was just a coincidence, but it turned left in the same direction as if it could be following her.

Martin had seen people being tailed before, he had even done it plenty of times himself and this person was most definitely following Marie. They were travelling far enough back not to be noticed, by Marie of course not by anyone else who may be onlooking, they were unaware of that. They were also aware enough to go slow enough so as not to catch her up. Whoever they were he had no idea, but his instincts told him Marie was in grave danger and he needed to act quickly before something serious happened to her, on top of whatever had possibly already occurred. He was starting to wonder genuinely if she was just an innocent victim in this and they had all been played or duped by the real criminal. He took down the registration number of the car and proceeded to the duty desk sergeant asking him to run it through the database and see what comes up. After only a few seconds the results came in as the car being the property of a Mr Charles Sharwell, "fuck" Martin shouted, "for one moment I had myself believing it could actually fucking be him". "Could be who" asked the desk sergeant, "That Colin Stevens guy, the one that is top of our suspects list in the Cotton Mill killer case." Bob Anderson the desk sergeant typed in the name Charles Sharwell and immediately it came up with known aliases and one of the four names that were mentioned was, Colin Stevens. "Well, you'll like this then Martin." He said as he turned the screen around so he could see what was on it.

"Bingo, eureka or whatever they bastard well say," Martin said as his eyes nearly popped out of his head with excitement. "Fucking got you, bastard", he shouted in an ecstatic tone of voice. But the smile on his face was very short-lived and suddenly turned sour as his mood changed rapidly with his thoughts once again switching quickly back to Marie. What was he doing following her, did he have some unfinished business with her and was she truly as he had guessed in grave danger? He needed answers and he needed them fast, there was no time to hang around and dawdle. He had to get after them and find out, he had to save her from possibly the most dangerous guy he had ever met, before the consequences affected all involved, him included with which would be another monumental fuck-up on his part, after all he had just released her, possibly straight into the arms of a murderer.

He left the building and headed as fast as he could to Aspen Avenue in the hope Marie would be there waiting for a bus, or shopping and oblivious to anything that may be going on around her. Alas, she was not and although he spent the next hour or so looking for her, in just about every shop or café he could. Not only had she disappeared into thin air, and he was becoming concerned for her welfare but also the black Toyota was missing, there was no sign of it anywhere either. This was not going to go down well with his superiors, within ten minutes of her release from custody, she disappears without trace and with him being the one that released her, it was all on him, it was his call therefore his responsibility. But just for now he would keep quiet and hope she will turn up.

When the evening edition of the Gazette was published, Grant had stuck to his word for all the good it did in the end, and the headline on the front page read 'Hero cop remembered as woman arrested on suspicion of his murder'. Well, that was a waste of fucking time he thought to himself, nothing to do with Grant as he had done all he promised but Colin now knew Marie was out and prior to the story making the paper. Granted she was only out on bail but if Colin thought for one moment that she had the information to cause him harm, then who knows what he may do. He has killed before, per say, so what is there to stop him killing again. Hopefully, that is where he comes in and sooner rather than later. Because later could well be just too late for Marie. It was going to take all his experience to sort this mess out, so he had better get started A.S.A.P and set about trying to work out where Marie was and how he could help

.

Marie was walking aimlessly down the high street not really caring about much except getting home and putting the kettle on. She'd had a terrible few days and was only interested in getting home for a nice strong mug of Decaf tea before she would climb into her own comfortable bed and catch up on at least some of the sleep she had lost the last few days, after a nice warm shower, that is. That's when she felt it, kind of like a poke in the back from a metal rod of some kind or another. She turned to see what it was and then she heard a familiar voice say "Hello Marie, guess who. I believe you have been trying to get me into trouble, that was not nice of you now, was it? Don't make a single fucking sound and come with me without a struggle or I will splatter your bitch brains all over the fucking pavement here and now and be done with you once and for all. You are starting to be the bane of my existence and I am running out of patience and excuses." She felt the blood drain from her body as she realised who the voice belonged to, it was him, it was Colin Stevens.

Marie believed her only option to keeping herself alive was to comply and so went along with his instructions and walked with him to his waiting car. He opened the passenger side door and ushered her toward it with the barrel of the gun, she climbed in and sat on the seat. The funniest thing she thought to herself was, she wasn't scared anymore, she'd had just enough of this jerk and wanted to be free from him at any costs. Anything he could do to hurt her he had already done, so why did she need to fear the worst, what else could be any worse than what has already happened. It was not long before she was sorry and wondered why she had opened her mouth and tempted fate, sorry that she had even asked herself the question.

After nearly an hour and a quarter of searching Martin gave up on the idea of finding Marie. He headed back to the station deciding now was probably the time to use the search warrant and check out Colin Stevens' place. Possibly a tad late, but he hadn't given up hope of finding her alive, maybe she could even be there. That is what he kept telling himself as he got the team together and ready to move off, whether he believed it or not was another matter. After all, this motherfucker had killed at least three times and Martin was in no doubt that he would again at the drop of a hat. Because once a serial killer commits murder he only stops when he is either caught or dies. There could be a break in between murders, on some occasions even years, but they never lose the urge, only keep it under control until one day it gets the better of them and resurfaces.

 He had read in a report he'd received from a mate of his who was an expert on serial killers after asking for some advice. He had asked him for a quick analysis on Colin Stevens given the information he had, and it came back that he was both psychotic and schizophrenic, but it was only his opinion as he hadn't had time to do a complete assessment or evaluation. Originally, Martin wasn't so sure but now he was starting to believe. This was something he already thought could be possible but at least now he had an expert's conformation, or at least thoughts on the matter.

Although he had no choice to release her and was practically ordered to, not only by both his bosses and Marie's lawyer, but also by law, he just wished he hadn't put her in such a position of danger. The poor girl must be at her wits end and petrified beyond belief, and who could blame her, especially with all the shit she had been through recently, in an unforgettable but not nice unforgettable sort of way. As Martin and the team were arriving at Colins' house with a search warrant in tow, Colin and Marie were arriving at a destination of their own about ten miles away. It was a lock-up garage Colin had been renting on a week-to-week basis for about five years now. It was known only to him, the mate he rented it from and now Marie. It was like his man-cave, kind of like an Aladdin's cave to him, it housed some of his secrets and had even acted as a hide out when he felt things were getting a bit too close in the past. He had stayed there a couple of times and slept in his car, just to enable him to lie low when things heated up that little too much for his liking during his past endeavours.

C.J.   "When you heard that Marie Calvin had been arrested for the murder of Jack Williams, how did it make you feel?"

C.S.   "It felt wonderful, as if my plan had worked, I tried to set her up and it was going great, apart from one small flaw."

C.J.   "And what was that flaw?"

C.S.   "I took the bloody gun with me instead of leaving it in her apartment. I had planned to hide it somewhere as evidence so the police would find it, and then that evidence would have been damning for her. I had gone to all the effort to make hers' the only fingerprints on it but like a dickhead I walked out with it in my hand completely forgetting to drop it."

C.J.   "Why not wait a while and then do it?"

C.S.   "I could've gone back in and planted it later as I still had a copy of her key, but the place had already been searched and it would have proved pointless and risky, so I just kept it for protection."

C.J.   "So, what went wrong at the lock-up if you were the only one to know where it was? How did they find you?"

C.S.   "You know, that was a mystery to me, but it was also the only time I admired him (Martin) for his detective work in finding me. Although he did kind of fuck it up completely after that by letting me escape. Swings and roundabouts."

C.J.   "How did he let you escape exactly, surely if you wanted to escape that was down to you, you said yourself if you put your mind to anything, it'll happen."

C.S.   "And I believed that, I still do, but it was just the way it happened. The way they set up was a complete farce and left me with an unexpected get out clause, but we will come to that after, before that though."

The gates opened automatically as Colin pressed the key-fob he held in his hand, and once the up-and-over door was fully open he drove in and came to a halt with the bonnet as tight up against the wall straight ahead as he could get without touching. It was a tight squeeze, but Colin looked as if he'd had plenty of practise and parked it expertly. He then pressed the fob once more and the door began to close. Once it was fully down, he edged around the car to the side where Marie was slumped down in her seat, opened the door, and dragged her out. She knew he was powerful from her previous experiences with him, but this time he seemed to have a kind of superpower and he picked her up as if she were light as a sack of feathers. He threw her across the part of the garage floor that wasn't blocked by the car, and she came to a halt in the far corner, landing up against a small chest of drawers.

She was weak, she was sore and more than anything she had no fight left in her, not for the moment anyway. For now she will just lay where she fell and hope he will get on with something else and leave her alone even just for a few minutes.

Chapter 21: The raid at Colin's.

I am glad I was out when they came to raid my home, if I was there, I would probably have done something stupid and gotten myself arrested or even killed after all I did still have the gun. If I had, then I would not be able to put into operation the final parts of my plan. I wasn't quite ready, but soon.

Martin rang the bell to Colins' place a few times and called out who they were, "It's the police, open the door, we have a warrant to search these premises and will gain entry by force if necessary". He rang it again and then banged on the door with his fist in a futile attempt to rile whoever may be inside. After a while it was quite clear that Colin Stevens was either hiding and not playing ball or else not at home. It was decided to use the door-ram to break the lock and gain entry for themselves.

 It took 3 attempts to smash through as the door was being ultra-stubborn and hanging onto its' hinges without wanting to let go. When it went, it sounded like an explosion as the jambs cracked and the door flew down the hall and thudded into the wall. Once inside the entire team split apart and went into the rooms they were assigned back at the office. Martin knew the lay-out of the place as he had been there before. He went into the bedroom and looked around, where to start and whatever it was he was looking for, he had no idea. He never did on these searches, they just hunted high and low disrupting as many items as they could until something showed up, and often did but occasionally, only occasionally nothing did. They had done this exercise countless times and were organised, but it looked more like organised chaos than anything else.

He checked each drawer in turn in the chest in the corner of the room and that turned up nothing whatsoever, so then moved to the bed, he lifted the mattress throwing it to the floor and looking under where it had lay, saw nothing but the slats and springs of the bedframe just as and where they should be. He then lifted the pictures on the wall in case there was a hideaway behind one of them but alas, there wasn't. He had almost exhausted his search when he decided to stomp up and down on the floorboards to see if there was a loose one anywhere that could act as a storage space for anything that Colin didn't want found, especially by the police. Apparently under the floorboards was the most popular hiding place for contraband, maybe it will turn something up.

He had been going for a few minutes and walking around testing the boards strategically when he got over by the chest of drawers and with one big stomp the bottom cover of the chest of drawers fell forward and landed at his feet on the floor. Shocked to find that his plan had worked, he Knelt down and reached into the hole left by the missing front piece and felt around. At first there was nothing, but as he reached further in his hand brushed up against something, he grabbed at it and pulled it out from its' hiding place, it was a small box, like a trinket box green in colour and about twelve inches long and eight inches wide. Reaching back in he found another box, this time a see-through plastic container just like the ones Chinese food gets delivered in and it had an elastic band wrapped around it to stop the plastic lid falling off.

He tried one more time but to no avail, he had retrieved everything there was. This stuff must be important if he is taking the time and effort to hide it Martin thought to himself and picked up the two boxes and carried them through into the front room, placing them on the table in the middle of the lounge. He had no idea of what exactly it was he had found but just knew it was going to turn out to be important evidence or else why would he try so hard to hide it. Once he had removed the elastic band from the transparent box and opened it up fully, what he saw brought a wry grin to his face if not on the other hand leaving him a little horrified at the same time.

Inside the box was a collection of buttons, all shapes, sizes and colours, there must have been at least 40 to 50 in it or possibly more. Knowing what he knew about the case and one detail in particular, he shook his head in disbelief, and said to jane Collins," This fucker is worse than we ever imagined, thank God, we found him and know what he is capable of.". He showed her the box of buttons and the colour immediately drained from her face.

 The part that had been deemed best to be omitted from public reports was the fact that the Cotton Mill Rapist/murderer had taken a button off all his victims as a kind of souvenir of his conquest. Martin knew about at least eleven and possibly twelve but up to and beyond fifty. It begged the question, how seriously fucked-up must this person, if you can call them a person, really be. This was way beyond what he thought, what they all thought.

If a question could ever be answered correctly then the seriously fucked-up person in question was in the process of binding Marie Calvin's hands together with duct tape and gagging her mouth with it also. Not the answer anyone would wish for especially for the poor unfortunate Marie, but the answer is no less true because we don't want to believe. Marie was once again starting to think she wasn't going to come out of this situation alive. But she had thought it once before about Colin and yet she was still here, just. So, she clung on to the faint hope that she could be wrong again.

After exhausting the search, Martin and the team gathered up what evidence they had found and took it to the station to be logged in, photographed, and then placed in the Cotton Mill operations room for further examination. It had been a very successful search and he could say without doubt now that Colin Stevens was indeed the cotton mill rapist and possibly a serial killer or at least a murderer. Martin was left scratching his head as he was just a little surprised that he hadn't found either the knife used in the attacks, or the gun used to kill Jack. That could only mean one thing, he (Colin Stevens) had them with him when he kidnapped Marie. This now made finding her a priority as she could be or was in dire danger, if indeed she were still alive at all.

Marie, still alive was pleading with Colin to let her go and said she promised not to say anything to the police. Colin laughed a hearty laugh and replied "How the fuck am I supposed to believe a word you say when you have already been to the police once, Marie. I have no doubt in my mind whatsoever that you will go to them again. I am just surprised you haven't shagged martin Jackson yet, isn't that what you do, find a man, fuck him, use him, and then toss him in the garbage. You certainly did it with me, so I do know what you are like and probably hundreds more do as well. Bitches like you deserve everything bad that comes their way, you are nothing but a fucking slut and that's all you will ever be." Colin then cracked her across the cheek with a flick of the back of his hand and as she fell to the floor with blood rolling down her face she started sobbing, only dry sobbing because no tears were coming out. She felt sad, she felt she needed to cry but she also felt she had cried enough over this moron. These were just crocodile tears, tears cried for herself really, just to sate herself and prove, that she was not just giving in and at least trying to put up a little resistance.

Back at the police station, Martin had exhausted his efforts in trying to gain access to the trinket box they had found at Colin Stevens' place. He shook it gently and could clearly hear a kind of rattling noise coming from inside, but he could not, no matter how hard he tried, get it open. He decided the time had come to find out what was inside once and for all, even if it meant he had to break into it. It was obvious by now that Colin either had the key on his person or had hidden it well, so well in fact that they may never discover its' true hiding place. They had already gone through his entire apartment with a fine toothcomb without success, so their chances appeared slim to middling at best and getting worse all the time.

Martin disappeared off to the kitchen and returned a couple of minutes later with a sharp kitchen knife. He was going to try and pry the box open hopefully to make enough of a gap that he could see its' contents without breaking it. Once he had the knife in between the lid and the base of the box he couldn't stop himself and with one sharp twist the two parts of the box separated and the lock holding them together shattered. He opened the box fully to reveal a key ring with several keys attached. They all appeared to be main front door keys and yet when he went back to Colins and tried them, not one fitted the lock to his apartment.

Who did they belong to, and why did he have them? There could be a simple explanation, maybe they were from his old houses, and he had kept them as souvenirs, but Martin felt there was a far more sinister answer that had not yet come to light. He was not going to rule anything out especially anything this motherfucker was involved in he didn't trust him, not even for one minute. Maybe if he had trusted Jack's instincts in the first place then Jack might still be alive but then who could have foreseen what Colin was capable of. If Jack had seen it, once again he may still be alive. It would have all just been guesswork and they worked off evidence, not one man's guesses on where he comes from, no matter how much he trusted him. During his entire career he had done things by the book so why change now? Why throw away everything that he believed in for a hunch or two.

Chapter 22: Back at the lock-up.

The money I spent on the lock-up must be the best money I have ever spent. Not only was it a hiding place for any illegal stuff I could get my hands on, and there was plenty, but I could store whatever I wanted there and nobody but me knew about it. I could also use it as a hideaway for myself, it wasn't ideal by any means, but in emergencies it was comfortable enough. It was also one hell of a torture chamber, if I needed it to be, and so far out of the way from normal life that nobody could hear a sound. I would say money spent wisely.

As Marie lay on the freezing cold concrete floor of the lock-up it was virtually impossible for her to get herself into any sort of comfortable position or sleeping pattern. Her hands were bound meaning she couldn't lie with them under her head as she normally would and then rest her head on her hands through the pillow, simply because there was no pillow. Her legs were also bound but they were done so tightly that her ankles were pressing and rubbing together feeling like they were chafing and with them resting only on the freezing floor, this too made it all just so uncomfortable. Thirdly, her mouth had been duct taped to stop her screaming but all it did was muffle the sounds slightly or make it hard for her to breath as she couldn't get the same amount of oxygen in through her nostrils as she could through the opening to her mouth.

On the few occasions she did drift off and wasn't woken so rudely by Colin she would come to with panic attacks and the feeling of not being able to get air into her lungs as quickly as she needed, due to the tape on her mouth. The panic attacks, the freezing floor and Colin's torture attempts were all factors in her getting next to nothing or at very most, little micro-naps for sleep. Although she tried as hard as she could she had missed so much there was never a chance of her catching up.

Every now and then Colin would relent ever so slightly and show he had a human side, however well-hidden it was the rest of the time. He would give her the nod as if to grant his permission for her to crawl into the boot of the car to lie down there but only for a few minutes. Just getting off the cold floor was such a blessing and the carpet in the boot although rough felt like a soft shag-pile carpet compared to the ice cold she had been experiencing, even for a short while until she was forced back to the floor. This was just yet another part of the cruel torture treatment she was receiving at the hands of this evil, sadistic psychopath.

As soon as she had settled and gotten herself comfortable in the boot of the car and felt as if she were relaxed enough to drop off, he would nudge her to keep her awake. He would then forcibly remove her from the boot, putting her back on the floor. Just one part of three-part torture plan he had for her. Keep her from sleeping for long periods to make her remain tired, bind her so she is uncomfortable and cannot relax and then lie her down on a floor so freezing cold it would be like sleeping in a freezer compartment. She was allowed to sleep but only in small doses and only when he permitted it. Keeping her in a disturbed sleep pattern meant she got enough sleep to survive but not enough to gain strength and enable her to have the power of the upper-hand and the strength to fight back. He was slowly but surely knocking the willpower from out of her, she was beginning to feel she had no spirit or at least next to nothing left.

He had learnt from the T.V. programme Who Dares Wins about SAS recruitment tactics that if you keep complete control of the situation and don't give whoever it is a chance to fight back through lack of strength or inclination then you win every time, and this was certainly proving to be the case with Marie. He could feel her resistance was at an all-time low and her spirit had diminished. She would be giving in soon if in fact she hadn't already.

If he did for any reason feel insecure or that she was plotting something, he would remind her who was in charge by pointing the gun at her and on the odd occasion striking her with the handle of the knife or the butt of the gun leaving a small cut or bruise on her temple. But this was mainly down to his own insecurities rather than her plans to escape, because although she wanted to, desperately she had no strength left in her body to fight him, but he wasn't to know it.

Colin decided for them both, Marie, and himself that they needed some sort of sustenance and knew by previous experience that there was a corner shop a mere five-minute walk away. He had visited it on a couple of occasions in the past when he had stayed at the lock-up to lie low from previous attacks. It stocked just about everything needed to hide away from reality for a few days, even weeks if needed, so thought it would be ideal to get in what he needed without having to travel too far to get it and risk being seen.

Colin ordered Marie to her feet, but she was having none of it, tired from lack of sleep and under-nourished she just didn't seem to care and simply refused, staying where she was, lying on the cold floor. He reached down and grabbed her by the hair picking her up by that alone. She winced with the pain as she was dragged to the back of the car and thrown into the now open boot. "You really aren't helping yourself here, Marie. Little bits of stupidity like that are just acts of defiance and I am fed up with being run ragged by cunts like you. You really are in no position to issue demands", he screamed at her, showing her both the gun and the knife, he was pointing them both in her direction once again. It was his way of letting her know that he had now been pushed well past his tether and slammed the boot shut without caring if he trapped any parts of her in it, lucky for her she had landed fully inside the car.

Marie heard the muffled sound of the garage door open and then close again a few seconds after. He was going somewhere but she had no idea where it could be. Her questions were answered about twenty minutes later although it seemed much longer to her locked in the boot as she heard the door to the garage open once again. The boot of the car opened-up almost immediately and there stood Colin in front of her with a blue plastic bag full of stuff it looked like he had just purchased.

She learned by her mistakes and climbed out of the boot when ushered to do so and flopped herself down on the floor where she had been lying before. She was parched and wanted or needed whatever he had got for her. Martin removed the tape from her mouth and handed her an opened bottle of Evian spring water, putting it into her taped hands and letting her drink it herself rather than spilling most of it while trying to feed her himself. She wanted as little contact with Colin as was possible but hadn't eaten or drunk for nearly three days and was famished so accepted it gracefully and began to drink it sip by sip.

Colin showed Marie the headline in the Evening Gazette, which he had also purchased 'Hero cop remembered as local woman arrested,' "How are you here if you are supposed to be there?" he asked her. "Is there something I should know? Are you hiding something from me?" Marie shook her head, then shrugged her shoulders, he could see in her eyes she wanted to say something so let her without interrupting. "It was nothing to do with me, it was all my lawyers' doing. He said they had to by law, either charge me or let me go. They had no real evidence against me thanks to you, so they had no option but to release me. They did however say I wasn't to leave town as I would certainly be brought back in for more questions".

"What the hell are you going on about, thanks to me, I have done nothing to help you and it just shows how fucked up the system genuinely is. Any man would still be locked up because we are not in the position to flash our titties or wiggle our tight arse sweet cheeks to get a fucking pardon like women can." He said to her in a rather derogatory way.

"The gun Colin," Marie replied." You forgot to leave it at my flat that night and in your hurry to get out you took it with you. If you would have left it as you planned, I would be well and truly fucked by now but as it is, you saved me, you fucking saved me and you are that dumb you didn't even know it, until someone tells you." She shouted. She felt as if she was pushing it a little calling him dumb but at this point really did not care what he thought, and if he did do anything then maybe it would put her out of her misery once and for all and she could be free from this nightmare.

He had also purchased some crisps and a packet of biscuits, both of which she took and stuffed into her mouth and ate like a pig that had just found the trough of food the farmer had left out for it. Colin looked at her with a disgusted stare, but once again she really couldn't care what he thought and just carried on as she was. After eating all she needed and probably more she settled down and lay by the chest of drawers ready for some much-needed sleep. If she could drop off to sleep with all that was going on, but the more she thought about it the less chance she would have, so she just shut her eyes and tried her best to block out everything that she possibly could. Eventually, although she had no concept of time or how long it had taken, she drifted into an uncertain stupor and slept for what felt most of the night but had in fact only equated to what amount of sleep that Colin had permitted her to, next to nothing but she needed it just the same, however amount of time it was.

At about the exact moment Marie was drifting off in the lock-up, Martin was saying his goodbyes to Jane and the rest of the team. He too was in desperate need of sleep as he had been working non-stop for nearly 38 hours. He needed the change of scenery that his own place could bring, a place that meant he had the chance to relax in comfort, the kind of comfort that the station couldn't provide. As he walked toward the door, he took one last look at the picture of Colin Stevens and smiled, I may not know where you are you son-of-a-bitch, but I soon will. But I now know what you are, a fucking good for nothing and woman hurting monster, the lowest of the low and total scumbag, he thought to himself. With that his gaze then turned to the photo of Rachel Masterson and he shook his head in disgust, a disgust he harboured and tried to keep in as much as he could. Not disgust toward Rachel Masterson in any way, but total and utter disgust at himself and his team for not catching the person involved. As he was leaving, he mouthed the words sorry Rachel in the direction of her photograph. He dipped his head while whispering his apology and felt slightly appeased that she would soon have that little bit of closure that she had been craving for ten years, ten long years.

Chapter 23: Too young to die.

The biggest blot on my existence was the killing of the young girl, If I had thought for one second that she was only that age I would never have done her. I am a lot of things, a killer, a rapist, a thief and a few more things to boot that we won't go into but a paedophile, never.

Yet, by that name I am always going to be tarnished and it haunts me to this very day.

In the prison Connie was still questioning Colin and decided to ask about the one thing that was playing on her mind. Something that had been bugging her for some time. She didn't want to push it too far just in case it made him recoil and refuse to say anything else, but on the other hand, she really wanted to know. She decided what the hell and to ask the one question that she knew was taboo and not to be brought up at any time. What was the worst he could do, she already had plenty to be going on with, enough to make a story, if he refused then so be it and went ahead anyway?

C.J.   "One thing that haunts me about you Colin is when it comes to the murders you have committed you mention four but there were in fact five."

C.S.   "I think I can guess where you are trying to go with this, but I don't want to go there, it's not something I talk about."

C.J.   "Go where with what Colin? You said you would talk to me no holds barred and keeping certain things back is not no holds barred, it is censoring. Surely a murder is a murder no matter what age they were. How old was she again, 13 years-of-age?"

C.S.   "She was 14 but looked so much older, still no excuse but I wouldn't have done her if I knew she was only 14. That was not the way I operated, not who I was at all."

C.J.   "The problem is you did and now the word paedophile is permanently on your criminal record, you can't get rid of that. It's a stigma that can never be erased and will always be associated with you."

C.S.   "I am no paedophile whatever the fucking record says, never have been and never will be. That was a mistake I must learn to live with and one I am very sorry for. I can be a nasty piece of work, I am not denying that but a child killer, no. I didn't set out to be or even consider killing anyone that young. When I heard the story of Bill Wyman and Mandy Smith, I questioned how he could not know how old she was, but after this one I saw just how easy it could be to feel duped and I started feeling sorry for him. I never questioned anyone after that. That would have made me a hypocrite and that was not who I was or am."

C.J.   "Where did you meet her, how did you let yourself get into the position to be able to murder her."

C.S.   "She was in the pub, dolled up like a tart and looked at least 18/19, she was acting all big and tough and had the confidence of someone older than her years. She acted as if she owned everyone in the place and to a degree, I guess she probably did, me included. They were all hanging off her every word and buying drinks for her, I could honestly say that she probably never had to buy her own drink, ever. I'd had enough of her lies and manipulation, and I thought I would teach her a lesson on what tough really was but went a bit too far, or a lot too far as it happens, by killing her. I only found out how old she was when they put her age in the paper. I was just as horrified as anyone else when I found out, I was disgusted with myself."

C.J.   "And by then it was too late to do anything about it, no matter what you did or said you had been labelled."

C.S.   "It was and no matter how many times you say you're sorry it makes no difference at all; it just falls on deaf ears. I can't blame them though, I just wanted them to know how truly sorry I was."

C.J.   "They wouldn't accept your apology?"

C.S.   "Would you if it was your family." Colin said shrugging his shoulders and showing her the palms of his hands while holding them out in front of himself. "Seriously I mean would you"

C.J.   "No, I don't believe I would now you come to mention it, I would have shunned you also."

C.S.   "Well, there you go then, and that is why I don't like to talk about that one in particular…. there is so much I have done that I don't regret but her, big mistake and one I rue so much."

The room went quiet and neither of them spoke a single word for a good five minutes. Eventually Colin broke the awkward silence when he started where he had left off before Connie had pushed her luck and in a vain attempt to try and get back on track.

Chapter 24: Varinder Jarvit...At your convenience.

The store where I got my goods was a nice little place and the owner, a very pleasant Asian dude by the name of Varinder Jarvit. I'd had a couple of dealings with him in the past and he had always been polite and charming as a shopkeeper should be, if they want to keep their customers. If I had known for one second that he was shopping-me out to the cops, I might have had a different opinion though. If I knew he was a two-faced motherfucker.

Martin was sat back at the desk in his office when his phone rang, he picked it up and answered with his usual gruff voice greeting, "Detective Martin Jackson how may I help you?" A voice on the other end of the line said, "Officer Jackson, my name is Varinder Jarvit, and I am the proprietor of the convenience store on Waltham Avenue. I think I have seen the man you are looking for". "What man?" Martin asked, "And how do you know I am looking for someone, sorry who are you again." By this time Martin was so confused that nothing anyone said made any sense to him. It just went in one ear and then straight out of the other. Even if they told him black was black or white was white, he wouldn't have cared until Mr Jarvit explained that he had seen the Photofit in the Gazette and a man that had visited his shop to purchase some items looked remarkably like it.

With everything that had gone on it had totally slipped Martins' mind about the photofit. All the effort he had gone through to get it sorted, only to forget it in an instant, was there too much on his mind or was his age finally catching up with him or could it possibly be a little of both? He had been too busy wondering when, where or how the next clue would be coming from that he had forgotten he'd already had the wheels in motion and the next clue was already up-and-running, just waiting to be solved. With this Martin apologised to Varinder Jarvit for the misunderstanding and asked him to proceed.

"A man that looks remarkably like the picture in the Gazette has been in my shop for the last two nights. The first night he bought some crisps, biscuits and 2 bottles of water along with a newspaper and then last night he purchased 2 more bottles of water, a bottle of vodka and a newspaper." Mr Jarvit explained. He had saved the receipt stub from the role and held it in his hand, so it was possible for him to reel off everything that had been purchased.

"Are you sure it was him? Have you ever seen this man before?" Martin asked, "Yes I do believe I have." Mr Jarvit responded. "I have a good remembrance of faces and he was in a couple of years ago, I only remember when exactly because it was the day after that girl was murdered on the village green. I was paying more attention to anyone coming into the shop then as I wondered with anyone new that I hadn't seen before that maybe it was them that could have done it." He spoke.

"And was he acting strange in any way on these two nights he came in, even a small detail may help us Mr Jarvit so please try to remember everything you can if possible." Martin asked. "No, not the first night, he just came in and made his purchases and left. But last night he came in said hello in a friendly voice and then headed off to buy what he needed. Something must have happened between the time he went to get his stuff and returning because his entire demeanour had changed. He didn't utter a single word on his way out, just threw the money at me and didn't even wait for his change. It seemed to me something had spooked him, possibly the picture but I am only speculating here Detective, but there was something that changed his mood, "Mr Jarvit went on.

"Ok, thank you Mr Jarvit, you have been a great help, I will get someone to investigate it, they will pop in to see you if not today then most definitely tomorrow. If he happens to return to your shop in the meantime, please ring me straight away and let me know won't you and don't try to tackle him yourself. If it is him then he may be armed and extremely dangerous," and with that put the phone down and headed to the operations room to speak with Jane Collins.

"Jane! got a minute please?" Martin requested. Jane wandered over and asked what was up. "May have a lead on our man, somebody fitting his description has been into a little convenience store on Waltham Avenue stocking up on essentials, may be him but may be an innocent shopper so we need to check it out. Guy that owns it, a Mr Varinder Jarvit reckons the guys' personality changed when he saw the photofit picture. He said he started all happy and joking with him but after seeing the picture, stormed out of the shop in a foul mood like he had been spooked or something." He didn't tell Jane that this was just an assumption by the shopkeeper, he felt he didn't need to relay that information to her, not yet anyhow. "Can you do a background check and see if Colin Stevens has any links to anyone out that way will you please?" He asked her. Jane looked at him and nodded without saying a word. She had a new task, a slight change from what was becoming the normal and she was going to do her utmost best to perform it well, as always.

Martin went back to his office and closed the door. He sat down at his desk, opened the drawer and pulled out a bottle of whisky and a tumbler and placed them on the desk in front of him. He knew he wouldn't be disturbed as it was an unwritten rule that if his door was open, anyone was welcome, however, if it was closed this was time he needed and wanted just for himself and if anyone dared then they had better have a good reason, or else the shit would really hit the fan, and it had in the past a few times. Once he had lost his temper and given a good rollicking to whomever it was that had disturbed him it didn't take him long to calm down, but at boiling point he was hotter than lava spewing from an erupting volcano.

He stared at the bottle on the desk, the one he had taken from the drawer in his desk, it was unopened, as it had been for two years. Ever since his problem times and his alcoholism, he had the bottle in his draw to remind him not to have a drink. It was a strange way of thinking, as not having the bottle there in the first place would no doubt have the same effect, more even as the temptation would be zero. But there must have been some method in his madness and his logic seemed to work just fine because apart from the small blip he had after Jack's murder he had done well and had been bloody proud of himself. He had always laughed at people that had said he had a problem until one day he woke up and saw the light, it had been shining on him for years, but he just refused to see it.

Since the day he'd had what you would call an epiphany and realised just how close he'd come to drinking himself into oblivion. So many just like him had come and so many just like him had gone down the same path and he didn't want to become just another statistic. But that was then, and this is now, there was no point in crying over spilt milk as they say and even more pointless dwelling on the past as he had done for most of his life and where had it got him? Nowhere, nowhere at all. He calmly picked up the bottle, took one last look at it and then placed it back into the drawer, unopened. He never used to have the willpower, he never used to have any control but had worked tirelessly with the A.A. on his addiction, and they had steered him in the right direction. There was nothing else that they could do but give him pointers, the hard work was all down to him. He did have a sober buddy who he should call if ever the temptation got too much but he never had and likewise, he had never been called to rescue them either.

The second night Colin had gone into the shop, he said hello to the owner Varinder Jarvit and after talking for a minute or two about the weather and other menial things, he had walked to the back of the shop to pick up some bottled water from the fridge and a bottle of vodka from off the shelf. He was on his way back to the till to pay when he was passing the newspaper stand and got stopped in his tracks for a second when he read the headline 'Man sought in Cotton Mill case' he was so close to dropping the vodka and water he had in his hand when he saw the picture that accompanied the story. It wasn't an exact likeness; they never are but the photofit picture did look somewhat rather like him. Was he just reading too much into it or had the shopkeeper noticed it also, no, surely it must just be a coincidence he had only seen the shopkeeper 3 or 4 times in his life, there is no way he would remember him, how could he, why would he?

He took one more glance at the newspaper, what the fuck, he thought to himself, that's impossible, how could anyone have managed to give a description and make it so real. He had been careful, or so he had thought, but, obviously not careful enough it would appear. He lost the plot but only for a second and stormed out of the shop throwing the money for the water, vodka, and newspaper at the owner on the way out and didn't even wait to see if he had any change to be returned. He did feel guilty when he had done it as the shopkeeper hadn't done anything to him, but by then it was way too late as he had left without so much as a goodbye. He wanted to go back in and apologise, but by now the time had come and gone, it wouldn't have served any purpose apart from his face to be seen once again and he continued on his way back to the lock up. He must have looked a right sight cussing and swearing to himself as he walked along, anyone that happened to be watching must have thought he was crazy, he was of course but they wouldn't know that. He would have looked just like one of the tramps or drug addicts seen every day on the streets, the ones that are seen but ignored, the kind you would cross the road to avoid encountering at all costs.

Colin had no idea, but Marie had decided she'd had enough and decided it was time to try something, to possibly fight back if the opportunity arose. She had somehow managed to scramble onto her knees, it took a lot of effort and shuffling back and forth, but she persisted and when she was there, she flopped down deliberately onto her face. She felt the pain as she struck the cold floor with the socket of her eye and immediately felt the flow of liquid running down her face. Although she couldn't see for sure because there were no mirrors in the lock-up, she knew it had to be blood. Her plan was starting to take full effect and the bastard would have no choice but take her to the hospital. Even he couldn't be that callous, surely.

Just to make sure she repeated the process another 2 or 3 times, at least that was what she thought, but had lost count. She just remembered the excruciating pain, necessary pain that could help her in the long run. In fact, it was more like 6 or 7 times that she lifted herself and fell and all her efforts had left her drained and completely exhausted. The last time she did she heard a noise as she landed, it was the sound of the garage doors opening. Colin was back and she was looking forward to seeing his face when he saw her. It was a picture and well worth it as he looked totally shocked and even ran over to her asking her if she was alright.

"Oh my God, what happened?" he asked." Sounding very sincere. "I tried to lift myself up but fell over. "Marie replied thinking she had got the better of him. But her joy was short lived as he screamed back at her "How many times, you stupid bitch, don't make me out the fool? You nearly had me, but only for a second. You must think I'm some kind of dumb fuck if you expect me to believe that hogwash, although I nearly got suckered in. I can see through your plan, and I am not taking you to the hospital. Is that what you thought would happen? Fuck me, give me a little credit will you, please? Did you really think that I would suddenly cave in and feel sorry for you because of a little bit of blood? Fuck that, you hurt yourself, you sort it out, unbelievable." I've seen more blood than this, believe me. A lot more. This is fuck all on the scale of things."

All the way back to the lock-up he was racking his brain trying to work out how and when he could have been seen. No matter what angle he came in from he could not find one solution to the problem so decided the only way was if it was a set up between Marie and Detective Jackson. That must have been the reason she was set free; she must have penned a deal. Yes, it all makes perfect sense now (but it really didn't, it was just guesswork) she had provided them with a description of him to both incriminate him and at the same time, secure her own release, what a bitch. What started as some sort of fairy story made up by him suddenly bordered on the realms of reality and before he could stop his mind transcending into over-active hyperdrive he started believing the utter bullshit he was thinking could be true.

Although it made no sense whatsoever, he convinced himself that it did and was what had happened. Nothing at all he tried to get into his head was able to alter his mind thought and he was now thinking only about how he was going to make her pay, to get even with Marie again, it seemed to be his lifelong ambition, blame her for everything and then get even. When he arrived back at the lock-up and saw her lying on the floor covered in blood he ran over to see what had happened genuinely concerned for her, until it was, he worked out her plan and that was a catalyst for him, he went berserk and just couldn't stop himself, he flew off the handle and Marie was at the brunt of it all.

She had seen plenty of mood swings in him at Allen and Co but this time he was different, and it was a different she didn't like one bit, his eyes were glazed as if he had somehow been possessed. She knew Colin in a bad mood didn't bode well for her and immediately had regrets about pushing him too far. That's when she felt the punch to the back of her head, she didn't see it coming but certainly felt it happen. She fell in a heap on the floor and as she did he came in for more and kicked her three times, once to the head and twice to the torso, while at the same time saying "I know exactly what you did you fucking bitch, I told you if you mess with me you will pay but you cunts never listen and do what you want anyway. If you want to hurt yourself, that's fine with me, go ahead but I hope you don't mind if I join in and kicked her again just for good measure."

He then left her lying semi-conscious on the floor, battered, and bloodied as he opened the door to the car and sat on the front seat. He opened the vodka and started drinking it neat, straight from the bottle. Why do they have to think they are better than us, he thought to himself, not just Marie but every goddamn one of them but especially the blonde bitches. All of them think they are a cut above and just because they were blessed with being born with a certain coloured hair.

Marie's pain was immense, she felt as if she had a broken a rib or possibly two. She remembers being punched and kicked by Colin but how many times she couldn't recall. It took a few minutes, but she eventually passed out with the pain and lay motionless on the freezing floor. Only this time she didn't care how cold the floor was as she couldn't feel it, she felt nothing at all as she drifted into the dark void she calls her safe place, hidden somewhere at the back of her mind.

Maybe it could've been considered a little presumptive of her, but she felt safe there, surely even someone of Colin's immorality wouldn't hurt her while she was being rescued by the sanctity inside her own mind. Although he walked past a few times and shook his head as he looked down on her, as he looked down on all women, he never hurt her again that night, he let her be, let her sleep. Possibly drifting into unconsciousness was the best thing that could have happened to Marie, and maybe, just maybe it saved her life that night, who knows how far Colin could have gone if she hadn't, when or if he would have stopped the onslaught. Her safe place had saved her just as she had hoped or at least prayed it would.

Chapter25: Tailing Colin.

All I was doing was walking back to the lock-up, just minding my own business and enjoying life in the moment. Oh yes and planning a bit of revenge on Marie. I had no idea whatsoever I was being followed. Why would I, nobody knew about me or why I was there, or so I thought. This was the one and only time I respected Detective Martin Jackson, as a policeman and for doing his job well. Little did I know it was pure fluke and a random call from Varinder Jarvit who called their hotline just on the off-chance.

Martin pulled his car up to the curb outside the shop owned by Varinder Jarvit, he turned the engine off and headed into the store to explain that he would be hanging around outside, just in case and more in hope than expectation that Colin Stevens' may return. He told Mr Jarvit not to worry about reputations, he knew that having a police car outside your place may drive a few people away so he told him he would be stopped about a hundred yards along the road and out of sight to anyone that wasn't looking out for him.

Martin assumed that colin would want a newspaper to keep himself up to date with any new information, it was a presumptive guess, but he had already bought two so a confident assumption. And if this was his only source of receiving news or information, then he was adamant that Colin would be there at some point in the day or night. He would put his life's wages down on it and was willing to sit and wait it out for however long it took. Two hours had passed without a sign and Martin was completely bored out of his fucking mind, there was nothing to do but stare at the shop and at one point Jane Collins had dropped by to ask if he needed anything, but he declined as he always did with a polite "No, but thanks anyway."

While on stake-outs Martin tended not to eat or drink as what goes in must come out and he had been caught out in the past. This one time he had happened to miss the person that he had sat there for 14 hours looking out for because he had been caught short and really needed to go. Who would have thought that they would happen to turn up at the precise moment that he was in the toilet relieving the discomfort he'd gotten from a soda heavy bowel? With hindsight he should have seen it coming as sods law states it and has done on numerous occasions. He swore that day never to let it happen again and although the criminal underbelly wished he would, he hasn't relented one bit.

After sitting there for nearly three and a half hours without a sign of Colin or Marie, he was starting to think of calling it quits for the night. He didn't think Colin would risk bringing her out into the open but then again nothing Colin did surprised Martin anymore. The shop was due to close at 9 p.m., a mere twenty-six minutes from now and most people who had needed any shopping would have already stocked up. But he thought he would wait and give it the full time he had allotted as Colin was not most people. Colin was an out-of-control killing machine and therefore a law unto himself. What he did next was anyone's guess, martin only wished he had seen it or at least believed Marie from the start. Although all the evidence pointed in the other direction there was always something about Colin. Jack had seen it; Marie had seen it; so why hadn't he.

It was time for the police to make a mockery of Colin's self-obsession and quash his laws to enforce their own, just as they have done since the formation of the Bow-Street-Runners in the 1740's, often referred to as the world's first ever professional police force. Who could have guessed how far things would have progressed since those early days. If the original guys from the Bow Street Runners came forward in time by 250 years and saw how things were done now, they probably would never believe what they were seeing and likewise if it was the other way round then their efforts would more than likely have looked very amateurish, for todays' standards of course and not for their own.

It was 20.48, the time was lit up on the clock on his dashboard. While he was looking at it, he was distracted by something else that was in his eyeshot. As his eyes adjusted, he noticed about 200 yards down the road there was the shadow of a figure walking along the pavement in the direction of the convenience store. As the figure got in a little closer, he could clearly make out by the build that it was a man, and he was alone. He had no idea yet, if it was Colin but if it was then Marie wasn't with him, but he would soon be able to tell for sure as he was heading straight for the part of the pavement lit up by the streetlamp. Once the unknown shadow emerged from the darkness and his face came into full view, Martin could see without a doubt it was Colin Stevens, he was one hundred percent sure. He couldn't forget that bastards face, not for one minute. He had stared incessantly at the photo of him on the operations wall enough to be sure and have no doubts that it was him.

He wanted to leap out of the car and arrest him there and then but stopped and thought for a second as to what good would it do. They needed to find out where he had been hiding and that could in turn lead to the possible safe return of Marie, so he held back and just watched him enter the shop. Colin was in the shop for about five minutes in all, and when he left, he was carrying a blue plastic bag with his purchased items inside. He then headed off in the same direction as he had come from oblivious to the fact he was being watched. Martin kept his eye focused on him until he reached the end of the road to see which way he turned. As soon as he disappeared around the corner Martin leapt out of his car and started to follow, He decided to follow on foot rather than starting the car and possibly alerting Colin of his presence. He walked as fast as he could to the corner where Colin had turned and looked down the road. Colin was about half-way down and walking along swinging his blue plastic bag back and forth as if he didn't have a care in the world, certainly not the actions of a psychotic killer that had recently kidnapped a girl and was now possibly keeping her against her will. But when do they ever look like what they really are, total and utter monsters?

Even the most prolific serial killers over the years had never looked like psychopaths, the Ted Bundy's, or Jeffrey Dahmer's of this world or even Britain's very own Denis Neilson just looked like the average next-door neighbour that nobody would ever suspect or think capable of doing what they were charged with, and Colin Stevens most definitely fell into the same category and had certainly fooled a lot of people for a very long time. If you looked at him you would never think he could be a killer or a rapist, he like them all looks just like the trustworthy neighbour next door. The neighbour that you would trust with your life or that of your family but how wrong can looks be. How wrong can impressions be?

When he reached the end of the Road, Colin turned right onto the Bowering Estate, which surprised Martin as he knew it was a dead end and there was no way out on the other side. He couldn't be taking a short cut through as there wasn't one. Had Colin picked up on the fact that he was being followed and was now leading him unawares into a trap and his own probable doom or was there another reason. So much was going through Martin's mind, but he was too far in to pull out now and carried on following Colin, trap, 'or' no trap, he had to take the chance.

Either way he was too far in to stop now, and he tentatively took the first steps onto the estate always managing to keep at least one eye on Colin to ensure he wasn't to become a victim in a new but deadly and dangerous game. The Bowering Estate was comprised of about 40 lock-up garages and was well known to the police as a drug addicts and sellers paradise, anything you needed you could get there, but mostly in the day, at night it became a secluded ghost town and very rarely would you see anyone.

At one point the garages stopped, and you had to turn the corner to find more, this is where Martin held back poking his head around the corner to have a quick peak. He saw Colin come to a stop about three quarters of the way down and pull something form his pocket. The door to a garage then opened and Colin took a criminals' look around before going inside and then Martin watched as the door closed behind him almost as if entombing him. A criminal's look being when someone who is doing something illegal stops to take a glance to both the left and the right of themselves and the surrounding area before proceeding on with what they were doing just to make sure they've not been followed or spied on, hence a criminal's look.

Chapter26: Escaping the lock-up.

You really do have to laugh at certain situations, but only if you don't fuck up an easy job and turn it into a fiasco, which is what the cops did. I never expected to escape from the lock-up but when I did, I was laughing all the way to the Travelodge. What I would have given to be a fly on the wall back at the police station when they had to explain themselves and their actions.

Martin rang Jane Collins to tell her about Colin and the lock-up, he gave her the address and said he would remain there to keep an eye on the situation and make sure he doesn't go anywhere else, thus giving her the chance to gather the team together, which she did quite readily and before long there were police arriving from all directions. Martin wanted things done on the quiet for now, as he didn't want to alert Colin to the fact that they had found him so most of the police cars remained on the edge of the estate and all of them had their blue lights turned off. All the officers in attendance and there were plenty of them walked onto the estate before taking up their positions.

Just about every angle was covered, Martin was sure, there were officers positioned on all corners of the estate and their cars were being used as barricades to block anyone from driving away. As soon as Martin was satisfied that he had all the bases covered he moved toward the door of the garage into which Colin had disappeared earlier and nodded to Jane. When she nodded back, he moved swiftly and with a loud bang on the door and the call of." Police open up, we know you are in there, come out with your hands in the air". he waited for the response.

After a couple of minutes of frantic commotion and movement from inside the garage, they heard a car engine starting and revving up. Believing they may be in danger from being rammed they moved to both sides of the garage door and away from its' direct line or exit route. The car seemed to be going backwards and forwards and touching the door without breaking through. Then suddenly there was a tremendous thud and an incredibly loud crashing noise followed by the sound of tyres screeching and a car speeding away into the distance.

A little shell-shocked at what he had just heard Martin called out "What the fuck was that, and more important where did it fucking come from?" Everybody was running around like busy ants and not really doing anything or going anywhere so nobody had an answer for him. Although they all felt they knew what it was, they were just worried about giving him information he didn't want to hear and being on the wrong end of his reaction, so they all just bottled it up and didn't say a word. Anything else would have been a mistake and would have led to unneeded attention as they all well knew. Martin could at times be a hothead, not as often as Jack was but if anyone pushed him too far, then God help whoever it was.

After resigning himself to the fact that the garage was in all probability now empty, Martin went about trying to get the door removed so he could see for himself. After a short wait and what seemed like an eternity someone eventually found a crowbar in the boot of their squad car and handed it to him. He shook his head in disbelief that anyone could be so dumb as to believe he could even begin to open it with such an item but began the process of trying to bend the door on its' hinges enough to enable a way in for himself anyway. He pressed on with it, more to prove himself wrong and not doing anything than trying to prove them right.

Once he felt he had bent it over enough, he then crouched down and looked in through the gap. What he saw certainly didn't make for good reading, the garage was as he had feared empty, and there was a giant hole in the wall at the top end of the garage directly opposite to the door. How the fucking hell am I going to explain this to the Goddamn chief he asked Jane? "He is going to have my bollocks on a plate and probably have me eating them for tea… probably washed down with a glass of Chianti too no doubt, fuck, this is a disaster." he added. Jane declined to answer as she believed there wasn't any right thing for her to say at that precise moment that could make anything better and so decided to go with the coward's option of remaining silent. At least that way she would be able to save herself from any ridicule that was coming his way and may be able to be passed over to her. She did have a sly chuckle to herself as she was walking away though. She pictured Martin as Hannibal Lector, munching on his own bollocks as he sipped Chianti…. priceless. This may have ended badly, totally turning tits-up but at least she had that image to keep in her mind at least until something better came along to dislodge it anyway.

Once Colin had heard the bang on the door of the garage and the warning from the police which all came as a total shock to him, he panicked, how had they found him? what could he do? He wasn't expecting it and it took him so much by surprise that he tried to bundle Marie into the car, but she had slipped and fallen face first onto the floor thus breaking her nose, to add to all the damage she had done to herself and was also added to by Colin's fit of rage. She was in agony and screaming when Colin decided he'd had enough and without a word he scooped her up in his arms and forcefully threw her into the boot of the car. He then started up the engine and drove at the wall of the garage a few times, weakening it before making one final and successful attempt to smash his way through what was left to get away.

Once he had broken free from the lock-up and after laughing to himself as he never felt it would work, Colin drove and just kept driving. He was going nowhere in particular, he just wanted to get away. He continued driving for about an hour or so, until he was out into the countryside and the towns lights were just a dim reminder somewhere in the distance. At that point he pulled off the main road and into a country lane where he parked up and prepared to rest for the night. He didn't even spare a second thought for Marie or her broken nose, or the fact she had been bouncing around in the boot every time he had taken a corner too fast or slammed on at red lights he had only noticed at the last minute.

He had no idea, either that she had dislocated her shoulder and even if he had, he probably wouldn't have cared as all he wanted to do was get away and if possible, get at least a little bit of shut eye. Both were proving tricky with the bitch in tow. With hindsight he should have just left her at the lock-up and make her their problem, but he just wasn't thinking clearly and now was in this thing more than he ever was, too deep to just drop it and move on. How he got here was a mystery, like a relentless whirlwind affecting everything in its' path.

Once that initial first step is taken, no matter how big or small it may be, there is just no turning back. Colin could see this and knew he was in deep shit, too deep to pull himself out, he could only see one plausible way out of the situation, but he wasn't ready for that, not yet anyway, soon perhaps, but not at this moment.

Chapter 27: Colin's place.

While I sat holed up down some country lane, the cops were running a fine toothcomb through my place, hoping to get that little spark of something that could lead them to me. Don't worry Martin and your team of clowns it won't be long before you don't have any more waiting to do. Maybe it's because I am ready, but it could also be partly that I feel sorry for you. Either way: I will see you soon.

 He adjusted his seat so it was lying prone, closed his eyes and before he could say supercalifragilisticexpialidocious, he had dropped off and was sound asleep. He had a strange dream about Mary Poppins and couldn't understand why she had made her way into his dream; she was getting really annoying being extra sickly-sweet and he'd had enough. He was just about to kill her when he came to, with such a start. He had no idea where he was and it took a few seconds for his eyes to adjust but when they had he remembered the events from the last night and although he didn't know exactly where he was, he knew why he was there and that was a bonus. Usually when he woke up in a strange place, he had no recollection of anything that had happened to get him there, at least this time he had some form of an inkling.

Remembering Marie, he got out of the car and went to the boot, he listened intently but there was no noise, so he unlocked it. When it opened and he saw Marie lying there even his heart skipped a beat, the poor girl looked in pain, her face was all red and swollen, with dried up blood, and her shoulder had dislocated out of its' socket. If anyone alive could look dead then this was Marie right here, right now. He told her not to move, as if she was in any fit state to go anywhere anyway and left the boot open for her so she could at least breath in a little fresh air. He wandered for a little while down the country lane to try and get his bearings if that was possible as this place was new to him and from that he would be able to work out exactly where he could be.

Marie's pain threshold was usually very high but at the point in her life where she was right now the agony was taking over and her threshold was subsiding, or it could have even disappeared altogether. She wasn't quite sure of reality anymore or if it still even existed. She was hoping she would wake up to find herself in her own bed and realise that this was or had been just a horrible dream, but before she could fully digest the idea, Colin returned, and it reminded her just how real the situation was, how real the danger was. Marie was not so sure she would ever be able to sleep peacefully again, or if she could manage it at least not for a long time, and all the unwanted memories she had now stored in her mind had been wiped completely from her memory.

Colins' little foray down the lane had reaped dividends, he now knew the name of the lane that they had parked on and after looking it up in his trusty if a little worn A to Z he worked out a route back to town. A lot of people were trying out these new Sat-Nav System things, which stood for Satellite Navigation, a trend that was just starting to break through. But Colin was more than happy to still use his book of maps, or atlas as it was more commonly known just as he had done since he had passed his driving test all those years ago. Apparently, sat-navs have revolutionised driving and made it damn near impossible to get lost but Colin didn't believe that for a second. They were also very expensive and for that reason alone he believed they would fizzle out before too long, but he had been known to be wrong in the past on a couple of occasions, especially as far as electrical goods and inventions were concerned.

If the police had managed to track him down to his lock-up, then chances were quite high that they had remembered his address and probably been there too, he was no detective, not by a long shot but he also wasn't a total moron. He was however a desperate man and in need of a few items and a shower, boy did he need a shower, possibly even some more cash so decided to make a little recon-mission to look and see if his place was being staked-out. He headed to his apartment and on the couple of drive byes that he made it didn't look as if it were being watched. They may have been good at their job and were waiting in hiding but he felt he had no choice but to chance it and so he parked his car up a few hundred yards down the road and walked cagily back to the building.

He was just praying that he didn't bump into anyone he knew and need to try and explain why his picture or rather someone that looked remarkably like him was in the Gazette and who was this new woman in his life. Some of his neighbours were nosey little bastards and had to find out everybody else's business instead of just minding their fucking own. On the most part it was before they had even learned their own stuff or knew anything about themselves at all.

Nosey little cunts, and then they had to search for someone else to talk to, anyone who would listen, and they would casually let it out as if it were nothing at all. Why the fuck can't people just do one and leave him to his own life as he does with them. He couldn't care less about them so why do they want to know every sordid detail about him, he laughed a sly laugh as he wondered what they would do if they knew the truth. Boy, could he give them a few sordid facts that would blow their mind but then that would just feed their egos and the shit would hit the fan, not for the first time. Best thing to do is not say a word, keep your lips tightly shut and not stoke the fires.

Colin grabbed Marie roughly by the arm and pushed her out in front, frog-marching her into the building after of course he had unlocked the door with his key. He had a quick glance around to check the coast was clear, it seemed to be all calm and quiet, but it was still early and a lot of them (his neighbours) would still be in bed or just starting to get ready for work. Some just waking to the sound of their alarms, others stepping into the shower to freshen up while some more may be finishing the last dregs of their tea or coffee, whatever their preference while taking a last bite of toast as they head out of the door in a kind of run/walk as they were now late. Time had elapsed, passing without incident before they could realise and now the morning rush was well and truly on.

 Thankfully, Colin thought to himself not even one of them is out and about now, he had the chance to ghost past without detection, keeping his fingers crossed the situation didn't change. Yet somehow expecting it to change at any given moment, sooner rather than later as that is how things seemed to be going for him at the moment. Everything is fucked up completely and no matter how you look at it, no matter how hard you try to think it out, it just stays the same.

They moved over to the lift and Colin pressed the call button, with a whirr of a noise they heard the lift start to descend to the ground floor from its' position on floor five. He counted down the floors as they changed and each number lit in turn,5, 4, 3, 2, 1 eventually coming to a stop on G denoting ground floor where they stood expectantly until the doors opened. He looked in expecting someone else to be there but luckily it was empty, and he pushed Marie inside before entering the lift himself and pressing the button for floor three, the floor where his apartment was. Marie gave him a look that said watch it dickhead, the look was enough to do it, she had no need for words and couldn't be arsed anyhow, enough was enough and he knew, he fucking knew. Colin shrugged it off, he didn't like it, but he just shrugged it off, all he wanted to do was to get them both into his apartment, unseen and A.S.A.P.

"Yoo-hoo, Colin, hold the lift please," a voice shouted. But he was trying his best to stop that happening by frantically pressing the door close button. The old lady from down the hall was getting ever so close and just when he thought his luck was running out, the doors suddenly closed before she had quite made it. "Thank fuck for that, she's a fucking nosy old bitch, that cow." He said to Marie as if she were his best friend and forgetting why they were both there. She just ignored him and refused to be drawn into ant form of conversation with him but understood perfectly well what he was saying as she had known a few people like that herself over the years.

Once they reached the third floor and he had watched the doors slide open, he had a very quick check around before they exited to the right and walked near to each other, but only because Colin had such a tight grip on her, and they moved down the corridor towards his place. He had just inserted his key in the keyhole when he heard one of his neighbours' doors starting to open. He turned the key as quickly as he could, and when the door opened, he pushed Marie in through the open doorway seconds before they were spotted, he pushed her so hard that she fell into the hallway in a heap. He slammed the door shut behind him and let out a giant sigh of relief before locking it in case Marie had any inclination to run but only then he noticed she was lying on the floor, nursing her pains, and wasn't going anywhere. If anyone had seen Marie then they would surely notice the cuts and bruises she had and may call the police, he was adamant that they hadn't been seen, or at least she hadn't anyway. He knew the old cow from downstairs had seen him, but he didn't care about that, he was seen around there all the time and there would be no need for them to tell anyone.

The inside of his apartment felt kind of different somehow, at least to what it usually did, anyway. If he hadn't noticed the small tell-tale signs here and there that someone had been in and disrupted the place, and then tried to put things back as normal as possible then he could certainly have guessed and been right. Give them their due though, the police hadn't done that bad a job of cleaning up after themselves but the differences they had left only the owner themselves would notice and Colin did, almost immediately, he had a keen eye for details and all the signs were that the details were all wrong.

Marie sat down on the sofa and just observed as Colin frantically darted from one room to the next checking them out strategically one-by-one as if he was looking for something and knew exactly what he was after. But it wasn't like that at all, he was just making an inventory in his head as to what was missing or what he could see was missing.

When he reached the bedroom, he looked and saw the fake front was still on the chest of drawers, Thank God he thought to himself as he moved across the floor towards it. He got down onto all fours directly in front of it and he removed the fake bottom, he then reached in his hand to try and retrieve the hidden items, there was nothing there. He reached as far back as he could and then to both sides but still nothing, "Oh fuck. Oh fuck, fuck, fuck he said to himself as he stood up and walked over to the wall. "Fuck" he said again as he punched the wall as hard as he could. It felt as if his knuckle had exploded, and he suddenly wondered why he had done it. His hand was shaking with the pain, there was some blood and he winced. He glanced down at his throbbing hand and thought well that was a stupid thing to do, wasn't it? But Colin is that sort of guy and he would no doubt do it again without stopping to think about how much it hurt in the first place.

He then had this paranoid feeling he was being watched, maybe that was the reason it felt so strange when coming in before. He had never felt anything like it in his own gaffe before, that's for sure. If they weren't watching and it was a big if, then no doubt they would be back sooner rather than later to check if he had returned. He needed to calm himself down and lose the feeling of paranoia that was eating at him from the inside, he was starting to lose the plot and no good ever came of someone losing their sanity when all they needed to do was remain relaxed.

He grabbed everything he felt he needed as quickly as he could and returned to the lounge to pick up Marie, his heart skipped a beat, the sofa was empty. He closed his eyes, shook his head, and then looked again just in case he was seeing things or not as this case proved to be. But no, she had gone, the sofa was most definitely empty. He had no idea where she could have gone or what he was going to do about it. He was just about to call her name when he heard a noise from along the hall; It was the sound of the toilet flushing.

He ran out of the lounge and into the hall just as Marie was exiting the bathroom. She could see by the look on his face that he wasn't best pleased with her, but she really didn't care one iota. She simply said to him," I was desperate, and you were busy running around all singing and all dancing, acting like a complete arse, what else was I going to do, shit in my knickers, I really don't think so, I am not a baby anymore".

Colin didn't utter a single word in reply as he didn't have a come-back answer to It whatsoever, well nothing that would seem clever and in fact he was just pleased to know she was still there when he'd thought that she had upped and bolted. I thought you had done a runner he told her. "Run, me? How the fuck could I run anywhere with my hands and feet bound?" she enquired. "It took all my strength and balance just to make it to the bathroom, running was not an option even if I wanted to." She barked at him. "Point taken, but it didn't stop me thinking it and giving myself a mini fucking stroke or heart attack." He growled back at her. Knowing this was probably going to be his last visit home in a while he picked up all the cash he had lying around and put it in his pocket.

He had no idea how much was there but felt It would come in handy if not at the least just to stop him using his credit card and basically telegraphing his whereabouts to all and sundry, making him so much easier to find. The trail he was leaving behind was an easy one to follow but only once they had started looking and had a starting point to begin their search from, which no doubt they would be by now especially after the incident at his lock-up. If anything, it would probably have made Martin Jackson more determined to catch him and he wasn't quite ready for that just yet. He had one or two more things to do, a couple more tricks up his sleeve before the time would come to surrender his freedom, but it was close at hand, he was looking forward to the rest that would come with it, all this running was taking it out of him, he was fucking exhausted.

On leaving his apartment he rushed Marie out and before long they were back at his car. He threw all the stuff he had picked up at the house into the boot, it wasn't even placed it was just thrown in all willy-nilly and Marie was put on the front passenger seat. Bloody hell she thought to herself, I have come up a long way in the world, not just allowed in the car but on the front seat as well, what a privilege, whatever did I do to deserve this. She wanted to say something but felt it would just add problems further down the line if she upset him again with derisory comments like that, so she just bit her tongue and kept quiet. Colin started the car and pulled away as fast as he could without drawing undue attention on himself from anyone that may be watching. He just wanted to be away from there pronto.

The screeching of the tyres as he drove away would have been more than enough to draw attention had anybody been around to witness it, Colin was both lucky and foolish at the same time. There was just something in his mentality that meant he always had to push the boundaries, no matter what he was doing. The easy option that a normal person would take was not even an option he contemplated but then again Colin Stevens was no ordinary person. Colin Stevens was about as fucked up as anyone could be, he was an antagonistic, moronic, psychotic sociopath and it was nearly time for the world to know, he was so close that he could feel the freedom being locked up could bring, that is exactly how fucked-up Colin Stevens was.

Chapter 28: Travelodge.

I don't stay in hotels very often but when I do, I am more than happy with a cheap and cheerful place rather than a posh hotel where you are afraid to move or touch anything. The kind of place where just walking down a corridor gets peoples fingers pointing and tongues wagging, it's like they know you don't belong there, treating you like an imposter. Well, fuck the lot of you this is The Travelodge, and this is my domain.

He drove about 3 miles out of town to where he knew there was a Travelodge motel. He left Marie in the car, handcuffed to the steering wheel, and he went into the reception and booked in under the names of Mr and Mrs Miles-White. He had no inkling, not a scooby doo as to how that name popped into his head, only the fact that he had always wanted a double-barrelled name and if this was the only opportunity to have it then by God, he was taking it." Cash or card, sir?" the receptionist asked, "Cash." Colin replied. "Ok sir, two nights bed only and no breakfast, at the rate of £55 a room per night that comes to one hundred and ten pounds exactly please."

Colin counted out the money and then handed it over to the receptionist who in turn counted it again before placing it in the till positioned underneath the front desk. He gave her such a discerning look that she said, "Sorry sir but I have no choice in the matter, anything missing at the end of the week is deducted from our wages, I am sure you would too under the circumstances. Here is your receipt and your room key you will be in room 236 today which is on the second floor. If you go up in the lift you will come out and go to the left but if you go up the stairs, then you will come out of the doorway and turn to the right. "She explained to him.

He thanked her and then headed off to the car to pick up Mrs Miles-White so he could take her to their honeymoon suite. That is what he had told the receptionist anyway, that they were newly-weds and were stopping for a couple of nights before flying out to The Maldives where the real honeymoon could begin, if they knew what he meant, which they did only too perfectly well. Once Marie was clear of the car he walked her along the wall of the hotel, and then entered through the exit furthest away from reception. The state Marie was in they could surely tell by her broken nose, black eyes, and bloodied face that there was something seriously wrong and although he had unbound her feet she still limped slightly as she adjusted to walking without them. Her hands were still bound, as he didn't want to relinquish any of the higher ground that he had fought hard to gain, because he knew that although he had won the last couple of battles Marie was still very much interested in winning the war outright. Although she looked a complete and utter mess, he really had to admire the resilience she was showing throughout this entire ordeal. Personally, he would have cracked well before now. He looked at her and smiled, she looked back with a frown and asked what he was smiling at. He didn't reply and just shook his head laughing to himself as he frog marched her into the hotel. You are my wife, for the next couple of days at least, so act like it.

It was at this point that he started having serious doubts about Marie, even though he admired her and thought how strong she was for someone that had gone through so much in a short time. The doubts he had meant although he couldn't help but admire her resilience and inner strength, he couldn't help but wonder how much she was holding him back. She was slowing down, mainly due to her injuries, most of which he had given her, so he only had himself to blame for that but most of all she was getting more and more rebellious. Her attitude was something he didn't want or need right now, he had enough on his plate without it. If he knew this from the start, that he was going to have such niggling doubts and problems then he would have probably left her well alone to rot and not taken her hostage in the first place. It turned out that Marie is expendable, and he was going to have to work out how and when to expend her, even if it meant letting her go, but not until his plan was in action and fully operational.

The room at the Travelodge was nothing special, in fact it was exactly what you would expect to get for its' £55 per room per night price tag. There were two single beds, each having its' own bedside table and lighting, a table which housed the tea and coffee making facilities (a kettle, 4 mugs & sachets of Coffee, Tea & milk etc), one chair as always between two people which Colin never understood, a 16inch T.V. mounted on a bracket on the wall and a large window that overlooked the car park. The bathroom was separate from the main room and comprised of a bath with shower attachment and a shower curtain that looked like it belonged in the 1970's. There was also a sink and a toilet, yes, just the usual standard stuff you would expect. None of it gold plated but well up to the standard needed for a short break away and just £55, that is only £27.50 each, a bargain really for anyone's money.

Marie sat on the bed nearest to the bathroom and Colin cuffed her to the headboard. It was uncomfortable but couldn't have been too bad as she managed somehow to close her eyes and slowly drift off into a deep sleep. Or else she was so tired that she really did not care one iota. She had no idea of how long she had been asleep but when she woke, she saw that Colin was not in the room. She tilted her head slightly and could see from the mirror positioned in the bathroom that he wasn't in there either. Where had he gone, what had he gone for and more importantly, what was he going to do with it.

Marie looked at her hands attached to the bed by the handcuffs and noticed something odd about them, not much but just something she hadn't noticed when they were placed on her wrists earlier. These ones were big and clumsy, not at all like the smaller more petite ones she had been wearing the last couple of nights. She felt that her small woman like wrists were capable of squeezing through the hole in them if she twisted and pulled hard enough.

Colin must have more than one set, quite a scary thought for someone that wasn't a policeman she thought and picked up the wrong ones' while being in such a hurry to get her to the hotel. Maybe this was just the break in her luck that she so desperately needed. Either Colin had not planned everything as meticulously as he would have hoped or the luck she was having, changed from bad to very good in a trice, and boy was it about time something went right for her.

Although they were still reasonably tight and rubbing her hand raw, she managed to wriggle her wrist back and forth and until it was halfway out of the handcuffs, she was ecstatic and couldn't help but smile to herself, her first smile since at least this ordeal started and maybe even before the incident with Colin at Allen and Co., there really hadn't been a lot else to make her smile but this was a small victory amongst countless defeats and she was accepting it with arms open wide (if she could free herself that is).

Eventually, after what seemed like hours but in fact was only minutes, she felt it happen. Her right wrist was free from the hand cuffs, and she pulled the other away from the wall and sat up on the bed. She shook her hands to get the feeling back into them as it felt like the blood had all rushed to the rest of her body and she got that awful tingly feeling for a short while before all feeling came back to her. She had seen Colin place the gun and knife in his bedside table before she had passed out with exhaustion and so, moved straight over to see if they were still there.

As she opened the drawer to his bedside-locker she saw the knife sitting on top of the Gideon Bible, but the gun was missing. He must have taken that with him, either as insurance or to do the unthinkable. The Gideon Bibles are supplied to just about every hotel room around the world that will accept them, but they are rarely ever read. They are probably used more as door stops than reading material, which is sad as religion is just not a topic people are comfortable talking about. Religion and Politics are two subjects that are barred from conversation on holidays and rightly so.

She grabbed the knife and started moving towards the door, but her timing couldn't have been more off if she tried for it to be. Just as she reached the door, she heard the sound of a key being inserted and then the click of it opening. She had no time to think and darted into the bathroom with seconds to spare before Colin walked obliviously into the room. He wasn't expecting anything untoward so just strolled casually into the room and by the time he realised Marie was not on the bed it was too late.

She ran out of the bathroom and thrust the knife into his back and stabbed him repeatedly while at the same time jumping on him and knocking him to the floor. He managed to pull the gun from his pocket and aimed it backwards toward her and pulled the trigger, but luckily for her the bullet missed and lodged in the wall. She then reached for the gun and tried to wrestle it out of his hands before he could fire it again. The next time she was sure he wouldn't miss. She wouldn't have even dared try if she hadn't weakened him with the stab wounds as she knew from experience that he was a very strong man.

The gun bounced toward the window and came to a rest against the wall, Colin had stopped moving so Marie assumed he was finished and went to pick up the gun. The second she bent down to pick it up she felt a hand grab hold of her by the hair and jerk her head back sharply and then throw her violently to the floor. She then felt him climb on top of her and put his two hands around her throat and start to strangle her. She had dropped the knife somewhere in the struggle and had no idea where, her only hope now was the gun.

As he was slowly squeezing out the life that she still had left in her, she was frantically stretching and trying to reach the gun. Colin felt empowered and now had the feeling of killing two birds with one stone. Not only was he getting rid of Marie once and for all, but he was also getting the sensation he felt when the urge to kill struck. What he hadn't noticed though was, that in his moment's lapse of concentration, Marie had managed to get her hand on the gun and pointing it toward him got off two shots. One hitting him in the chest before the real killer blow struck, the one that tore through the matter of his brain as it entered and then a fraction of a second later exited through the back of his head.

He was blown backwards by the shot and landed about a foot away from her with a pool of blood forming like a halo around his head. Weeping she picked herself up off the floor and sat on the edge of the bed to try and compose herself when she suddenly jumped out of her skin as a voice behind her said "Are you ok". Then it asked again "Marie, are you ok. Come on wake up, wake up,".

With everything that had just occurred she didn't quite click on to exactly what was said by the voice, only the fact that it was talking directly to her and whoever it was knew her by name. She thought she must be in shock and that it would soon subside, and hopefully she would return to normal before too long. Until that was, she twigged, and everything came together all at once. Only at that point did she remember who the voice that she was hearing belonged to.

Colin Stevens had walked into room 236 of the Travelodge Hotel to find Marie in the middle of a nightmare and thrashing about on the bed. He was worried that she may do herself some more damage and tried to wake her by calling her name. It had no effect whatsoever, and if anything, she was probably getting more out of control, so he shook her a little and called out again "Marie, are you ok. Come on wake up, wake up."

As she came to, Marie couldn't believe that Colin was standing in front of her and she was lying prone, handcuffed to the bed as she had been all along. She looked at the handcuffs to find they were the small, petite woman sized ones and not the clumsy large ones she had been wearing a matter of minutes ago, but all in her dream. Still unwilling to believe it she looked over by the window to see nothing but an empty floor. No knife, no gun, no halo of blood and certainly no dead Colin. Yet it had all seemed so real, how could this be? Why could she not catch a break even when she catches a break, happy just for a second or two until reality strikes with its' heart piercing knife.

Colin asked once again only this time shouting at her "Are you ok,", he was used to getting his own way, especially as he was the one with all the power, the gun, the knife and both his hands free and was getting really pissed with her not answering his demands. "Yes" she finally snapped back, "Just having a nightmare but that may not come as any surprise to you Mr Colin 'fucking retard' Stevens as I seem to be living one fucking long one with you at the moment" she carried on." Without you it would just be a dream, you are the reason it's a fucking nightmare, I hate you with everything I've got or ever had and can't wait until I get a chance to fucking kill you once and for all." she finished, sobbing uncontrollably.

With hindsight maybe she should have left it at yes, she knew she had made a big mistake but in the end what could he do to her that he already hadn't done. Why oh why did she have to ask that one question. Colin pulled the knife from his jeans pocket, his favourite knife, the one he had found when he was just 3 and a half years old, the one he had used to skin the dead cat when he was just seven. The same knife she had dreamt she had found in his drawer just sitting on the bible and moved in close to her. Smiling, he pulled her head back by the fringe of her hair and looked right into her eyes so she could see his pure and total hatred of her. Then with one swift uninterrupted slashing move of the blade he cut her throat from ear to ear.

Earlier on and when he had realised that Marie had fallen asleep on her bed, Colin assumed she would be there for a while and decided to take his chance to use the time and dispose of his car or at least get it somewhere that was not so obvious and would lead them (the police) straight to him. He went down to reception and asked them, because they appeared to have no signs to hang on their door, could they not disturb his sleeping wife for the next few hours at least. He made up a bullshit excuse that she had a headache and was resting. The girl on reception apologised and said they would get some to them as soon as they could, but he told them not to worry so long as they didn't wake her and walked out of the building and got into his car.

He drove the few miles back into town and while there he kept his eye out for the perfect place to leave it. Somewhere not too obvious where they would find it too quickly, but also somewhere it didn't look as if it had been abandoned in a hurry. The idea he had in his head was, if they believed he was close by to where it was parked then they would concentrate their search in that area and not look for them in the actual place they were hiding out. Once he had picked the perfect place, just a few streets away from his apartment, if they thought he was there then that would give them more time he thought to do what he wanted to achieve before he finally handed himself in. He then parked the car up and starting walking into the centre of town.

While walking along a hackney carriage passed on the other side of the road so he held out his hand to flag it down, after driving past it then did a U-Turn about twenty yards down the road and came back to where he was standing. He opened the door, climbed in, and asked the driver to take him to the Travelodge. It was a short journey and the fare only £5.80 but they could have been a million miles away as far as the police were concerned. On arriving at the Travelodge, he gave the driver a ten-pound note and told him to keep the change, considering it money well spent. He then went back into the hotel and up to the room where he heard a strange commotion coming from within. When he had unlocked the door and entered, he found Marie asleep and in the middle of a nightmare and the rest as they say is history.

Chapter 29: Mr Chester's car.

When is a car, not a car? When it turns into a driveway. It may be a stupid little joke, but it always made me have a giggle or two in the past and still does today. Then afterwards, seeing the faces of people puzzled and wondering just what it is that I am laughing at gets me even more. I never said I was normal, did I?

A car is a car no matter what make, model or size. A Porsche or a Ferrari can get you from A to B, just like a Mini or a Focus, it just comes down to taste, or snobbery. Poor Mr Chester's loved his car, and I had no right to take it but with all the other options available to me it was an easy choice. I mean it was not like I was keeping it and he would get it back eventually.

Martin Jackson had not long come out of a meeting with the big chief and possibly the biggest rollocking of his career so far and was in no mood to be messed around by anyone else. So, when he received a telephone call from someone claiming to be Colin Stevens, he was more than just a little bit sceptical to accept it. "Like what you found in my bedroom Detective Jackson" he asked "If pictures can tell a thousand stories, then buttons can tell so much more" he continued. "Where you at Colin," Martin asked. "You made me look a total cunt the other night and that won't be happening again. Make the most of your freedom because I am closing in. Your arse is mine dickhead, you hear me, your fucking arse is mine"

Colin already knew the game was just about up but said to Martin, "The only one that made you look like a cunt was yourself, I simply eased you into it, but you jumped with both feet. I am nearly done anyway and ready to give myself up, it's been a long ten years. But I have one more thing to do before that happens, are you easily shocked detective?" he asked. "I am not easily shocked Colin, you of all people should know that. Whatever you are planning, give it your best shot but keep looking over your shoulder as you do". Martin warned him. "We'll see" came the eery reply "We'll see. "And with that the phone line went dead.

Colin moved toward the door to room 236 and opened it saying goodbye to Marie as he passed her, only to be polite of course and with a sly grin on his face as he walked out into the hallway, she never replied. Ignorant bitch not answering he thought to himself but you're not my problem anymore. He so wished he could have been a fly on the wall when she was discovered though. Some poor innocent sod just getting on with their daily routine will suddenly come across one of the most gruesome sights they are ever likely to see. He felt so much sorrier for them than he did for Marie, and she was dead. Although it was just a reaction that he had no control over, she got what was coming to her and in his eyes, she deserved it. He was trying to vindicate himself but how on earth can anyone be vindicated for carrying out such a heinous crime. He was done caring and had a lot to do before he could finally settle down to the new chapter in his very eventful if a little complicated life.

When he got down into reception Colin paid for one more night but had no intentions of using the room but at least Marie was making the most of it by having a nice long lie-in. This fact he kept to himself as he said goodbye and walked out of the front door to the hotel and into the car park. His thinking was that it would give him more than enough time to do what he had to do before they find her and come looking for him. By this time no doubt, he would probably already be locked up in the police station or as close to damnit as possible after handing himself in, it was nearly time.

His intentions for now were to steal a car from the car park and drive into town. While there he would tie up all the loose-ends that needed sorting before walking into the police station and handing himself in to Detective Martin Jackson or if he happened to not be there then he would hand himself in to second in command in the case, Jane Collins. He would rather it was Martin Jackson, because he'd already had dealings with him, but beggars can't always be choosers. He was doing things this way as he wanted to be in control of the situation right up until the end.

He could have carried on but by then he would have lost the initiative, they were closing in and fast. Things had already started to go a little skew whiff lately thanks to the meddling cops and they had got in much too close for his liking. This way he was caught when he said he was getting caught and that was the way it had to be just to restore some clarity to the situation for himself more than anything.

Colin strolled through the car park eyeing up all the cars before deciding which one he would take. He had been stealing cars since he was a kid and had stolen just about every make and model that were on offer to him today. He walked right past and ignored the Porsche 911 and the two Jaguars as they would only bring undue attention. They looked out of place in a Travelodge car park let alone out on the open road, and he headed straight for the Red Volkswagen Golf parked in bay 26. Somebody had once told him that

VWs were the best cars ever made but he couldn't recall who it was, he just remembered their words and so he had always had a liking for them. He had no idea that the person in question was his real father and had said it to him when he was just a toddler and he had remembered the words all these tears only to forget it was his father that had said them to him or indeed who his birthfather actually was.

It took him only seconds to pop the lock, he opened the door and climbed in and sat in the driver's seat, it felt good, he felt alive as if it were made for him. He removed the casing from the steering column and pressing two wires together had the engine running in no time at all. What he had failed to notice while he was busy stealing it was the girl from the hotel reception had just finished her shift and was walking out of the Travelodge doors and into the car park at exactly the same time as he had got it started. On hearing the noise of the engine revving she had looked over expecting to see Mr Chester's from room 167 sitting in his car but instead she saw Mr Miles-White from room 236 and thought it a little odd.

 He saw her too, but tried in vain to avert his gaze, but it was too late, she had seen him and was walking over to the car." Oh Fuck" he thought to himself, "Walk away, please just walk away". But she came closer and eventually was standing by the driver's door where he was sitting and knocked on the window. "Where is Mr Chester's'"? she asked, "Isn't this his car". "Yes, it is" Colin replied "He was going into town and offered me a lift when I told him I needed to pick my car up from the garage. He forgot something and went back to the room to get it. Told me to look after the car until he returned".

"That's odd, I didn't see him go past" she said in an accusing kind of tone "I will wait here for him to return, I had rather wanted to say goodbye to him anyway, he is off home in the morning, and I am not back in till the afternoon."

Colin stepped out of the car and walked to the boot, opening it he asked her if she could give him a hand with something to save Mr Chester's feeling he had to oblige when he returned. Explaining it was heavy and he may struggle, to which she reluctantly said "yes". As she got to the boot, she looked in and saw nothing," what is it" she asked "This." he replied as he hit her on the back of the skull with a tyre iron, knocking her unconscious immediately and then picking her up after she had hit the concrete of the floor with such a thud and throwing her into the boot.

"You couldn't just walk away could you," he said half to her but talking to himself. She of course didn't hear a word as she was out cold." You had to try and be clever when playing dumb was easier, that is the problem with you stupid women. You should have left the detective work to the police you stupid cow." He slammed the boot shut and got back into the car, driving away while screeching the tyres through the car park as if in defiance to the entire world, but especially women, as he went. The screeching of car tyres seemed to be his trademark at the moment he thought to himself, he really has to stop before he is noticed before his time is up and he doesn't get the chance to fulfil his self-imposed obligations.

When he arrived in town he drove directly to where he had left his Black Toyota Corolla and reversed up to it, so the two cars were back-to-back or rather they were boot-to-boot. He opened both boots and transferred the girl into his own car, he bound her hands and feet with rope he had in the back of his car and then placed duct tape over her mouth before locking it again.

Looking into Mr Chester's red VW he could see some blood stains in the boot, for a second, but only a second, he panicked before realizing he could probably use it to his advantage later if he needed a bargaining tool with the police. He could maybe pretend it was Marie's blood and keep them guessing until they could run tests and prove it wasn't, it was their prerogative to prove otherwise not his to help them in their investigations.

Although he knew he may be tempting fate, Colin then went to his apartment where he had a shower and changed into some fresh clothes before making himself some toast which he washed down with a cup of tea, his first in three days. He usually drank at least five cups a day, so this one was probably the best one he had ever tasted, and he savoured it. He wasn't so worried this time about being caught as he planned to hand himself in anyway, so he just relaxed and watched a bit of daytime T.V. Like the kind of programmes that you hate to watch but find yourself watching religiously every day when you are home, just for something to do, to help pass the time between lunchtime and teatime.

After half an hour or so he decided it was time and he was serving no purpose by putting off the inevitable, so he went back out to Mr Chester's car, he drove it the short distance to the police station and parked it directly outside part on, part off the kerb before heading into the building. Once inside he asked the desk sergeant if he could see Detective Martin Jackson. "Who shall I say wants him" he asked. "My name is Colin Stevens, but you can tell him the button killer is here, he will understand."

The sergeant disappeared for a minute or two before returning with another guy, although he had only met him on a couple of occasions, he recognised him right away and said, "Hello detective, we meet again at last" To which Martin Jackson replied "Come through Mr Stevens, you have proved one tricky little mother fucker to pin down, and then even harder to fucking catch. I can't tell you how relieved I am that you are finally here." With the pleasantries over, if that's what you can call them, Martin led Colin through to the interview room and they both sat down in silence wondering what the future held for them. Two men obviously heading in total opposite directions.

Back at the prison, Connie who had been listening intensely to Colin for a while felt she should speak up and butted in by asking him.

C.J.   "Sorry to butt in Colin but why choose to hand yourself in then, after all that time?"

C.S.   "I just felt the timing was right, I could probably have gone on for ages if I had run but then I would have been looking over my shoulder at every rustle in any bushes or any sounds out of the ordinary and I didn't want that, not being in total control. I knew that they knew who and what I was, and it would only be a matter of time before they found me and came for me so I thought I would save them a job. Things were already starting to slip away from me anyway. I wanted to be in charge and dictate my own future, not have someone do it for me."

C.J.   "You knew it would lead only one way, and that was to jail."

C.S.   "Of course, from the very start I knew it would more than likely end up in me going to jail or ending it all, but I really didn't care which, I never did, and I was ready for any consequences. My life had run its' course and I was faking it just to survive. I had at one point even contemplated suicide, but I didn't want posthumous fame, I wanted the glory I was due while I was still alive, suicide would have to wait, for now anyway, it was not the time."

C.J.   "You wanted your moment of fame, you felt you had earned it, it was what you craved, so you were taking it while you could still have the chance to enjoy the occasion."

C.S.   "I wanted people to know who Colin Stevens was and what he had done, even if they didn't understand why he had done it. That is why I am doing this now after a couple of years. I don't want to be forgotten but that is what was starting to happen. I was rotting away and floating out to sea like a piece of driftwood, nobody cared, just left to bob up and down on an unending journey to nowhere with nobody even noticing."

C.J.   "But, by losing your freedom though, being locked away is a big price to pay."

C.S.   "Was I ever free really, I saw myself as a slave to evil and nothing else. Just an envoy carrying out its' will when it wanted me to. I was going nowhere or to hell and getting there fast, in fact I think I had arrived, it sure felt like it anyhow."

C.J.   "Do you think you would have killed again if you hadn't decided to stop yourself by taking the temptation away?"

C.S.   "I am not sure on that but I reckon I was capable of anything so I would have expected me to yes but whether I would have is another matter, maybe it was too late for me."

C.J.   "Too late, what do mean by that?"

C.S.   "By handing myself in I was going out on my terms and not theirs. If I'd have carried on the chances are, I would probably have tried to fight my way out and been killed in the process thus missing out on the few moments of fame I felt I had merited."

C.J.   "I can see why but I just can't see when it could ever be the right time."

C.S.   "Simple, my choice and my choice alone, I felt it was time and that was it really…….. I am strong in character and was never going to play the weak persona in the story."

Colin had been sitting in the police station interview room, the one he had become accustomed to for about 15 minutes. Martin was sat opposite to him and barring the occasional clearing of the throat, cough, or sniffle there was deadly silence. They had both been thinking of this moment for a long time and now it was here they were both dumbstruck, no words were forthcoming.

Eventually, and well beyond the time it was due, Martin decided to break the awkward silence by asking Colin about the blood in the boot of the VW Golf. "We know the car belongs to a Mr. Chester's," he said, "but whose is the blood. It is obviously fresh so I would say it has only been in the car for a few hours at most, where or who is it form" "that'd be too easy if I just give you answers without making you work for them Detective, time for your police brain to do a little bit of work and try to solve it. Who do you think the blood belongs to?"

"The most obvious answer would be Marie, you kidnapped her and now she is missing, maybe I am just jumping to conclusions, but I would have to guess at the blood being hers. And I would like the opportunity of getting help to her if she is in pain or discomfort, should I call for an ambulance? He asked Colin.

"Sorry to say Detective an ambulance is much too late for Marie. "As he said it, he could see Martin's head drop in a resigning kind of way. "And would it throw a spanner in the works to know that the blood is not hers anyway. She has had her blood spilt but not in Mr Chester's car, she is somewhere else just waiting to be discovered." Colin replied in a cynical kind of way.

"It erm, kind of erm, would yes actually," replied martin "I had it all decided that it was erm, her blood, Marie's blood and the chances are she was probably dead anyway. Is it Male or female, Colin, I mean the blood in the car, is it male or female?"

"One out of two is not bad." Colin told him. "And in answer to your other question female of course, what did you really expect me to answer to that."

Jane Collins knocked on the door and when ushered to she popped her head in through the doorway, "Got a number for you to call. Mr Chester's again, wondering if you have found his car yet, he needs it to get home. Also, may be nothing but a car on the high street, someone said they thought they heard a voice coming from the boot but when they called back there was no reply. Could've been hearing things but seemed pretty sure it was a voice."

"What colour and make of car is it, may be a wise idea to send someone out to take a look, just in case. After the fuck up last week, we don't want to arm them any more ammunition to use against us. If we check everything and then double check it then we have done what we can, we can't do any more than that. If we are wrong, then it is fate, and we really are as shit as they say."

"It was a Black Toyota, didn't give the model but the reg. is", She was stopped in her tracks as Martin told her not to bother as he was quite certain he could guess it. Could even ring a bell to Mr Stevens here as well. What do you say Colin? If we go down to the high street now, would you say we could possibly find the owner of the blood from the VW Golf." he asked." "Who knows detective? Stranger things have happened in life, it's possible, then again anything is possible." Colin replied.

The interview was suspended at that point as Martin was in a hurry to get to the black Toyota himself and as fast as he could, somebody's life just could well depend on it. Colin was returned to the cells for a break and to prepare any more answers that were needed by Martin and the team from future questioning and Martin was heading off to check out the Toyota.

The pair of them, Martin and Jane jumped into Martin's car and sped as fast as they could to the high street. It didn't take long as it was less than a mile away as Colin had mentioned to him during the interview earlier. When they arrived, they parked up a few yards away from the black Toyota and got out of the car. As they did, they were they were greeted by a police constable from their precinct, and he introduced them to a man sitting on the little wall by the car showroom. With him was a well behaved, black Labrador lying patiently at his feet. The dog had no idea why his walkies had been suspended and was looking bored, kind of if he just wanted to get on with things before going home again. It took all his energy to get ready to go out, he expected to be walking not sitting at his owner's feet, he could do that at home all day. On the plus side he was being inundated with doggy biscuit treats, he usually had only a couple on the entire walk, but he had already been given 5, obviously bribery to help him forget his boredom.

Martin went over to the man and introduced himself before thanking him for his observance and reporting it. "I thought I was hearing things at first and if I didn't report it and it turned out to be something bad then I would never be able forgive myself," came the reply. Occasionally, when things like this happen the obvious choice is to pin the blame on or at least question the first person to have contact. But Martin was pretty sure just by his demeanour, by the way he was acting that he was totally innocent and as he had said, he was just a by-passer that may have stumbled on something or not as the case may turn out to be.

After speaking to the man on the wall, who was called Brian Maylor for a few minutes and stroking the dog called Butch while he did so, he told him he could be on his way but to leave his number with the police officer in case they needed any further information. This he did and no sooner had he done so, then Brian Maylor with Butch in-tow went off and continued with their disrupted walk. Martin watched them until they had disappeared around the corner seeing Butch's tail wag as he followed his master, thinking there is innocence, how it must be great to not worry about anything other than the simplest things in life, walking, eating, shitting, and getting stroked.

Martin was in a bit of a lull as he waited for the special force to come and open the boot. He knew he could do it by himself, but things had to be done properly and by the book or the shit would hit the fan as it had already, numerous times. All it took was one person from the special force saying somebody else had done their job before they'd arrived, and he was fucked. Being in charge sometimes is not as glamourous as it is made out to be. Ten minutes later and they turned up with all the tools and equipment you are supposed to use, not a crowbar to yank it open as Martin would have done and then got on with the job of finding out for sure if anyone was inside.

While he was waiting for them to arrive Martin did keep trying to contact whoever it may be or indeed anyone that could be inside by calling in," This is the police, shouldn't be long now we will have you out in no time at all. Just hold in there you are doing good" whether his words fell on deaf ears or not he didn't really care as he was only interested in keeping whoever it was as calm as he possibly could. He didn't bang on the boot as he felt any noise would be at least doubled and possibly trebled inside and could possibly cause more stress than it may prevent.

When they finally turned up Martin stepped aside and let them do their work, to work their magic if you wish and they had the lock drilled out and the boot open within two minutes of arriving. As he peered inside, he could see nothing but space, the boot appeared empty, and he thought of what he was going to do to Colin Stevens when he got back to the station for sending them on a wild goose chase. But just as he was about to move away, he heard the faintest of words, "Help" came the quietest voice he had ever heard so he moved forward and leant into the boot and at the top end under where the rim opens, he saw the figure of a young woman. She had managed to crawl into just about the only place she could have hidden, maybe in an attempt to ambush her abductor if given the opportunity.

He told her he was with the police; she was now safe, and he couldn't hurt her anymore. He then reached in to help her out of the boot but not before asking if she was hurt or unable to be moved. She told him her head hurt still from the whack it had taken but apart from that she was OK. He took her over to his car and sat her on the front seat as there was more room there for her to stretch out. Looking at her he noticed something about her, something that made him think hard, she was wearing the uniform from the Travelodge. Why was that a thing he thought to himself and then it kicked in, "The Travelodge".

"Jane, here a minute. "He called "Where did Mr Chester's have his car stolen from" he asked her. "The Travelodge," she replied. They both made the connection at the same time and the words fuck me escaped from their lips in unison, "As soon as this darned ambulance turns up, we can be on our way. Who knows what we may find there, I am guessing Marie, in some condition or other hopefully alive but I am not going to hold my breath over it, especially after what he said before? "Martin said. "Why what did he say before?" Jane enquired. "That her blood had already been spilt but not in the car." He replied to her. "Shit." Was all Jane could muster in response.

Chapter 30: Inside room 236.

What was waiting for them at the Travelodge would probably test anybody's tolerance to throwing up, it was not a nice sight. But what was done was done and I couldn't go back so I had no choice but to leave her there for them to find. They found her a lot quicker than I had imagined they would, and it nearly put my entire plans into jeopardy. I got away by the skin of my teeth, once again. Was I invincible or was I just lucky?

Martin could not believe how quickly their luck had changed, one minute they were scratching and scraping around for even a morsel of a clue and the next, giant case-crackers seem to be falling into their laps without even having to stretch themselves. It is one of only a handful of things that have gone right for them in the whole investigation and long may it continue. It took a little while for the ambulance to turn up but once it did and the girl from the Travelodge had been checked over, passed fit and had been loaded and taken to hospital, Martin turned to Jane and said," Right then let's go, we won't hang on this hey Jane, done that too many times and where has it got us, down shit creek without a fucking paddle."

There is only one Travelodge in the area so even if the girl hadn't said where it was it really wouldn't have taken too much working out. Especially for cops but for anyone in fact. They both jumped into Martin's car, and he drove the three miles or so, to the Travelodge where he pulled into the car park and stopped in one of the spaces closest to the main door. After getting out of the car Martin just stood by his door and looked around the car park. "What is it?" Jane asked inquisitively. "Oh nothing, the way our luck had changed I expected to see her standing here just waiting to be rescued" he replied. "By her I take it you mean Marie Calvin, but didn't he say he had killed her," she asked "Not in as many words, he implied it without saying. I kind of hoped he was bullshitting us again it has been known of him to string us along."

They both walked into the hotel lobby and introduced themselves as police officers to the girl working in reception. "We need some answers to a few questions if that is OK, "Martin told her. "Of course, whatever you need" came the reply. "Do you have a Mr Colin Stevens booked in at the moment" he asked. "The name doesn't ring a bell to me unless he has booked in on someone else's shift. No sorry nobody by that name is staying here. "She replied after checking the name in in the register.

Martin looked blankly at Jane and said "What the fuck is going on, he has to be booked in here, how can he not be, there isn't a Travelodge that I don't know about is there? Everything put together has led us here. He can't be that clever, surely that he has set us up for another fall. No, I am not having it there must be something we have missed." He turned back to the receptionist and asked "How about in a different name, is that possible. How many people have you got in at the moment" he asked her? "Twenty-four rooms are taken between thirty-eight guests" she replied after checking once again in the register.

"On a different subject we have another guest that had his car stolen from the car park and he keeps asking me to ring because he thinks the police are fed up with him calling, but in the end, he just wants his car back" she said. "Ah yes, Mr Chester's we also need to speak to him at some point, if you could call him and bring him down for me that would be appreciated." "Have you found his car, he will be so made up, I will call him down to reception now" she replied. Martin never replied as it wouldn't be in his or Mr Chester's best interests to say yes. Either way he wasn't getting his car back any sooner due to it being involved in a kidnapping, so instead he just watched her pick up the phone.

She dialled his room extension and waited a few seconds for him to answer, "Hello Mr Chester's we have a couple of police officers in reception that would like to talk to you, any chance you could come down to reception" she asked him and then put the phone back on its' receiver. "He is on his way down, shouldn't be more than a couple of minutes. He is old but he is quite nifty on his feet. Goes in the gym every day he is with us and talking to him he has a treadmill at home as well." She said" He's very fit for his age."

Mr Chester's arrived at reception a little over 3 minutes later and Martin took him off to the side to explain that his car had been confiscated for forensic tests due to it being involved in a crime. He also said that if he needed to go anywhere to use a taxi and claim the fares back by getting receipts for his journeys. Although he wasn't happy about it, who would be, he was man enough to understand and thanked Martin for his honesty before heading back up to his room.

Martin turned attention back to the receptionist and asked her," Anything strange or out of the ordinary happened in the last few days, something odd or peculiar that didn't quite make sense," "This is the Travelodge detective, not the Ritz. That could relate to over half the guests we ever have staying with us even the ones' in at the moment." She replied in a cheeky but joking way. "Yes, I guess it could and I don't doubt it for a second," he responded, "But if we could stay serious for a moment, anything at all no matter how small it could help." He continued.

"The strangest thing I can really think of is the couple that booked in on their honeymoon, we have been taken pretend bets on how long the marriage will last," she said "What is so odd about a married couple on honeymoon and why would their marriage be at risk" he asked her, hoping it would solve all his problems in one, but not counting his chickens, he really didn't expect much. "Well, that's the odd thing they are on their honeymoon, but they booked into a room with two single beds. I mean if they aren't sleeping together now then what chance will they have in the future. We wondered if they'd had a fight so soon in their marriage. We were all guessing though and doesn't look like we will get find out anyway." She spoke.

"Why not" Martin asked "Why would you not find out. I would love to know myself now you have said, it sounds intriguing". "Because he hasn't been back since he left yesterday, and she hasn't left the room at all during their stay," she replied.

Alarm bells rang in Martin's head and Jane heard them too, that's how loud they rang. They looked at each other and put one and one together… "What name are they booked under and what room" Martin asked the receptionist. "Mr and Mrs Miles-White and they are staying in room 236. But they are a couple, and you wanted a man on his own" she enquired. "Where is the room" he asked. "Second floor" she replied as Detectives' Martin Jackson and Jane Collins disappeared through the doors leading to the stair well.

They both ran up the two flights of stairs at full pelt, their legs were feeling the burn but that didn't stop them, only slowed them down slightly. They just had to get to room 236 and as fast as they possibly could. When they got to the room Martin knocked on the door and called out "Marie are you in there, it's Martin Jackson from the police" but there was no response. So, he called out again only a little louder, "Marie are you in there, it's Martin Jackson from the police," yet again there was no reply. He never called out a third time and decided not to wait for the key to unlock the door either.

He raised his size nine shoe as high as he could and with all the force he could muscle-up Martin kicked the door to room 236. It broke full off its' hinges and flew halfway across the room and landed just by the desk housing the kettle and mugs and all the tea and coffee making equipment.

They could see some light coming from the room on the right, the bathroom which looked promising as they edged slowly into the room. Looking in Martin could see that the bathroom was empty, but further ahead he could see a bump in the bed under the covers. Either this was Marie or Colin had taken her and stuffed pillows to make it look like someone was sleeping. Anyone coming in to clean would see the bump and quickly vacate the room so as not to disturb them from their well-earned slumber.

As he moved forward and closer to the bed, he could feel his heart pounding, getting faster and faster and faster with no signs of slowing or stopping. Something like a like a runaway train thundering down the track on its' way to oblivion. He reached his hand out and shook the figure in the bed, but it just shook and made no attempt to move at all. By the way it felt he knew it wasn't pillows and most certainly a person and although he didn't like to admit he felt there was only one person it could be, Marie Calvin.

He reached out his hand once again but this time instead of shaking the figure he grabbed the covers. Then after inhaling one long deep breath for strength and courage (needing all he could muster) he pulled back the covers to reveal the dead body of Marie with her neck sliced open so deeply she was nearly decapitated. Only a few strands of tissue were keeping her head attached to her body. The blood was thick and congealed and the darkest shade of red you could imagine, practically black in the light or dark so to say.

Martin took a step back and turned away, he had seen all he needed to and far more. He walked out into the hallway, composed himself by raising both his hands above his head and placing them on the wall leaning into it. He breathed heavily and eventually regained his composure before re-entering the room and placing one hand on Janes' back, rubbing it gently to calm her as he could tell she was just as anxious as him. In all his years in the police he had never seen anything as bad as this and hoped he would never have to see it again. Jane turned around and leant into his shoulder, weeping. She was an excellent and tough cop, but everyone has their limits and she had just reached hers or even gone beyond it.

They decided enough was enough and to call it a night. If they went back to the station, it would involve paperwork, a hassle they really didn't need right now. They just wanted to go home to try and rest if that was at all possible after what they had just seen. Colin was in the cells and going nowhere so they chose to let him stew overnight and start their inquisition first thing in the morning. Martin dropped Jane off at her house on the way home and said, "We'll rip that mother-fucker to pieces in the morning, see you then but try and relax as best you can," To which she replied, "Goodnight and thanks." He had no idea what for and opted not to find out pulling away and heading off into the darkness and off towards his own home. He had no time to be nursing her and doing his job.

Colin Stevens sat upright on the bed in his cell using the wall as a backrest. He just stared forward into the space of the room and eyeing one spot on the wall, he rocked gently back and forth. He was totally unaware of anything going on outside and as far as he was concerned Marie was still undiscovered at the Travelodge. He knew his car had been discovered but never thought for a second that the connection to the hotel would be made so soon.

As far as he was concerned, Detectives Martin Jackson and Jane Collins should be running around in circles like a blue-arsed-flies trying to make the clues they had come together, just as he had planned for them. They should be miles away from any answer to any question about him or his time with Marie, or so he thought. It was a very muggy warm night, and he felt a lump in his exceedingly dry throat so called out to the guard for a cup of water. A paper cup was brought in and handed to him, then filled from a jug of ice-cold water also brought in by the guard. He gulped it down post haste and asked for another. This one he took with him and nursed in the palm of his hands as he sat back on the bed in the exact same spot he had been before. The heat made it impossible for him to sleep and he was becoming increasingly impatient with the beads of sweat trickling down his forehead, feeling like the tingling of a tiny spider's legs as they did.

On arriving home Martin headed straight for the kitchen, he hadn't eaten for at least 12 hours and was ravenous. His stomach had been growling at him like a tiger for hours and though he tried his best to ignore it at some point he just had to give in to its' pangs, which was now. He looked in the cupboard and although he had plenty in, he wasn't willing to put the effort in to cook anything over-demanding and instead opted for the simplistic, yet very satisfying and tasty fried egg sandwich. It took a little longer to construct than it did to demolish it and he washed it down with a mug of coffee. He grabbed the TV remote control and pressed the red button to turn it on. He then flicked his way through a multitude of channels and all that seemed to be on were shopping channels or adverts. Over one thousand channels and still fuck-all to watch he thought to himself, "I really have to cancel my sky package," he said out loud before turning it off and going to bed.

Within ten minutes of his head hitting the pillow he was deep in a sleep that even a nuclear bomb couldn't have woken him from and feeling more relaxed than he had for over months. Two men with two different ideals, one relaxed enough to be sleeping like a baby while the other sits awake and restless. Ladies and gentlemen, I give you the ever-differing lifestyles of a cop and a criminal. Who knows what the future may bring as tomorrow is another day, and the roles may well be reversed as diversity takes its toll on existence once again?

The next morning Martin woke as fresh as a daisy and for the first time in forever he was rather looking forward to going into the office. After a quick refreshing shower followed by a few sips of a coffee he had made earlier but left to go cold, he headed off to his car in preparation for the shortish journey to work. There were a couple of things on his mind about yesterday and the way it all unfolded but nothing major as the main point was, they had that murderous mother-fucker Colin Stevens locked in one of their cells at the station. And unless there was any major turning point then he was going nowhere but prison and hopefully sooner rather than later.

When he arrived at the office, he walked up the flight of stairs to the first floor where the operations room was positioned and walked in nodding his head to the other members of the team that were already there. He didn't say a word at this point but instead just brushed past them and over to the writing board where he added Marie Calvin's name to the list of victims of the cotton mill killer. He also drew a circle around the name of Colin Stevens then another circle around the cotton mill killer and then a symmetrical line between the two circles, linking them together. He wrote in capital letters one and the same, got him.

He was felling slightly jaded this morning thinking over the events of the last two weeks or so but was also in a buoyant mood due to the results of yesterday. In a reserved but firm voice he said, "OK guys gather round if you would please." Everyone that needed to be there was in by now and the eight of them all came over to where Martin was standing and formed a semi-circle around him and the writing board which he was standing in front of.

"In case any of you have just got back from visiting Mars and don't know Colin Stevens is down in the cells, for some reason he handed himself in to me last night. Only thing is it wasn't soon enough to save Marie Calvin, he had already topped her at the Travelodge and left the gruesome find to Jane and myself. Her throat had been severed to a point her head was left hanging on by only a thread of tissue and ligaments. We, and by that I am referring to Jane and myself again will conduct an interview with the bastard later, where he is going to be charged with 5 counts of murder, 6 counts of rape also kidnapping and possession of unlicenced weapons. This hopefully should be more than enough to put the cocky wanker away for a long time. I don't want any excuse for him to be wriggling his way out of this somehow and don't ever want this cunt walking our streets again. Understood?" he asked. "Yes sir." came the response in unison from the entire team. "What Jane and I saw last night was not very pleasant and will stick with me forever and also Jane I think," he said looking directly at her. "Yes," she responded with a sad look in her eyes. Martin continued "And I know it's not just us it has been a hard time for us all in one way or another, but I believe we are closer to the end than the beginning now so just bear with it for a little while longer and we will get the results our hard work has merited. Also, we need to keep serious and professional by dotting our I's and crossing our T's, and in doing so give no quarter to them in their attempt to secure bail for him. He is locked up and that is where he must remain, behind bars."

He dismissed them and they all went their own separate ways leaving the operations room empty barring himself and Jane. He never realised how the room echoed until everyone had left and then heard it immediately as he spoke. There wouldn't be too many more chances for them all to get together as the case was practically solved. Only on the occasions when they needed to compare notes and most of them had already been filed in waiting, ready for the expected court case. Martin has assigned one person, Steve Thompson to be the one responsible for cataloguing and transferring everything onto file from the very start and to save time having to do it all in one go at the end. His decision had proved to be the right choice as over ten years of evidence would have taken an age to catalogue and transfer. Steve had proved very efficient and didn't involve himself too much in the workings of the case unless he saw something so blatantly obvious that had been accidentally overlooked by everyone else as does sometimes happens.

At least by doing this they had a good base to start their proceedings for a trial and everything was together and labelled for when they needed it in the order of how the trial would go. If they had left it then it would have been at least another six months before they could even begin to think about court, now it could be up-and-running in as little as three weeks depending on court availability of course.

But for now, they will just bide their time and do things correctly and by the book. Dot their I's and cross their T's just as it should be. The time will soon pass, and his entire sordid event will be done with, and Colin Stevens will be locked up for good.

Chapter 31: Souvenirs.

The souvenir buttons were a personal choice, I just stumbled onto it by chance, but it seemed like the right thing for me to do, at the right time. Over the years the collection grew, as did the list of victims. Even I was shocked by how many. In the end it became commonplace for me to just open the tub and throw a button in, I never counted them, ever.

C.J.   "From what I have worked out about you Colin you are a man of impulse would you say that was fair?"

C.S.   "Yes, that's very observant of you and I think that would be fair to say. I did a lot of things on impulse, things that weren't planned like killing Jack Williams and attacking him in the supermarket. With hindsight I should never have done it, but impulse is another thing altogether. Again, with Jack Williams I never planned on killing him, but the opportunity arose to help myself at the same time, so impulse made me take him out of the equation. And then Marie, she was starting to be very grating and really starting to piss me off so, when she said one thing too many I just reacted, again on impulse."

C.J.   "Did impulse make you hand yourself in, were you ready for it or did you have regrets afterwards?"

C.S.   "Maybe it played its part, but I never had any regrets, not in anything I did. What was done was all for a reason and that included handing myself in at that precise moment. I was ready to be caught and I was ready to welcome the fame I was to receive because of my actions and of what I did over the years."

C.J.   "From what you are saying it sounds to me like you got bored, maybe you had done everything you could to quench your desire and simply got fed up."

C.S.   "Wow, I never really looked at it like that before, I think you know me better than I know myself. You could be spot-on with that assumption. I reckon I was bored with the killing side of it but interested to hear what everyone was thinking or even saying about me and the only way to find out was to call it a day."

C.J.   "I am taking it that you read the papers each night to see how things were progressing in the case."

C.S.   "I did buy the papers but not to see how the case was progressing, I just wanted to read about myself. I know I wasn't mentioned by name per say but I knew it was me that it was about, and it gave me such a thrill. I was kind of famous like a movie star and for a while afterwards I was buzzing with the adrenalin."

C.J.   "So, why did you change your plea at the trial. You were all out to say not guilty and then suddenly your lawyer said you had amended your plea to guilty on all counts."

C.S.   "Impulse, I really didn't want to fight anything anymore. I couldn't prove my innocence because I was guilty and what would be the point in dragging out the process any longer than was needed, for myself or anyone involved. At least that way there was no strenuous daily trips to court and back., I could just settle in and start my life over. Bed and board for the rest of my life, what could go wrong?"

C.J.   "Do you hold any animosity or hard feelings towards Detective Martin Jackson? After all, if he hadn't got in so close you may not have decided as you did, you could have carried on with your murder spree?"

C.S.   "No, none whatsoever in fact I respect him more than I did originally when he was fucking things up, but once he got going and got all his shit together, he was quick as lightning in getting things sorted. Every corner I would turn he would fucking be there without fail and I have to admit, finding me at the lock-up was a touch of genius. Yes, I think I underestimated him too much and he was a better detective than I gave him credit for at first."

C.J.   "But you escaped from the lock-up and he took one hell of a rollocking for it I believe."

C.S.   "Nobody could have known I would break through the wall with the car, even I only knew it about 2 minutes before and then I was surprised it worked. I honestly thought it would wreck the car and I would be caught anyway. I just got extremely lucky, maybe I hit a weak spot in the wall or something but that didn't stop me having a good laugh about it though."

C.J.   "Must have felt like all your Christmas's had arrived at one time."

C.S.   "Something like that."

C.J.   "Tell me about the buttons and their significance."

C.S.   "Souvenirs, nothing more nothing less. Just a little token reminder for my own personal memory bank."

C.J.   "A little reminder? there were 57 buttons in total, are you saying you attacked 57 women?"

C.S.   "I would say it was slightly more to be honest, I only started taking a souvenir after about the 5th or 6th."

C.J.   "And what was it that made you start?"

C.S.   "By accident really to start with. The first time I didn't take a button off her, it just popped off with the force I used and fell on the floor. I decided there and then that it was a good idea and I picked it up to have as a keepsake or souvenir and did every time after. I didn't realize there were 57 in there though. If you asked me how many I would have said 25 or 30 but 57, wow no wonder I was starting to get bored."

C.J.   "You are acting like it's all one big joke. Some of the girls you attacked have been traumatised for life and a few even worse than that and you are just laughing it off as if it doesn't matter."

C.S.   "What can I do or say that could possibly appease you or them. If I was in anyway worried about what they thought then surely, I wouldn't have done anything to them in the first place. What happened, happened, and you, I, or they can't change a damn thing so getting all gushy and gooey won't help anyone in the slightest."

C.J.   "OK, you obviously have your thoughts on the matter, and I have mine, we are of different opinions and are obviously never going to get close so let's not fall out over it. How about we change the subject and switch to when Detectives Jackson and Collins told you they had found Marie and you were being charged."

C.S.   "I knew it was coming sooner or later but I really did not expect them to find her (Marie) so quickly, caught me a little off guard, it really did."

Chapter 32: Breaking the news.

I always knew I would either be caught or die in the act of escape so the predicament I was in was no surprise to me. I had given them the slip for over ten years and now was their moment, it was their turn but only thanks to me, always on my terms. As I sat in my cell waiting for them to come and get me, so much had gone through my mind that I found it hard to sleep. Thinking on though, it was the time, and I was ready and prepared for the new pathway my life was taking.

Detective Martin Jackson had just finished his third coffee of the morning when he decided to call Jane Collins into his office. On arriving she rapped twice on the door and walked right in without waiting for Martin to reply. The door was open, and this meant anyone was free to enter whereas a closed door meant enter at your peril as anyone with half a brain would have worked out.

"I think it's time now Jane" Martin said. "Let's go and give this mother-fucker the good news," he continued. "He has had plenty of time to stew things over and must be wondering why the fuck we have not gone in yet, so let's put him out of his misery." "Sounds good to me, boss," Jane responded and the pair of them took a walk to the cells where Colin Stevens was waiting impatiently in cell number 3. He had been pacing for a while and was indeed as Martin Jackson had implied been stewing things over and wondering why they hadn't been to see him yet.

Once the door to cell 3 had been unlocked they both walked in to find Colin sitting on the edge of his bed as he had been most of the night. Martin said to him in a stern tone of voice, "We can either do this here or in the interview room Colin, what would you prefer?" Colin replied by saying. "I would prefer the interview room if you wouldn't mind as I have been in here all night and could do with a change of scenery." "Fine by me, it's your ass," Martin replied and the three of them headed off. Colin just wanted it done, Martin wanted it done and so did Jane. "Let's not put off the inevitable any longer." Martin said. He was looking forward to this.

The three of them after leaving the cell block, headed up the stairs to the interview suite and although he didn't know it yet for sure, he guessed the "it" of let's get it done referred to him being officially charged. This was an exciting development for Martin and Jane as it meant all the hard work had paid off, but not just themselves, the entire team. It would also give them a little closure on this and more time to work on other cases they were behind on. It would also give a bit of peace and retribution to the victims and their families, not before time may I add. At least it would until the time of the trial when every last detail would be dragged up before the court once more. For Colin he was heading into the unknown, it was a welcome unknown though. He knew it would end up in him going to jail but for how long. He reckoned on twenty years, but it could possibly end up twenty-five to life with no parole if the prosecution had their way Who could blame them, not him for sure.

He was hoping the judge would be lenient as he had given himself up and was also willing to assist them in any way they required. But sometimes even all that didn't matter a jot if the judge was in a foul mood, you just had to take what you could get on the day and suffer the consequences or not as the case may turn out.

When they had settled down Martin looked at Colin and said, "We found your car and the girl in the boot who is alive and well, no thanks to you, and she led us to the Travelodge. Would you like to hazard a guess as to what, or rather who we found in room 236?" "Possibly a lady by the name of Marie Calvin, I do believe that is where I left her and I'm not so sure she was in any fit shape to try and escape on her own fruition detective."

Martin looked at him with contempt and all the disgust he could muster, making a joke at a dead woman's expense while she has no means of defending herself was unacceptable in his eyes. "Colin Stevens you are under arrest for the murder of Marie Calvin and four others, you are also charged with raping at least six women and kidnapping with intent. Two further charges of possessing deadly weapons, both illegally will be added at a future date bringing the total to 14 counts, how do you plead?" "Guilty as fuck and proud of it." He replied. "Get this fucking prick out of my sight and put him back in the cell before I do something I regret," Martin screamed.

"You've got to learn to chill out a little at times Martin," Jane ordered. "We all want this fucking prick to suffer as much as he has made others' suffer, but this is not the way we go about it. One wrong move could mean we don't get to trial, and he could walk free on a technicality. Then we will have to choose to drop it or rebuild our case, but in the meantime, he walks the streets doing what the fuck he wants, and to who." She continued. "If that happens then I am not sure I can start again, I will be done with it."

This is the first time Jane had acted up to him and he was taken aback, but just a little. He was always telling her to grow a pair but not literally of course and she had finally done it. She did apologise but Martin told her there was no need, everything she said was right. He himself was close to bailing as well and didn't want to screw things up for himself but especially not any of the team that had worked so hard to bring it to this point. He wanted to bring it to a conclusion as much as the next man or woman but only if it was the right conclusion. And by that, meaning Colin Stevens was incarcerated for as long as he could be and not a day less.

With only a few minor setbacks and plenty of toing and froing they eventually managed to get the case to court which was a major achievement in itself after the position they found themselves in early on in their investigations. In court, things were going just as Martin had expected them to. Colin was fucking them around as much as he possibly could but what was new in that, and his lawyer was playing on his insanity claims at every given opportunity. The jury appeared to be falling for the story and Martin felt they were starting to lose the upper hand until the third day of the trial when Colin Steven's lawyer asked to approach the bench. This was unconventional and took everybody by surprise. It is virtually impossible to prove someone is not insane when they claim they are but easy to prove they are so what happened next perplexed the fuck out of the entire prosecuting team.

It only took thirteen words to throw the entire case wide open. "My client Colin Stevens has changed his plea on all charges to guilty" he said to the judge. Everything was turned on its' head by Colin Stevens deciding enough was enough and changing his plea from innocent due to insanity to guilty on all charges and totally going against all his lawyer's advice. Once it had been proved that he had not been coerced into the decision in any way and had in fact just had a change of heart, it was over, easy-as. The case was done and dusted and wrapped up pretty smartish. All that was left to do now was to wait for the sentencing which had been decided with court commitments as they were, would take place in the same courtroom and be scheduled for 3 weeks' time.

After three weeks in a prison cell, plenty of time to sit and stew and just contemplate what may happen, the rest of his life was decided in just a quarter of an hour. On returning to court, he was given twenty years to life with no possibility of parole as Martin and his team had hoped for, in an arraignment that lasted just 15 minutes. The journey from the prison lasted longer than the time it took to sentence him. Afterwards he was whisked away as quickly as he had arrived and returned to prison to start his new life away from everyone but the select few that would be given the job of guarding him for as long as he was in their charge.

C.J.   "I was wondering if you could put the way you changed down to one specific thing or was it a culmination of other things that caused you to lose it and make you do what you did."

C.S.   "I guess it was a culmination of events of sorts, but it was all sparked off by one event and that was me finding the knife. Although I don't remember a lot from before I found it, I was content, I had to be. There was no reason for me not to be, but as soon as I found it and I mean immediately, I started to be devious which I never had been before. Firstly, by hiding it and then by smuggling it into my room and after that doing anything that I had to so it wouldn't be discovered. It was almost as if it was in charge, and I was just there to carry out its' will."

C.S.   "Are you saying that if you didn't find it then you wouldn't have gone off the rails."

C.S.   "That is impossible to answer Connie, because no matter what else could've happened, I did find it."

C.J.   "What I am trying to say without sounding conceited is, I have seen things in you that lead me to believe you may well have turned either or."

C.S.   "Things like what?"

C.J.   "Your temper for one, there has been three times you have lost it with me already and I have only known you a few hours. Although you haven't physically hurt me, I did feel worried enough to stand my ground and keep alert, ready to run if I needed to."

C.S.   "If you remember I told you I wouldn't hurt you before we got started and no matter what else I am, I am not a liar. I pride myself on being truthful."

C.J.   "Everybody lies at some point, even if it's just a little one from time to time but they are still lies, no matter how well intended they are. Telling someone they look good when you know they look like shit for instance, still a lie but an acceptable one."

C.S.   "I see no point in lying and I never have. If I feel you look like shit, I will tell you, and don't worry you don't."

C.J.   "Thank you, I think. Yes, anyway. When you handed yourself in you had the gun with you but there was no sign of the knife, what happened to it?"

C.S.   "It's in one of the last places that you could imagine it would be, but I know exactly where it is. If I ever feel generous enough then maybe one day I will let you know, but I wouldn't hold my breath."

C.J.   "Still not willing to give up on it, even now?"

C.S.   "It's all I have to keep me going, maybe one day if I ever get out then, well who knows stranger things have happened."

Chapter 33: A mother's Love? Really!

I am sure she must have had love for me at some point but in the end, it was so well hidden that even the best detectives in the world would find it hard to locate in her blackened heart. It was so right and then it went so wrong, maybe part of it was my fault, I have no idea and I stopped caring after the multiple beatings, but she had no right to do what she did and I'd had just about enough to last a lifetime .

Adele Stevens sat on the edge of the bed in her cell. She had tried all week to avoid coming into any contact with news on her son's trial and had warned everybody not to talk to her about it or give her any information they found out for fear of reprisals. She just stayed in her cell, even at mealtimes she would collect her food and then promptly disappear back to her own confines. She would not watch the T.V. in the lounge or read any of the newspapers that were brought in by other inmates and their families in order of not finding out anything at all.

Alas, some of the other girls found it hard to keep their mouths shut and just loved to wind her up by talking about the case loudly just outside her cell knowing only too well she could hear. In prison there really is not much else to talk about so when a story like this hits the news, they are going to talk about it until the subject has been totally exhausted, no matter who it is about. She could have cried but that is something she hadn't done in 20 years finding it impossible to let her emotions out. She still had feelings for Colin but she didn't love him, those emotions had died out years ago.

Ever since she had found out about his arrest, which was a while ago, she couldn't help but wonder if she was responsible for the way he had turned out. It was impossible to avoid the news as it was all anyone was talking about at the time. She wondered if she hadn't been such a bitch then would things have ended differently. What a strange group the Steven's were turning out to be, one member murdered and two serving prison sentences, not your average everyday loving family.

There was always something special about him and by special she meant weird, she just wasn't sure of what exactly he was capable of, until now that is. That had been spelt out clear to her and she hated hearing it.

One woman that couldn't help herself was Sandra Bulworth, she hated Adele and just loved to tease her. She would often walk into her cell and tell her everything. One day she pushed her too far and tipped her over the edge by saying," I never thought I could ever know anyone more fucked up than you, but it turns out it runs in the family, your kid is fucking worse." This sent Adele flying into a rage and she grabbed Sandra in a headlock, smashing her face several times into the concrete wall of the cell.

Sandra tried to fight back but Adele's grip was too tight and by the time she had been dragged off her by the two guards she hadn't even seen enter the cell Sandra's face was more like a scene from the movie 'Carrie' where Sissy Spacek had all the pigs blood poured over her, only it wasn't animal blood it was her own. Sandra's face was beyond any recognition, and she was rushed to the hospital where she spent the next two weeks recovering. Adele however was rushed down to solitary and some solo time, which suited her just fine.

Solitary at this point was probably the best thing for Adele as it gave her the perfect opportunity to avoid all forms of contact with anyone. No contact, no news, no bullshit. She sat in her solitary cell content with her days work and laughed as she pictured Sandra's bloodied fat face, that bitch won't try that again in a hurry she thought to herself.

She only hoped this latest intervention wouldn't harm her chances of parole, it was due to be re-assessed in the next six weeks or so. Surely, they would be able to see she was provoked, O.K. maybe she had taken it a little too far afterwards, but she hadn't started it or even wanted any trouble, why would she if it could affect any chances of her freedom being granted.

C.J.   "Did you know your mum had heard of your arrest."

C.S.   "Somebody mentioned something to me on the subject, but I couldn't have been less interested in anything, ever."

C.J.   "So, it wouldn't interest you to know that your mum has since been paroled and is out free."

C.S.   "No, it wouldn't although it is funny when you look at it, one in one out, keep moving isn't there a song about that. She will be back in one day sooner or later. But I would hazard a guess at sooner. Anyway, that's more than enough time wasted on her let's get back to me and the trial."

C.J.   "O.K. Colin, for two and a half days in court you claimed insanity so, what happened to change your mind."

C.S.　　　"Personally, I never wanted to go with it, that was my lawyer's call. I am a lot of things but as I have said, one of them is not a liar, I knew I wasn't insane. I guess you must be at least a slight bit mad to do what I did but insane, no, I knew only to well what I was doing and that it was wrong, but it still didn't stop me."

C.J.　　　"What did your lawyer when you told him you were changing your plea?"

C.S.　　　"I don't know really as I never gave him much of a chance to have a reaction. I came in that day ready to do it and only told him about 10 minutes before. Of course, he tried to talk me out of it but by then it was already too late, my mind was made up."

C.J.　　　"Finally, a bit of decency, I didn't realise you had it in you."

C.S.　　　"That's a tad harsh isn't it, everybody no matter how bad they can be, has at least a little decency in them and yes, I include myself in that. Just because you have not been around to witness it for yourself doesn't mean it didn't happen. Same as everybody that claims to be good has at least a little evil in them, correct me if I am wrong, have you ever been evil Connie, done something you are not proud of or are you honestly squeaky clean like you make out?"

Connie had no response as whatever she had to say would no doubt have incriminated herself. She chose instead to remain silent on the matter. Colin accepted her silence as an admission of guilt and as an unspoken apology. He sniggered to himself in a knowing sort of way.

C.S.　　　"Thought as much, we all have it in us but with some it is easier to find and bring out. But with others it is so well hidden you may never locate it however hard you look, or they have it tamed and can control it, thus stopping it escaping."

C.J.   "You know what I think we have covered just about everything there is to know. It has been a real eye-opener for me, and I have found it very fascinating, but I think it is time to call it a day."

C.S.   "We have covered some ground today but if you have forgotten to ask anything or there is something else you need to know then you know where I am. I am quite sure I am not going anywhere."

Connie was starting to pack up her stuff in preparation of leaving when she turned to Colin, looked him in the eye and asked, "Can I be honest with you here Colin?" to which he replied, "Of course, go on what is it?". She continued, "When I first heard you wanted me to run your story, I was a little bit wary of coming and putting myself into such a vulnerable position." "In what way?" he asked her a little shocked at what she was trying to say. "I felt you were trying to go with a swansong and were planning on killing me as one last chance to hit the headlines, prison or not. I was thinking that possibly you got me here under the guise of an interview to satisfy your needs."

"So why did you come if that is what you thought?" he asked. "Curiosity." Came the reply. "All the way here, I was on the verge of pulling out, or turning around and heading straight home but curiosity is a strange Phenomenon and even stranger to explain," she went on.

"You are perfectly safe Connie I never have or ever will have intentions of killing you. You are doing me a big favour here, I mean who would write my story, no, don't you worry about a thing. As a matter of fact, there is only one person I would ever kill now, if given the opportunity of course. This one person has been the bane of my life and without them who knows what I could have achieved. Obviously being locked away and under guard on my one-hour free time doesn't assist me in any way, but when they slip up or have a lapse in concentration, who knows what could happen?"

"And who is that person." Connie asked looking at him inquisitively. "I am not at liberty to divulge that information yet but be rest assured as soon as I am ready to say then and only then will I let you know. It will finish my story off with a bang and it will be memorable, I can assure you of that. Just hang tight and wait for it, Connie." He replied.

By this time, she had finished packing up the few items she had brought in with her and said thanks and goodbye. He shook her hand and said, "Thank you and drive safe." She was escorted by Steve the prison guard back through the prison and all the clanging doors once again but this time she wasn't at all hesitant or nervous as he took her back to the car park where they had first met. He said goodbye and she thanked him for his help and then watched as he turned and disappeared back through the giant wooden prison doors. She breathed in the smell of freedom and thought it was not a job that she could ever do but I guess if it pays the bills, and someone must do it then why not Steve or any of them. When she reached her car, she opened the door and sat on the driver's seat letting out one of the biggest sighs she had ever done. She had done it and was very pleased with her day's work.

She sat in her car in the prison car park for about twenty minutes, she didn't even turn on the engine of her car and thought about the last few hours and how close she had been to a murderer, she went cold for a second. Eventually she decided she was ready and inserted her key into the keyhole and started the car up and then pulled away and exited the prison grounds starting the two-hour journey home. She was thinking of going into the office and getting started on her article but eventually thought it was a bad idea and headed straight home. It had been a long day, very productive but a long day just the same and she decided to call it quits. What are a few hours she thought to herself and Andrew would be waiting for her at home, she had only been away a few hours but needed him now more than she ever did?

It was one of the most remarkable bits of work she had ever had to do but she enjoyed it immensely. Every aspect, from finding out what made him tick to who he was and what he had become she found fascinating if at times a little bit daunting and scary. Colin Stevens was certainly a complicated character and she now had to use her nous and notes to unravel the mystery and finish the story.

Colin had given her the OK to write in her own words when she needed but she didn't want to make him look or feel like a hero because that he wasn't, she just wanted to do the best job she could with the information she had collected. It was going to be a challenge without question, she had no qualms about that, but it was a challenge she was looking forward to undertaking. As they said in her favourite movie "Tomorrow Is Just Another Day", well how true, tomorrow is another day, and it could be the start of the rest of her life and hopefully a stepping-stone giving her a giant leap forward. A woman in a man's world but feeling she could hold her own with the best of them without looking out of place.

Chapter 34: The final draft.

It was like I had been waiting an eternity but when it arrived it was worth every second. What she had written was so good that if I had to do it for myself, I wouldn't have done anything differently. I read it from cover to cover and then again and again. Knowing it was about me and that everyone and anyone would be reading it gave me such a buzz, I was riding on the crest of a wave once again and I just wanted to stay there forever.

Three weeks is a long time to be waiting for something you really want but must feel even longer when you are locked up in a cell for 23 hours a day. Colin will never be released, that's for sure but he knew he would not even be released into the prisons' general population because of the nature of his crimes, for his own safety he is in solitary confinement as some other prisoners don't take too kindly to rapists and women murderers, but especially paedophiles, and no matter what Colin could or would insist, he was one by law.

 Every day he would look at his bunk on returning from his hours yard time, more in hope than anything. Hoping to see a package waiting for him, but it didn't seem to be coming. He was permitted one hour a day in the yard for some well needed fresh air but only under guard supervision and when all other prisoners were locked safely back up in their cells to avoid any contact or risk. Each new day was the same, just a carbon copy of yesterday.

There had not been so much as a word from Connie Jones about the article she was writing about him based on the interview they'd had just over three weeks ago. He had rather hoped it would be out by now and was even starting to question the fact if Connie had welched on the deal. She had given him no indication that she would do any such thing, but it did seem to be taking a long time, too long in fact. Just to have something else to read, other than the scrawled messages on his cell wall, some of which had been written or carved years before he even arrived at Salworth.

It had taken Connie far longer than she had expected to sort the contents into chronological order, before she could fully commit to writing the article. The first draft had been completed and handed in to her editor for approval and she just needed his say-so before it went to print. Hopefully, and in media terms that could mean anytime it should only take a couple of more days to complete so she decided not to tell Colin and just let him sit it out until it was ready. He couldn't do anything about it so what harm would it do to keep quiet, he had waited 3 weeks so what was another couple of days. If she could have seen the way he was fretting, she may have had a different tune but for now she would wait and so would he.

Colin needn't have worried as just 3 days later he arrived back to his cell to be greeted by a parcel resting cosily against the pillow on his bed. He wasted no time in ripping it open but was surprised to see it was not a newspaper at all, but a copy of the full transcript addressed to him by Connie. He had wanted to read it in tabloid form as it would look more genuine and make him feel like others were reading it too, this way it felt personal between them and that was not the way he wanted things to go. What the hell he thought, I may as well read it anyhow, now it's here and he made himself comfortable on his bed and then began reading. He read it cover to cover without a break and overall, he was mightily impressed with the result. His original assumptions of Connie had proved correct, she was very professional and thorough and had not left anything out, she had even added in a few paragraphs in her own words', and it worked, it complemented what she'd managed to get from him.

Sure, there were a couple of times that she had made him out to appear well, not nice shall we say, but altogether understandable because of the subject matter. All-in-all though, it was a smart and professional article by an up-and-coming reporter who was at that moment on top of her game, but one day she had her sights set on being top of not just her game but the entire class.

There was also a small postscript note from Connie explaining that the story would be in The Independent each night for the next five issues, starting tomorrow. Although he had just read everything that was to be printed, he was super-excited to see it in print in the paper as he knew that was what everybody would read, and this was just a private copy for his own personal use. He wanted to see it as everyone else would see it and not in a biased way at all. Finally, after nearly two years of being left in the dark Colin Stevens was about to see the light once more. Or at least emerge out into it once more.

Chapter 35: Two years later.

Two years later...

Detective Martin Jackson was sitting at his desk for possibly the last ever time, retirement was less than 24 hours away and he couldn't wait for it. He loved his job and always had but he loved fishing more and that is what he planned to spend his free time doing. On his desk was a freshly opened bottle of whisky that had been sitting in his drawer for several years, unopened until now. In one of his hands, he held a tumbler half full of whisky from the very same bottle. Anyone that entered the room was given a glass and the chance to offer a toast to him and his future. If ever there was a time to finally open the bottle then this was it, so he did and was glad he had. To share the contents with his mates and work acquaintances made his last day worthwhile and a little bit special.

In his other hand Martin held a letter addressed to him by his good friend Brian Smedhurst a serial killer expert that had helped him on countless cases throughout his career. It had been sent to him during the Cotton Mill case and he had kept it as a reminder ever since. The letter read as follows,

Dear Martin,

A serial killer will remain a serial killer either until they are arrested and incarcerated and have the chance taken from them to kill or otherwise, they disappear due to their own death. It is an incurable disease, and they can never be changed or altered from their murderous course, (i.e., no treatment would suffice or alter their habits, they will never stop, just lie dormant for a while until the urge gets too big to refuse).

Even if there has been a while since their last kill, maybe days, months or even years, they will kill again given even the slightest window of opportunity. Life should mean life as they will vent up their anger over this time and unleash hell on some poor unsuspecting victim if they are freed.

Many serial killers do not try to hide their tracks and in fact leave more than enough clues while waiting to be discovered. Others on occasions leave DNA or fingerprints knowing one day they will be found. Hearing or reading about their own crimes and knowing other people are reading them, gives them a buzz and they will even brag about them to anyone that will listen.

From what you have told me Colin Stevens sounds like he is prone to outbreaks of psychotic behaviour and could well fit the bill as your killer. This is of course only my opinion and not fact.

Hope this helps, your friend Brian.

P.S.   So sorry to hear about Jack, I couldn't believe it when I heard the news. We will have to get together and remember him over a drink at some point, stay strong buddy.

Martin was reminiscing partly due to his retirement but also because of the shocking news he had not long received from the prison where Colin Stevens had been housed for the last four years. It was customary for them to make known any new developments and without a doubt, that is what this most definitely was.

Connie Jones was drinking coffee from a mug on which the words 'Ich Dien' were printed, they translated into English as 'I serve' and she found it very apt. for her especially as she certainly did. They were also the motto of The Prince of Wales and had been since their adoption along with a crest of three white ostrich feathers after the battle of Crecy in 1346 in remembrance of John of Luxembourg, King of Bohemia who was killed in the battle. This she only knew about from reading it in a book about the subject in question. It was all a part of her enthusiasm for having to know everything she could about anything. If she heard one fact she had to know, how, when, why, what and who with and generally anything that related to anything in any possible way, she just couldn't let it go until she knew everything. It had stood her in good stead at quizzes which she enjoyed and just when she had a few spare moments. It was kind of a hobby that took her away for a little while from the daily routine of normal life.

The postboy walked through the room with the trolley at 10 a.m. as usual but this time instead of walking past he stopped and reached in taking out a letter, he placed it on her desk. "Thank you" she said surprised as he went on his merry way but not hearing her as he was listening to Iron Maiden through his headphones. He was listening to the album 'Powerslave' and blasting out such classic tunes as 'Run to the Hills', Aces High' and the title track so loud that if you concentrated hard enough you could hear the words clearly.

She had no idea who it could be from as she was not expecting any correspondence from anyone and just stared at it hoping she would recognise the handwriting, but she didn't. She stared at it for a few more minutes before finally deciding to open it, what she should have done in the first place to enable her to find out who had sent it.

She opened it and read it, then she read it again. What the fuck, she asked herself? What the fucking hell she repeated while reading it a third time to take in the reality of its' contents and make sure she had read it correctly, she had. This is the letter:

Dear Connie Jones,

Colin Stevens here, the last time I saw you was two years ago when you interviewed me over the Cotton Mill rapes and murders, you produced a wonderful article about me and my life. I can't thank you enough for all the hard work you put in and the professionalism that you showed.

I don't know if you remember what I told you as you were leaving that day about killing one more time but only if circumstance allows it, and how it would be the one person that has been such a bane on my life. Things have gone very lapse at the prison, and I have seen and seized an opportunity to carry out the wish I never thought was ever going to be possible.

I am sure you think the person in question is my adopted mum, Adele Stevens as I know you have been in contact with her warning her of the fact, but you could not be more wrong. I bear her no ill-will anymore and hope she lives a long and fruitful life.

The one bane on my existence is and always has been Colin Stevens, or myself. As Karol Jovanovic I am told I was always happy but since becoming Colin Stevens things turned sour somehow and my life got messed up. I see only one way of stopping it and that is to say goodbye. Maybe you could let the world know that I am no more or at least will be by the time this letter reaches you.

Sincerely,

Colin Stevens, Button Killer.

P.S.   Don't throw the envelope away it may hold more than you think. Good hunting, Colin.

Connie wasted no time in checking all the news feeds she could find and eventually came upon a story about convicted rapist and killer Colin Stevens. Dubbed The Cotton Mill Rapist by the press and how he had taken his own life by cutting his wrists and throat with a shiv fashioned and sharpened from the handle of a toothbrush, he wasn't joking about the lapse of security if he could manage to do what he did.

She sat back in her chair and wiped a lone tear from her eye, why it was there she had no idea as she had only met him once and although he had left a remarkable impression it wasn't in that way, it was a professional arrangement and nothing else. Maybe it was just the idea of death she didn't like, full stop. She had always found it hard to accept no matter who it was or how it happened. It was just something that she had always found hard to come to terms with.

Meanwhile, sat at his desk in a different office, in a different town, Martin Jackson finished the last of the whisky that he had poured himself and said goodbye and good riddance as he toasted the demise of Colin Stevens, "and about fucking time too," he thought to himself. There had been a few people that he had come to detest over the years for one reason or another, but this cunt had to be top of the bill without a shadow of a doubt. Slimiest of the slimeballs, nastiest of the nasties and just about the most fucked up of the fucking lunatics he had ever had the pleasure or mis-pleasure in his case to ever meet.

Chapter 36: Andrew Coulson.

What a great idea, do-it-yourself envelopes. Whoever invented them, I thank you. Now I had the means I knew exactly how I was going to let Connie know of my movements in the few weeks leading up to my arrest. She was going to be shocked and wouldn't like it, but she has the right to know. Posthumously, I will tell her all she needs to know.

Connie stared at the envelope and then back at the letter, 'Don't throw the envelope away it may hold more than you think. Good hunting, Colin.' What the hell could that mean? she asked herself. It obviously meant something, or why would he say it, but what? She had slipped her hand in and ran it around the inside and found it to be completely empty, there was nothing left in there but empty space it just didn't make sense, so why say it. It was vintage Colin Stevens, taunting and teasing even after his demise. The only thing that had been occupying it was the letter that she now had grasped firmly in her hand. Had he meant to put something inside but forgotten, if so, she was never going to find out now with him being dead, it was all a mystery to her but one she was determined to solve.

She picked up the envelope once again and looked at it carefully, still nothing. So, she squeezed the two ends together to make the hole at the top where the letter goes in a little wider. When she peered in, she could see something inside, it was there alright but very faint, it looked like pencil markings and they were easy to miss unless you were searching specifically for them. Reaching over she grabbed the letter opener from her desk tidy and carefully sliced the two sides and pulled the envelope fully open and placed it flat in front of her. It was kind of like what you do when you butterfly chicken, slice it down the middle and open it flat out before you cook it and place it on someone's plate.

Now she knew exactly what Colin meant by it may hold more than you think, there was a crudely drawn map, obviously drawn by hand, and rushed but she could make out what it was meant to be. There was a building in the bottom left-hand corner and a tree in the top right corner, between the two there was a dotted line and the words five paces leading to a letter X. In the middle there were three circles that could pass for stepping-stones and up close to the top left corner there was a rough sketch of an animal, she wasn't exactly sure, but it could be a tortoise and if that were the case then, oh fuck me she thought to herself nearly losing her breath and totally taken aback as the shock kicked in.

 It wasn't just a drawing of any old field or just any old garden, it was a picture of the lawn in her garden at her home. She took a deep breath in to try and compose herself, but it wasn't working as her heart was beating ten to the dozen and showing no signs of slowing. What the fuck, how? why? and more importantly, why? and when? She had so many questions to ask but not one single answer, at least not one feasible one anyway. "Damn you, Colin Stevens." She shouted at the top of her voice waving both her fists in the air as if trying to reach out to him, but if that was the case maybe she should have waved them at the floor because there was only one place he went when he died, and it certainly wasn't heaven.

Once she had cottoned on to what she was seeing and had concluded that it wasn't some kind of sick joke played on her by someone bearing a grudge, she froze. Because what she had cottoned onto however crazy it may seem was a diagram of her back garden drawn onto the inside of the envelope that had arrived from Colin Stevens. She kept passing her eyes over it just in case she had made a mistake, but every detail was there, right in front of her. The revelation was shocking as it would have to have meant that he had to have been there and seen her garden for himself, but when? He has been locked up and how? She had been there. This wasn't over, not by a long shot. Playing tricks was always his game but now his game was becoming reality and she wasn't ready for it.

The shed was in one corner with the apple tree directly opposite, the three stepping-stones and even the tortoise or at least the clay figurine of a tortoise she had named speedy after Speedy Gonzalez, the fastest mouse in all of Mexico. Yes of course she knew a tortoise wasn't fast but that just makes the name funny and inventive and not boring like Tommy or Trevor or any other name beginning with T, because that would be too easy and just shows how some people have no imagination whatsoever.

The dotted line however was not there in the garden, it had been added on the sketch by whoever had drawn it and it led from the tree heading directly toward the shed but stopping halfway across the garden by a giant X as in X marks the spot or so she believed. She picked up the letter and the flattened envelope and decided to take them to her editor who would know exactly what to do. He had been in so many different situations both dangerous and amusing and come out of them all unscathed and if there was anyone she trusted, it was him. He was one of the brightest people she had ever met and knew a lot about a lot. Most people know a something about something or little about a little, but he knew everything about everything or that is the way he came across, full of confidence.

He was onto it straight away and said, "Isn't that your place Connie?" She replied "Yes, that's what I thought, and it is correct in every detail, scary isn't it." She continued. "I'll say, that means this fucked up freak has at the least been in your garden but where else, inside your house possibly?" he asked. "I hadn't thought of it quite like that but now I am, thanks you damn bastard." she shouted at him in a serious-yet-joking kind of way. Luckily enough he saw the funny side and just let her comment pass. He may be her boss and head of the paper, but he is human after all. "You must call the police and get them involved right away, or earlier if that is possible. I would do it yesterday if that was an option but obviously can't be." He ordered her. "I am getting onto it now," she replied and was given the rest of the day off to try and get it sorted.

She was told that the police would meet her at her house in about fifteen minutes, even if she drove at 70 miles per hour all the way it would take her at least 20-25 minutes so she said she would be there when she can. When she arrived, she saw the police were standing waiting for her, which is not surprising really as they had their blues and two's going all the way, but she had to stop at just about every red light on the journey, as is always the case when you are in a hurry. She opened the door and let them in, there were about 8 of them all in and they all trudged through firstly the hall, then into the kitchen and finally after Connie had unlocked the kitchen door out into the back garden. She informed the head detective or at least the guy that seemed to be in charge that she would unlock the back gate as there would be too much dirt and mud being trampled through the house, he agreed and said, "Thank you."

Andrew Coulter, the lead detective or at least the first in the queue when they had arrived and the one Connie had spoken to first, had the envelope in his hand and when he got out into the garden, he held it up looked at it and then looked at the garden. "There really isn't much doubt about it being this one is there it's an exact match." he said. He moved over to the tree and pointed himself in the direction of the shed, wasting no time he took 5 steps forward and stopped. He was handed a shovel by one of the other policemen and started to dig. He placed the head of the spade into the earth and keeping hold of the handle pressed down on it with his foot, the earth was softish and squelchy and it sunk in easier than he thought it would. He removed what earth had been dug out and went in again and again. He had no idea how far down he had to go but it wasn't long before his questions were answered as the spade came to a clanging halt as it struck something, 'here we go' he thought to himself. Everybody heard the noise at the same time, and they all stopped their little conversations or whatever they were doing to investigate the hole in anticipation of maybe finding secret treasure.

"What do you think it could be Connie?" Andrew asked. "I have no idea! I could guess but I would rather just find out than playing a game of I-spy." She answered. "It's both intriguing and petrifying at the same time and my heart is bouncing like a trampoline. How did he get to bury something in my garden without me seeing or even knowing he had been here at all, that has really knocked me for six and not a lot shocks me or at least I didn't think it did? I feel violated, not in the same way as his victims mind you but still violated just knowing he has been in my private space, and I have this picture in my mind of him laughing in my face while he is doing it. All nice and friendly while he is looking me in the face but all the time knowing he has been at my house."

"People find a way to do whatever if they truly are that desperate and if nothing it does answer one question?" he said to her. "And what is that one question, "she enquired. "The reason he wanted you to do the interview in the first place, he was trying to get you involved in more of a way than you thought you were."

Reaching down into the hole Andrew pulled out an old kitchen tea towel that had been wrapped around something and then tied with chord to secure whatever it was. After untying the chord, he unravelled the tea towel and, in his hand, he held a knife, a black-handled hunting knife with the image of a galloping stallion on the handle. The blade looked brand new as if it had never been used but they all knew that was not the case, it had been used alright on more than one occasion, on over 50 occasions to be honest.

"Before I left and after I had finished interviewing him, he said he had hidden the knife somewhere I would never think of looking and only he knew where to look for it. He said he had hidden it in case he was ever released and then he would retrieve it and continue his destructive pathway or else otherwise maybe one day he would let me know where it was. I never expected him to divulge the information freely, but I guess he has no use for it now and that is why he has chosen to let the secret out."

"He seemed to have been a tenacious little bastard, if he wanted something doing nothing was going to get in his way, they are the dangerous ones, the ones you have to be wary of." Andrew warned her." Yes, but he has gone, and I am just glad that he let me know now where it was. I could have been sitting on that for years without knowing, at least this way it is over with now and not a few years down the line being raked up all over again and dragged through the mud." Connie said.

"The only thing that stumps me, "Connie spoke wonderingly, "Is how did he do it. How did he get in without being seen and even more so than that, how did he manage to dig a fucking hole in my garden without me even knowing he had been there, surely I would have seen a freshly dug hole I am always out here not a week goes by that I'm not tending to my plants or lawn in some way or another?" She finished.

"That is a question we may never get the answer to, only one person knew for sure, and he is dead. Speculation is our only option on this one I am afraid. It's all going to be about guesswork so just accepting that it happened and forgetting about it is the easiest way." Andrew said to her. "There really isn't anything else to do in the situation."

"You are probably right detective, but it will never stop me wanting to know the truth, I am a reporter after all and finding things out is what I do for a living. I certainly won't let something as simple as a dead witness stop me from finding out. Connie never did find out how Colin had done it, all she knew was that she had been manipulated by this conniving, nasty bastard. He suckered her in, buttered her up and used her entirely for his own gain. After what she had done for him, she felt in return that he had let her down. But over the years he had let so many women down in one way or another, so why should she be surprised. That is just the fucked-up piece of shit he is and even if he was alive today it wouldn't change a thing.

She did another article on Colin Stevens explaining how much of a manipulating, conniving murderous serial killing machine he really was, and it won her a 'British Journalism of the year Award'. It appears that Colin Steven's legacy lives on through Connie Stevens and the award that takes pride of place over the fireplace in her front room. She puts it down to all the hard work she put in but still can't help but wonder, was it her hard work or his decision to get her to do the interview that won it for her, what a bastard he really was and still is, but that is how he wanted it, he has got his way and his memory is living on, fuck you Colin Stevens, you bastard.

Chapter 37: The end.

There comes a time in everyone's life to say goodbye to something or other, for me the time is now. Thanks for listening, thanks for reading and see you in hell my friends.

Two years earlier.

Connie Jones had a giant beaming smile on her face as she walked up the steps leading to the airplane that would take her to her most favourite place on earth, Italy's Amalfi Coast and Sorrento in particular. She had two weeks off work and was going to enjoy them immensely. She loved her job but needed the break to recharge her batteries and freshen her up and prepare her for whatever the future may bring. Whilst there she would take in Pompeii and Herculaneum, two of the cities destroyed by the volcano Vesuvius in AD 79 and may even take a trek to the top of the volcano and admire the stunning view of Naples, it's bay and the island of Capri. Little did she know that as she was boarding the plane about 50 miles away a stranger was climbing the wall to her back garden and preparing to dig a hole to bury something he wanted to hide from the police. The item he was burying was a black handled hunting knife that had been used in at least 3 murders and countless rapes and the stranger in question was a man by the name of Colin Stevens. She knew nothing whatsoever about him, he however seemed to know everything about her.

 He knew she worked for the Independent Newspaper, he knew where she lived and her boyfriend's name, he even knew she was off on her holidays, where she was going and for how long. He had done his homework and made it his point to know everything he possibly could about her while making sure he stayed hidden from her view, and she didn't suspect a thing. He also knew that he had more than enough time to bury a weapon in her garden and she would be none the wiser as the grass would have grown back before she returned from Italy, her chosen destination, Sorrento, a lovely scenic place he had visited himself in the past. While there he had even attacked another victim that would never be known about and taken a button off her blouse as a souvenir. He had made it his point to keep up to date with all that he needed to know about Connie while keeping himself out of view and was about to put in a request form to meet her at the prison in which he was incarcerated. He had no idea if she would be willing but felt she wouldn't turn away such an opportunity. One thing was for sure, he was ready, and the time had come. It was time to spill the beans and let the world know Colin Stevens was alive, for the time being at least. He was alive for as long as he wanted him to be. After that who knows, only time will tell.

Souvenir (in A Killer's Words).   by Paul White.

Printed in Great Britain
by Amazon